Taggart Family Values

Other Books by Lexi Blake

ROMANTIC SUSPENSE

Masters and Mercenaries
The Dom Who Loved Me
The Men With The Golden Cuffs
A Dom is Forever
On Her Master's Secret Service
Sanctum: A Masters and Mercenaries Novella
Love and Let Die
Unconditional: A Masters and Mercenaries Novella
Dungeon Royale
Dungeon Games: A Masters and Mercenaries Novella
A View to a Thrill
Cherished: A Masters and Mercenaries Novella
You Only Love Twice
Luscious: Masters and Mercenaries~Topped
Adored: A Masters and Mercenaries Novella
Master No
Just One Taste: Masters and Mercenaries~Topped 2
From Sanctum with Love
Devoted: A Masters and Mercenaries Novella
Dominance Never Dies
Submission is Not Enough
Master Bits and Mercenary Bites~The Secret Recipes of Topped
Perfectly Paired: Masters and Mercenaries~Topped 3
For His Eyes Only
Arranged: A Masters and Mercenaries Novella
Love Another Day
At Your Service: Masters and Mercenaries~Topped 4
Master Bits and Mercenary Bites~Girls Night
Nobody Does It Better
Close Cover
Protected: A Masters and Mercenaries Novella
Enchanted: A Masters and Mercenaries Novella
Charmed: A Masters and Mercenaries Novella
Taggart Family Values
Treasured: A Masters and Mercenaries Novella

Masters and Mercenaries: The Forgotten
Lost Hearts (Memento Mori)
Lost and Found
Lost in You
Long Lost
No Love Lost

Masters and Mercenaries: Reloaded
Submission Impossible
The Dom Identity, Coming September 14, 2021

Butterfly Bayou
Butterfly Bayou
Bayou Baby
Bayou Dreaming
Bayou Beauty, Coming July 27, 2021

Lawless
Ruthless
Satisfaction
Revenge

Courting Justice
Order of Protection
Evidence of Desire

Masters Of Ménage (by Shayla Black and Lexi Blake)
Their Virgin Captive
Their Virgin's Secret
Their Virgin Concubine
Their Virgin Princess
Their Virgin Hostage
Their Virgin Secretary
Their Virgin Mistress

The Perfect Gentlemen (by Shayla Black and Lexi Blake)
Scandal Never Sleeps
Seduction in Session
Big Easy Temptation
Smoke and Sin
At the Pleasure of the President

URBAN FANTASY

Thieves
Steal the Light
Steal the Day
Steal the Moon
Steal the Sun
Steal the Night
Ripper
Addict
Sleeper
Outcast
Stealing Summer
The Rebel Queen

LEXI BLAKE WRITING AS SOPHIE OAK

Texas Sirens
Small Town Siren
Siren in the City
Siren Enslaved
Siren Beloved
Siren in Waiting
Siren in Bloom
Siren Unleashed
Siren Reborn

Nights in Bliss, Colorado
Three to Ride
Two to Love
One to Keep
Lost in Bliss
Found in Bliss
Pure Bliss
Chasing Bliss
Once Upon a Time in Bliss
Back in Bliss
Sirens in Bliss
Happily Ever After in Bliss
Far From Bliss, Coming 2021

A Faery Story
Bound
Beast
Beauty

Standalone
Away From Me
Snowed In

Taggart Family Values

Lexi Blake

Taggart Family Values
Lexi Blake

Published by DLZ Entertainment LLC
Copyright 2021 DLZ Entertainment LLC
Edited by Chloe Vale
ISBN: 978-1-942297-57-4

McKay-Taggart logo design by Charity Hendry

Foreword

So this book was a long time in the making. It was written over the course of several years and represents many of the milestone events for this fictional family I started back in 2011. That was when Ian Taggart first walked onto the pages of what would become probably the most important series of my career. Even back then I knew Ian would become the center of this universe and he would need a woman who could handle him. Enter Charlotte Denisovitch. I could have ended the story there and everyone would understand that they went on and had kids and were happy. That's how romance works, right? We see the fun parts—the sex and the first love and dates and then the wedding.

But I'm old and I've been married for 28 years while I write this, and I know that some of the best "scenes" from my marriage didn't happen in the beginning. So often we view the wedding as the end of the story when it's really the start of what becomes a whole life. I've never been able to leave Ian and Charlotte alone. They're in my dreams at night and in my mind during the day. Likely because they're the couple I feel closest to in real life. Every author puts aspects of herself in her characters, and those two have a lot of me and my husband. So hopefully I can be forgiven for indulging my love of these characters.

I cannot quit them.

So here are some stories beginning with the first day and ending with a glimpse of the future for this family I love so much. Many of them have been published before in various places. "Paradise City" was a newsletter extra. "Sweet Child o' Mine" was given away for years to newsletter subscribers. "Rough Night" and "Make Lemonade" are stories in the cookbook collections. "Countdown" originally appeared in a charity anthology. "Stuck at the Office" and "Homecoming" are brand new because I thought Travis and Natasha needed their own stories. They're all here in one place now, a glimpse into one fictional family that hopefully resembles the love we all share.

This book is for the families we have and the ones we find. Because everyone we love is family.

Thank you for being part of mine.

Much love,

Lexi

1

Paradise City

Paradise City takes place before The Dom Who Loved Me.

Part One

Ian Taggart sat back, glancing around the lounge area of The Velvet Collar with all the subtlety of a lion selecting his evening meal. Not that he had to be subtle. After all, the women here wanted someone to make a meal of them.

So far Paris was pretty sweet. Far better than his last assignment. Ten Smith had come through.

"Your Scotch, Sir." The blonde smiled at him, her eyes going submissively down. She wore a corset and a tiny thong, both in an angelic white with pink embroidery. She had the innocent thing down.

"Thank you." He took the glass out of her hand. One drink now and then another when he was done playing, and by playing he meant after he was finished spanking a pretty sub and then fucking her hard until they were both satisfied. Then he would have his second Scotch. Alone. Like he would sleep tonight. He would play all he liked, fuck all he wanted to, but at the end of the evening he would go up to the apartment that served as his base of operations here in Paris and he would be alone.

That was how he liked it.

"Is there anything else I can do for you, Sir?" She said it with a breathy tone that let him know she wasn't merely talking about snacks. She wore no collar that would indicate she had a Dominant partner.

She was pretty and submissive. He hadn't fucked her yet. She would do for the night. "I'm looking for a play partner. How long is your shift?"

She could say yes or no. It didn't matter much to him. He would do his best to bring her some pleasure and then he wouldn't go back for seconds. It wasn't anything against her. It was simply how he lived. He was in Paris for a few weeks, watching a Russian who might or might not be selling enriched uranium to any number of assholes who weren't planning on using the shit to power their lights. After that he would move on to London and then Dublin and meet up with his G2 contacts, and he wouldn't come back for a while. Ten would likely send him to some shithole after that, so he was going to plow his way through as much submissive tail as he could while he had the chance. The only reason he was here now was the fact that he'd recently saved Ten's ass and wanted a European assignment as payment.

Her eyes slid shyly away, though he didn't miss her satisfied smile. "I'll be available in a few minutes, Sir. I would love to play with you."

He winked her way. "And hey, if you've got a friend, bring her along."

Her lips curled up in a playful smile. "I think I can help you out there, Sir. You know you're already a legend. Every sub here wants to play with Master Ian."

Well, it was good his reputation had preceded him. He watched her walk away, ass swaying. She was slender, graceful. She walked up to a brunette, whispering something in her ear that had the friend blushing and then looking his way.

Yeah, he was going to have some fun tonight.

"Could you leave a few for the rest of us poor Doms, Taggart?" Rene DuBois sank down into the chair beside him. He was a tall, elegant man whose lean body belied his strength. He had a thick French accent, but Ian knew that in the field Rene could sound as American as he did. Accents were important to an operative. "I swear you've been here for a week and you've left a trail of subs panting after you. What do you do to them?"

Well, he had a really big dick and he knew how to use it for one. "I'm exotic. You know the American accent thing works for some women."

But it was mostly the really big dick. And the fact that he could eat pussy for hours.

Rene chuckled and sat back. "I'm sure it's the accent." He sobered a bit. "Do you have everything you need?"

The Frenchman wasn't asking about his sexual needs. Rene was

14

mostly a club owner and a businessman, both of which were a front for his real job—French intelligence.

"I'm good. The contacts are all in place, and I read your report on the O'Donnells. I've worked with Liam on a few minor ops. He seems solid. By that I mean he's a dipshit, but a solid one. His brother causes me concern."

Rene nodded. "I talked to Ten about it. I have the same concerns, but Rory O'Donnell is perfect for this op. I don't think Leonov buys it if we send the elder O'Donnell in by himself. Rory is the one with real IRA ties. I'm not sure Liam knows what his baby brother is into, but I'm fairly certain we can trust him to stop it if Rory tries something. This is a gamble."

He liked Li O'Donnell. He would have to figure out a way to let the man know his brother was sliding into trouble.

"But the reward is worth the risk." The reward being keeping the world safe from dirty bombs. "I agree with your assessment, and I can't tell you how much I appreciate the logistical support. My last contact put me up in a motel room I shared with a goat. I'm not fucking joking. A goat wandered in and I couldn't get the fucker out. I finally named him Sir Goats A Lot and he became my roomie. That goat had gas. Lots of gas. I like it here better."

"I can only imagine." Rene took a sip of his own Scotch. "It's much more comfortable here."

One day he would have his own club. When he closed his eyes he could see it. Industrial, with clean lines and moody lighting. He liked The Collar, but it was old school, done up in reds and golds, velvet lining some of the walls and some incredible art. He wasn't into art. He wanted the subs of his club to be the artwork.

Of course in his more morose moments, he knew he would never have that club. He would go out in a blaze of glory and then be a random star on a wall at Langley. Because that was how operatives went out. There was a bullet with his name on it waiting somewhere out there.

Or a knife. Or some poison. God, when he thought about it, he kind of craved that bullet.

The blonde was back along with her brunette friend. They waited a few feet from him, and he rather thought they would have stood there a good portion of the night. Well-trained subs. He wanted to be done with business. He wanted to not think for a while. When he went back to his room, he would have to think about what had happened with Alex and Eve, and how John Bishop was dead. He had to consider the fact that his younger brother thought he was somewhere in the Middle East because Sean had no idea he'd been recruited into the CIA.

When he was alone, he would have to try to sleep and dream of all that blood on his hands.

So he waved the subby duo over. Yes, they would do. He could have one sit on his face while the other sucked his cock, and that would be a lovely way to end the day.

Until the nightmares kicked in.

He patted his lap and suddenly he had one on each knee. So much soft skin and soft voices and perfect obedience. Why was it starting to get boring?

"Dare I ask for names, or should I call you slave one and slave two?"

The brunette giggled. "You may call me anything you wish, Sir."

"You can call me yours," the blonde replied, putting an arm around his shoulders. "Bridgette and I will do anything for the Master."

He bet they would. They wouldn't question him for a second. They would follow all the rules and never think to defy him.

Wasn't that supposed to be what he wanted?

The music shifted from an industrial beat to something that had Tag sitting up a little straighter. That sweet guitar riff followed by the thud of a drum always called to him. "Guns N' Roses. Sweet."

Paradise City. Well, the grass did seem greener and the girls were pretty. He agreed with Axl on that one.

"I heard you were a fan. I had the manager put several of their songs into the rotation," Rene replied. Then the Frenchman's eyes widened and he sat up straighter. "There's trouble on two legs."

Tag looked up, and it seemed like the whole room had gone perfectly still. Every person in the lounge had turned, their eyes on the newcomer. He could hear the music playing, but his whole focus had shifted to the woman who'd just walked into the lounge.

Five nine or ten, with breasts that would be more than a handful and hips like fucking Jessica Rabbit. She wore a black corset and thong, her dark hair brushing the tops of her breasts. He would bet her hair wasn't naturally so dark, but it looked good on her and contrasted with crystal blue eyes. And she wasn't playing innocent like the other subs. No, she boldly looked around the lounge, her eyes searching for something.

Sub? She was likely a Domme with that stare, and for the first time in his life he considered bottoming if it meant getting into that woman's thong.

"I wouldn't, Tag. Her name is Charlotte Dennis, but she's got ties to the Denisovitch syndicate. I think she might be a daughter," Rene warned. "I let her in so I could watch her. There are several rumors about her I find troubling."

"Not my problem." Leonov was his problem, and he wasn't getting close to the man. The O'Donnell brothers were. Denisovitch had nothing to do with his op, so the man's daughter was absolutely in play.

Charlotte. The name played around in his head even as he felt the subs shifting on his lap.

Charlotte didn't suit her. No. That was a Charlie right there. If she was his, he would call her Charlie, a pet name between the two of them. He would tug on all that hair and call her his pet and she would sit at his feet, proof that he was the Dom of Doms because that was the single hottest women he'd ever laid eyes on.

Not that she would be his for anything but a night. Or two. Maybe three. Or one. That would be far smarter. A one-night stand, but he would take all night with that particular woman.

She looked around and suddenly settled on a target. Those clear blue eyes found his and flared. He could practically feel her will, and it was all focused on him.

Fuck yeah.

Except he had a problem. He'd invited these two, and now he'd definitely changed his mind. He didn't want a third. No. He wouldn't invite her to join them. He wanted that one all to himself.

Charlie strode over, bold as brass. "Bridgette, Giselle, I'm afraid you've been misled. I'm sure the Master didn't mean to disappoint you, but there it is. That man is mine tonight. I suggest you remove yourself or we'll have a talk."

Just like that, they fled like a couple of gazelles. His lap was suddenly empty, but he had prospects. Charlotte Dennis stared at him with bold eyes, and he felt his interest rise. He wasn't going to be bored tonight. No way. No how.

It looked like this lion had found his mate.

For the night at least…

Part Two

Ian felt his cock harden as Charlie sat on his lap. He didn't miss the way the two dismissed subs had sent glares her way, but that would be her problem and not his. His only problem would be how to get inside her as quickly as he could. "I don't usually let subs take control so early in the game. I don't usually let subs take control at all."

She draped an arm around his shoulder, but there was something stiff about the way she held herself. She wasn't as comfortable as she wanted him to believe. "I didn't know we were playing a game, Master Ian."

"It's always a game, Charlie, and you look like you've played a time or two."

Rene sighed and stood up. The Frenchman stared down at him. "There is no way I can talk you out of this?"

Not a chance in hell. "I think I can handle her."

Charlie's mouth had become a flat, stubborn line, and she watched as Rene strode back toward the bar. "Why would he talk you out of taking a sub for the night? I thought that's what you were here to do. And Charlie? My name is Charlotte. Charlotte Dennis."

He needed to start setting some clear boundaries. If she was going to bottom for him…tonight…she needed to understand what he required. "You're Charlie to me, and I would like to know why you came in and decided to send two subs away, leaving me with only you."

Not that he didn't want her. God, since the minute she'd shown up, he'd known damn well he would have her no matter the consequences.

She was quiet for a moment and then she bit that full-as-fuck bottom lip. "I've watched you for a couple of days. I stayed in the shadows. You made me want to come into the light. I sent them away because you're mine. You just don't know it yet."

It was odd. He was always the pursuer. In this particular world, he had to make the decisions, and that included whom to top. He'd had plenty of submissives flirt and try to cajole him. Not a one would have walked in and boldly stated that she was the one for him.

She wasn't. There was no magical "one." He wasn't some dumbass, romantic kid. But the idea that she'd decided he was worth making that statement for was intriguing. "I think you're definitely going to have to prove that."

Her spine straightened. "All right. What do you need, Sir?"

What did he need? So many fucking things. Her mouth on him. His cock in her. Maybe a little information. "Why are you here in Paris?"

Her eyes were suddenly steady, looking right into his. "I had some business."

Oh, she would be an excellent liar. She might not be lying now, but he'd been an operative long enough to know that the way a person answered questions told him a lot. She met his gaze head on. "How long have you been a member here?"

"Not long. It's only recently I figured out what I need sexually. I'm going to be honest with you. I only like to submit in the bedroom. Outside of it, I'm rather difficult."

Then it was good he didn't plan to date her. "I can handle that. I'm rather difficult myself."

"So I've heard."

Now her eyes drifted. He looked up and she was watching a couple stroll into the lounge. He recognized her as a famous French actress and the man as a producer. Not that he would ask either about their jobs if they didn't bring it up. Here they were simply a Domme and her much larger submissive partner who apparently liked having his balls tortured. The guy could wail. Charlie had the evilest grin on her generous lips. Damn, those lips were hot, but he had to admit the evil grin did something to his dick, too. "You know something."

Her eyes went wide. "What do you mean, Sir?"

"You know something about Mistress Marie and her sub."

20

"I know a lot of things, Sir. I've learned that information can be an important resource."

Oh, they would get along. "Information or gossip?"

She clammed right up. "Gossip isn't allowed in the club."

He arched a brow.

Her smile nearly lit up the room, and a thrill went through him when she leaned in and whispered into his ear. "He was supposed to cast her in the new action film he's producing, but he decided to go with a younger actress and yes, she's at this club, too. She's walking up to them right now."

He couldn't help it. People were funny as shit, and he loved a good train wreck. No one ever shared that with him. The Doms were all pretentious fucks who thought they were above it all, and the subs were too subby to admit that they watched the other club members like they were the best soap opera in the world. But they were. Who needed TV when he could watch As the Dungeon Turns? He simply never had anyone to watch it with.

He thought the second actress was a submissive named Helene. Rene had many influential people in his club. Not a one of them knew he was French intelligence, of course. There were politicians, important businessmen, creative types. They all came to The Velvet Collar to indulge and play. He wanted to play, but right now in a different way.

"They look awfully chummy for rivals." The two women had done that bullshit air kissy thing and looked delighted to see each other. It was boring.

Charlie looked at him. "You want to see something more fun, Sir?"

"You going to cause trouble?"

Her eyes suddenly went soft, and it did a funny thing to his...eww...had he just thought about his heart in a way that wasn't something like—*hey, did that shot hit my heart?* He shook it off. He must be getting old.

"Only if it pleases you, Sir. I would like to point out that what I'm about to do is nothing more than polite. I need you to understand that I'm essentially a nice person."

"But if a nicety happens to bring about a chaotic result?"

She shrugged slightly. "Is that really my fault? She's going to find out sometime. They have to start production soon. I'm sure he thinks he'll call her from somewhere far away so she can't lose her shit on him in anything but a vocal way. I'm merely giving her a potential physical outlet. When you think about it, I'm kind of doing the world a favor."

She was definitely doing his world a favor. She amused him. He liked the way her eyes lit up when she was plotting, and he absolutely adored the way she justified herself. How long had it been since he'd had fun with a woman that didn't involve sex? Oh, this would involve sex eventually, but he was enjoying talking with her.

He wanted to get to know her.

"I think you should go and congratulate your friend."

She winked and gracefully rose from his lap. He watched as she walked away and was aware of the satisfaction he felt that she was relaxed again. When she'd first sat down on his lap there had been a stiffness that belied her brazen attitude. Was she shyer than she seemed? Or was she working him for some reason?

He couldn't discount the fact that she apparently had ties with the Russians and he was currently investigating a Russian. It would be smarter to keep his distance.

Or smarter to get in bed with her as soon as possible. How exactly could he find out what she was doing if he kept her at arm's length? He would probably have figured out that big smelly dude who ran the underground bar in Morocco was actually running a terrorist cell if they'd been cuddling every night. Not that he would. Because of the smell and the extra dick in that scenario, but figuring Charlie Dennis out would be far easier if he was fucking her.

Damn that woman had a juicy ass. Firm and round, that backside was made for spanking. Her hair was down, the long tresses brushing the top of her cheeks. He would be able to control her with that hair. He would be able to sink his hand into it and guide her to his dick.

Yes, he should stick close to her to find out if she was playing him in some way.

His dick was talking. Luckily his dick was actually quite the strategic thinker.

She smiled as she greeted Helene and Marie, nodding Durant's way. Charlie then turned to the bartender. He couldn't hear her, but the bartender immediately went for a bottle of champagne.

Such a bitch. Thing was, he liked a bitch. He was kind of a bastard. Okay, he was an asshole bastard SOB most of the time. A strong bitch was the only kind of woman who could handle him.

Did he want to be handled?

The question floated out of his mind, and his whole attention was focused on the way Charlie moved and smiled and laughed. Marie said something that had them all smiling as Charlie started to pass out the glasses, and then the gorgeous French actress looked up at her expectantly.

Oh, she was good. Charlie raised her glass and then turned to Helene, saying something that made the younger actress go a lovely pasty white shade. It also made the subby producer's shoulders slump.

Charlie proved she could keep up with the rest of them when it came to acting skill. She glanced around as though shocked at the reaction to her perfectly nice toast. She was mean, and that kind of got his...nope. He wasn't going to play this sucker down. His dick was hard as a rock and twice as stubborn. It didn't matter that she likely had another agenda and had just proven how good she would be at playing the game.

He was going to have her.

Marie tossed that probably expensive champagne right in her sub's face and then went after Helene in a flurry of ridiculously dirty French. She pointed and screamed and suddenly there were dungeon monitors involved.

Charlie was a gazelle. She leapt over the now crying and on his knees sub, barely avoiding the crop that was suddenly in the Mistress's hands. She dodged the dungeon monitors and found her way back to him.

He patted his lap. There was no need to go anywhere right now. Not when they had a show to watch.

She sank down and wasn't so awkward this time. Her arm floated around his shoulders and she leaned in, her lips brushing his ear as she whispered. "Was that fun for you, Master Ian? Because it was for me."

She was a bad, bad girl. He turned his head slightly. He made it a habit to not kiss subs. Too intimate. A kiss, he'd found, promised far more than a fucking ever did. A good fuck was a biological function but a kiss...a kiss was an indulgence. He hadn't kissed a woman since

23

his high school girlfriend.

He stared at her, their mouths so close together. Chaos reigned around them, drowning out the music that pulsed through the club in favor of shouts and cries. Something flew by his peripheral vision. It might have been a butt plug. He couldn't be sure because all that mattered were those eyes.

All the reasons he didn't kiss a woman flew right out along with that probably over-lubed butt plug. Suckers could be slippery.

But she wasn't. She was real and here, and his hand found its way into her hair. So soft. He couldn't take his eyes off her lips. He leaned over and pressed his mouth to hers, feeling the satisfied sigh that came right before he covered her.

He was in her web now, and he feared there might be no getting out.

Part Three

Three hours after the incident in the bar, forever to be referred to as the *French Flying Butt Plug Fight,* Ian closed the door on the privacy room and looked back at Charlie. He locked the door, wanting to shut the world out. He'd been patient, but it was time to be alone with her. She was seated on the bed, her eyes seemingly innocent as she stared up at him.

Her breasts were thrust up, the corset shoving them to impossible heights. It also made her waist tiny and gave her outrageous curves. He had zero idea how she wore that sucker for hours and never complained. The same with those wicked fuck-me shoes with the red soles. They made her legs look a mile long, and he couldn't help but think about how they would look propped up on his shoulders as he fucked her long and hard.

But first he had to slow his roll because he had some questions.

"Did you enjoy the evening?" After the dungeon monitors had broken up that awesome fight Charlie had started, he'd decided to walk her through some of the scenes planned for the evening. He'd discovered watching other people play together could tell him a lot about what a submissive needed sexually. He preferred to learn through body language rather than question and answers since so often the sub lied, rather out of politeness or ignorance.

"Some of them," she replied readily. "Though I was disturbed by the one with the cellophane. I don't like tight spaces."

Of course, the sub in question this evening didn't seem to have the same issues as the ones he'd topped before. He was surprised she would admit her fears to him. If she was the instrument of chaos Rene claimed her to be, she should play this whole seduction thing close to the vest. Instead, she'd been open and real with him all night. Right up until they'd hit the mummification scene. That had been when she'd closed in on herself. When they'd watched that particular scene, her shoulders had tightened and her hands had balled into fists. Yet she'd stood there and if he'd only been looking at her face, he would have thought it didn't bother her at all. Her expression had been perfectly placid. She hadn't reached out to him, begging for comfort.

He'd been the one to put a hand on her shoulders, dragging her back against his chest. He'd been the one to whisper in her ear that everything was all right and they could go at any time. And he'd been the one to thread their fingers together and lead her away.

The fact that she'd called it a cellophane scene and not mummification confirmed what he believed. She wasn't an expert. She might have played around a bit, but he would bet she'd never taken a collar.

He needed to figure this woman out or he might go crazy. It was time to see how far she would go. He would take her answers tonight and check them out. Likely she was lying.

Or she'd figured out that the truth was often the best way to play a man like himself. Either way, he was intrigued.

"Why are you claustrophobic?" He would call her issue what it was despite the fact that the submissive in the scene involved hadn't been in a small room. She'd been on the main stage of the club. The sub had been wrapped in yard after yard of cellophane until she couldn't move a muscle. The sub herself had relaxed the more her top had restricted her movement, but it had bugged the hell out of Charlie.

"Any number of reasons," she replied, her eyes steady on him.

He forced himself to move toward the opposite side of the room from her. He had to force his legs to work because every instinct he had screamed out to get her on that bed and make her his.

That wasn't going to happen. He took a deep breath as he looked around the room. Rene kept things elegant, even in his sex spaces. The privacy room was decorated as beautifully as a suite at the Ritz, though he doubted the suite was stocked with condoms and lube and an array of torture instruments.

There were three ways out. The door to the room. The window in the bathroom. The air ducts. Rene had shown him that he'd had the air ducts specially made in case he or his friends required a quick exit. Still, the first night he'd stayed here, he'd tested it out. Trust but verify—even his closest allies.

"How about you tell me one of those reasons," he said.

He opened the armoire, leaving the doors wide so Charlie could see the collection of canes and paddles and the different types of rope he could potentially use.

He expected her to tell him about a time when she was young and got trapped in a closet. Or that she wasn't sure, simply hated small spaces.

"My father used to lock me in a coffin as punishment. Sometimes he would leave small animals in there with me. Once he placed a snake at my feet and locked me inside for twenty-four hours."

It took him a moment to process her words. "What?"

"My father is the head of the Denisovitch syndicate, though I'm sure you already know that," she replied, as simply as if she were telling him the sky was blue. "Rene told you, I suspect."

"Yes." He forced himself to answer calmly because his heart rate had ticked up at the thought of the woman in front of him being tormented by her own father. His had been a shitbag, but he certainly hadn't been physically abusive.

A soft expression crossed her face. "It's fine, Master Ian. The snake wasn't poisonous. I figured out a way to kill it and I survived. It's in the past."

"Did you know it wasn't poisonous?" He was still trying to wrap his brain around what she'd been through. It wasn't that he didn't understand torture—of all types. He simply couldn't understand putting a child through it.

"I figured it out after a few hours," she admitted. "It bit me many times, but I was still alive. It's funny how logical a person can be even when they're terrified. But seriously, Sir. It's over. With the exception of hating tight spaces, I don't think about it much anymore."

"Do you still live with your father?" How could he kill her father? It would be a fun weekend project. How long did it take a man to die from having his balls squeezed in a vise?

"We've reached a standoff, my father and I. I do the occasional job for him and he leaves me alone for the most part. I would love to simply walk out of his life, but that didn't work out for my mother."

He could imagine. Now was the time when he should shrug and fuck her and move on. And yet the words that came out of his mouth didn't even vaguely resemble what his ruthless brain was thinking. "I'll get you out."

He could kill the whole syndicate. It wasn't like he wouldn't enjoy it. His handler, Ten Smith, might have a problem with it, but he could deal with Ten.

Her eyes had warmed, her body relaxing. "Like I said before, I'm comfortable where I am now. I can't change the past, but I can live for the now. Are you thinking about using one of the canes on me?"

He didn't like the change of subject. It made him suspicious. Of course her boobs made him horny, and his mind and dick were contemplating war on each other. Still, suspicion was an old friend. "Why are you here, Charlie? Am I one of those jobs you do for your father?"

She shook her head. "I'm not working for my father."

That wasn't a complete denial. "But you are working."

"Aren't we always working, Master Ian?" She hadn't moved from her position on the bed.

He suddenly wanted more control. It was odd since she was so perfectly calm, but he could feel himself losing command because he wanted to do exactly what she'd asked. He wanted to play with her. He wanted to forget his every suspicion and sink into top space and spend the rest of the night with her. "If you're here to distract me, Charlie, it won't work."

He couldn't allow it to work.

"Then you don't have anything to worry about, Master Ian."

His brain was working overtime, trying to find its way out of the trap. Because his brain knew she was a trap, a gorgeous, perfectly baited trap of some kind. He simply wasn't certain why she wanted to trap him. "We don't have a contract."

She considered him for a moment. "Do we need one if you're only planning on spending one night with me? I have a contract with the club. That covers us. My safe word is lemon."

"Interesting choice. I'm not crazy about lemon." Not that he'd had a lot of it. His mom hadn't been big on baking. All he knew was he hated it in iced tea, and it had been super funny to watch his kid brother suck on one when he was a toddler.

He probably shouldn't have been allowed to be in charge of Sean when they were kids.

"You would be if you ever had my lemon pie," she replied with a smile. "It was my mother's. I don't make it often, but when I do it's spectacular. If we ever meet up again, I'll have to make it for you."

Meet up again? She said it like she was going to disappear tomorrow and he might or might not see her again. He didn't like that thought. It played around on the edge of his brain, the idea of keeping her close while he was here in Paris. "Charlie, I'm on a job. Like you said, we're always working, people like us. I won't be distracted."

"And like I said, if that's true, then you don't have anything to worry about. Would you like me to leave?"

Hell, no. His dick shut that shit down and fast. Questions were one thing. Her walking out the door was completely another. He was going to have her. He merely needed to figure out how carefully he needed to handle her. "I'd like you to properly introduce yourself, sub. And then I'll make a decision as to whether or not I have anything to worry about. Knees, Charlie."

With a mysterious smile that went straight to his cock, she got to her feet. Rather than dropping to the floor where she stood, as almost any sub would have done, she crossed the space between them, her eyes coming up to meet his before she began to sink down slowly. Though she kept careful inches between them, he would have sworn he could feel her sliding down his body, their chests touching, her lips coming dangerously close, right where he wanted them to be.

Something about this woman. He didn't understand it, this wild attraction he felt for someone he'd known for a few hours. It was precisely why he should dismiss her and move on.

Dude, you have a job to do. Remember the CIA gig we signed up for? His brain was working overtime. *This is the job that will take us to the next level. Go America. Rah, rah, Team USA, and after you've done this job you can tell everyone who thinks you're a dumbass because you came in via the Green Berets to suck it. All you have to do is focus.*

Eyes on the prize.

His dick was less eloquent. *Boobs. Boobs. Boooooobbbbbs.*

"If you're still nervous about me, perhaps you should question me, Sir." She licked across that bottom lip he wanted to suck on and looked up at him. "You could tie me up and make me tell you the truth."

And just like that his brain shut off.

And he knew he was in serious trouble.

Part Four

Ian looked down at the woman kneeling in front of him and wondered if there was any blood left in his brain. His dick seemed to have taken all of it. He was supposed to be interrogating Charlie Denisovitch, but all he could think about was tossing her on the bed and shoving his cock in.

If his friends could see him now...

He was the Ice Man. No one got to him. *Down, dick, down.* When he knew what her game was, he would decide if he would play.

Yeah, because you're going to walk away from that, Tag. Sure, you are. She could have a gun to your head and you would still try to fuck her.

"Master Ian?" Charlie's big blue eyes stared up at him. Her dark hair flowed around her shoulders, brushing the top of her corset. Those silky tresses would likely curl around her nipples when he got her naked.

That was a bad idea. The better plan would be to tie her up, torture her a little, break her down and ask her the questions he needed to know. When he had her so desperate for an orgasm she couldn't think straight, she would tell him the truth or he would be able to see through her lies. He would bind her hands and use a crop on her, touch her through those clothes so things didn't get too personal.

Sex didn't have to be personal. It could be an itch one scratched and then moved on. He tended to keep his "relationships" light and purely transactional.

Yes, if she proved somewhat trustworthy, he would push that tiny thong of hers out of the way, fuck her hard, and send her on her way.

"If you've changed your mind, I can go," she said quietly. "I understand. Your job requires a delicate hand, and I'm not exactly clean. I'm an assassin, Master Ian. I'm sure the Agency has a file on me. You should read it. I'm here in Paris for a few weeks. If you're still interested in playing, you can look me up."

She started to stand.

He put his hands on his hips, glaring down at her. Apparently the look was enough to get her to sit her pretty ass back down. "I didn't give you leave to go, and you didn't say your safe word. Are you so ill trained that you don't have a patient bone in your body? Tell me about your past Masters."

"I was only saying..." she began.

He wound a hand in that soft as sable hair of hers and twisted. "I didn't require an explanation of your actions. I gave you an order to tell me about your past Masters. I'm going to explain this to you because apparently they did not. I'm the Dom. In this club I rule. You do as I command or you safe word out and we can be done."

It was how all of his D/s contacts worked. And yes, he called them contacts because they weren't girlfriends, and he didn't take permanent subs. He played and fucked and everyone went their separate ways. He didn't explain himself. He didn't have to.

Tears shimmered in her eyes. "I don't...I wasn't...uhm, I've had two Doms. The first was a training Dom and I didn't have sex with him. It was a club in Moscow. We were...are friends. He's a nice man."

Now they were getting somewhere. "And the second?"

She flushed prettily. "Uhm, I had to assassinate him. It was a perfectly clean kill. It was honestly the easiest breakup I've ever had."

He released her hair as the laughter bubbled up, easy and bright. It wasn't a feeling he was used to. The only people who ever made him laugh were Alex and Sean, and that was mostly when they were doing something dumbass. And the women he'd been with, god, they would never admit to assassinating an ex. Probably because none of them would have assassinated an ex. Well, most of them. He'd tangled with a chick from MSS who'd tried to murder him right after he'd given her a killer orgasm, so she counted.

Her lips tugged up in a sweet smile, and her eyes had begun to clear. He didn't want to think about how those tears in her eyes had made him feel. "So you're not intimidated by my job?"

Her job was the problem, but it didn't intimidate him. He kind of wished it did. It would prove he had a brain in his head, but no, the fact that she knew how to kill a couple of hundred ways did it for him. "Did you assassinate this guy because he was bad in bed?"

Intent was important in this case. He let himself touch her, brushing his fingers along the planes of her face and moving to her neck.

"No, though he wasn't all that great," she admitted, and he could feel her relax as he touched her. It made him wonder how often she received physical affection. "He was in my father's syndicate, and he screwed a bunch of the brothers over. It wasn't like he was a good man. I don't know many of those. You have to understand that I do my father's dirty work, but only within the *Bratva*. I wouldn't take out a witness. No innocents. He knows that now. I paid the price."

He probably didn't want to know how much that had cost her. He ran his hand along the long scar on her shoulder. God, that did something for him, too. She wasn't delicate or perfect. Her skin showed the tale of her life like his did. She was fucking damaged, and it was somehow beautiful to him. "No one's innocent, Charlie. Not in our world."

She was in his world. She knew exactly who he was and who he was working for. It would be good to know how Denisovitch had come by that knowledge. Yeah, that was why he would sleep with her. Sure.

He moved behind her, and she stiffened slightly. Damn, she didn't like not being able to see him, but she kept her position. How many men had come at her from behind, wanting to take what wasn't theirs? How sweet would it be if a woman like this trusted him, gave to him? "Do you have a contract on me?"

She shook her head and then sighed as he moved her hair to the side and traced the line of her spine down to the top of the corset. "No."

"Are you going to use me for information?" He couldn't help it. He was going to do this, and there wasn't a reason to wait. He pulled the knife from his boot. He always kept one there. "I'm going to take off this corset now. I would offer to pay for the laces, but I think you

33

can buy new ones. I bet your dad pays pretty well. Answer my question."

He eased the knife under the bottom of the laces and carefully drew it up, releasing the corset.

Her body shuddered as though deeply grateful for the relief. "I'm not using you for information. At least not the kind from the CIA."

He pulled the corset off her and stared at her back, fascinated by the scars he found there. The corset had been laced tight, and it left grooves in her skin, red marks that told him she could handle discomfort. The angry scars told him she'd handled pain before. Like he had. Had he met his natural match? The female yin to his yang? "What other kind do I have that you would be interested in?"

She seemed to think about that for a moment. The lucky thing for her was despite the fact that his dick was hard as a rock, he could be patient. The patient man tended to win the prize. He moved around to face her again. Yep, those tits were phenomenal. He hadn't been making them out to be more than they were. They were big and soft, and her nipples were pink and brown and hard as pebbles.

"I want you to teach me."

He could barely breathe. She was the sexiest thing he'd ever seen. "Teach you what?"

Her eyes met his. "D/s."

He reached over and picked up the crop he'd placed on the end of the bed moments before. He wouldn't give her new scars. He would never do that, but she would still be able to feel him tomorrow. Every time she moved, she would feel the ache he'd given her, and it would remind her of the pleasure he intended to give her as well. When they'd both earned it. "You've had two Doms."

"Only one I've had sex with." Her eyes were on the crop, and she licked across her lips as though she couldn't wait.

It made his cock pulse in his leathers, but he wanted plain language from her. "D/s doesn't require sex. What are your really asking me to teach you, baby?"

He had a feeling. All those scars didn't add up to anything good. She'd known pain. She lived what had to be an insulated life. What could he teach her?

"I heard you're good in bed," she said, her eyes on the floor in front of him. "I want to know what's it like. I want to know how it feels to have a man bring me pleasure. I'm not saying he didn't try. Well, not very hard. He was a *Bratva* man."

He brought the crop up to touch the bottom of her chin, gently easing her up to meet his gaze. "Charlie, are you here to distract me? Is that your job?"

"My job is to assassinate an enemy of my father's." Her voice was deep now, her eyes meeting his boldly. "My target is going to be here in two weeks. I'm setting everything up. The man I'm going to kill doesn't touch your world in any way except to cause you trouble. I'm not here to kill you or anyone you know personally. I'm here for a while, and the subs talk about you."

"What do they say?" he asked, moving the crop along her neck.

She took a deep breath, her head moving to the side to give him access to her skin. "That you know how to please a woman."

"What do you want me to teach you, Charlie?"

A bit of hesitance was back on her face. "I want you to teach me how to enjoy it."

"Enjoy what?" He had an idea, but he wanted to hear her say it.

"Sex."

He traced the crop down her breastbone to the middle of her chest. "Then ask me properly. What do you want me to teach you?"

"I want you to teach me to come." Her voice was breathless.

"That I can do."

He was ready to begin.

Part Five

I want you to teach me to come.

A single sentence had damn near brought him to his knees. Something about this woman. He couldn't put his finger on it. Well, he could, and he was about to—put his fingers everywhere, put his mouth and his cock everywhere.

His first instinct was the caveman one, to fall to the floor beside her, shove her down, rip those barely there undies off her, and claim her in the most basic way. Luckily he had a crop in his hand, and that reminded him that he wasn't a caveman and he had a different way to claim her.

Consent was a beautiful thing. Any asshole could take a woman, but it took a real man to convince her to give herself to him, to open herself to his dirtiest, darkest fantasies and share them with him. Sometimes he was certain he'd gotten into D/s as a way to shove that caveman down where he belonged. The woman in front of him couldn't be claimed by right of strength. She was the fucking alpha female and she would choose.

He would make sure she chose him.

For tonight. Maybe tomorrow. He was here for a little while. What would it hurt to hang out with her?

Yeah, he had a wishy-washy bastard in there, too, and he shoved that fucker deep. He and the caveman could play cards and shit.

The alpha male had a job to do. He stood in front of Charlie, pleased with the way her eyes came up. He hadn't told her she should stare at the ground submissively. There would be time to play that way later. For now, he loved the way she looked at him—like she could eat him up, like he was the hottest thing she'd ever seen.

Could she be that good at her job?

He let the thought float away. It didn't matter tonight. He brought the crop down to that place where her legs were spread, knees gracefully in a *V* and palms on her thighs. He let the tip of the crop, the tongue-god—it would be his tongue there soon—find her pussy. It was still covered with the silk of her thong, but that was all right. He could be patient.

Patience. That was the key.

He let the crop caress her lightly. "What did you like about your previous sexual experiences?"

She caught her breath, and he rather thought it was a challenge for her to stay still. Good. He wanted that. He wanted her to want.

"I liked feeling close to someone. I worry that I've used sex to try to make a man love me when I should have used it to feel good."

"No man is going to love you because you have sex with him. We're not wired that way. I'm not saying it can't work to bring a couple closer. I'm sure it can, and sex can be a bonding agent."

"Have you ever loved a woman?"

He hated the touchy-feely crap, but he got the feeling Charlie needed a bit of it. Beyond having sex with her, it was suddenly important to give her what she needed. Even if he found it distasteful. "I was engaged." He let the tip of the crop drift up to the slight swell of her belly, but his eyes were still on her pussy. "Her name was Holly, and I thought I loved her. I think mostly I didn't want to go off to the Army alone. I wanted to go knowing someone was waiting at home for me."

Fuck, he'd never admitted that to anyone.

"I think I'm the same way, Master Ian." Her breath caught when he ran the tip over her left nipple and then moved to her right. "I was lonely, and I was looking for something to save me, someone. I figured out I have to save myself. But I want to know that it can be good. I want to know why other women giggle and glow when they talk about sex."

He brought the tip up to caress her neck. "Is that all?"

"No. I want to not be afraid of it."

37

He'd rather worried that was in there. Growing up in the Russian mafia couldn't have been the safest, most secure youth. Most of the women he'd known had dealt with some form of humiliation or abuse at some point. "Charlie, I won't ever hurt you in a way that doesn't bring you pleasure as well. I promise you that. But I will push your limits."

She nodded. "I want you to do that. I need it because if you don't, I'm afraid I'll be in my shell for the rest of my life. I put on a good show, but I have my insecurities. I have my fears. I want to overcome them. I want to enjoy this part of life."

Brave sub. It made her all the sexier to him. It was one of the things outsiders didn't get about the lifestyle. It took courage to ask for help. Charlie had identified a part of her life that wasn't satisfying. She'd made a plan, and now she was asking for help. She wanted to see if sexual submission could work for her. It was a beautiful contradiction and the exact one that called to him. She was strong enough to ask the right questions, and that meant she'd likely be strong enough to bottom for him. They might be able to get what they needed from each other.

Even if it was only for a few days.

He thought it was time to shock her a little and see if she was truly interested. God, he hoped she was because his whole body was practically vibrating with need. He eased the crop back down to her pussy, lightly teasing her there. "All right, then. Tell me what turns you on. Do you like dirty talk? Kissing? Spanking?"

He flicked his wrist, and the tongue of the crop slapped at her pussy. It would be a hard, fast pain that should do nothing more than send a thrill of sensation through her, but she would need to be in the right mindset. Some women wouldn't ever like the sensation. Some could be persuaded to.

Charlie's whole body tightened and then relaxed, those hands on her thighs quaking. Her eyes had dilated and if her nipples got any tighter, they might implode.

Yes, she liked a bite of pain. Luckily that turned him on, too. His cock was probably as tight as her nipples were.

"That worked pretty well," she admitted.

"Move forward. Onto your hands and knees." He kept his voice even, and it was a true sign of his maturity. He was going to make this last for as long as he could handle it. She hadn't come here to get thrown onto her back.

That could come later, after he'd proven to her that he could give her what she needed, after he'd taught her what a pleasure sex could be.

She moved obediently, and the pretty globes of her ass were in the air. Sheer perfection.

He could hear the music from the club below. It thudded through the walls and added a low hum to the room. It gave him a rhythm to flow with.

"I'm going to explain what will happen tonight, Charlie. If at any point you get scared or worried, you tell me you're at yellow. We'll slow down. If I go somewhere you don't want to go at all, you'll tell me red and I'll stop. That doesn't mean the session is over, merely that we both need to take a break."

"You're not what I expected," she said.

He was sure she'd expected a hardass, and he could be that. "A good Dom is flexible. At least that's the kind I want to be. I want to give you what you need, and you don't need a hard hand. Not yet. I assure you I can be a bastard when I need to be. I can be an asshole of the highest order when the occasion calls for it. Tonight I want to be the man who fucks you so well you want sex more than you want your next breath."

"I'm perfectly green right now, Master Ian."

He brought the crop down on her ass. "That's for sending away my two playmates for the night."

She gasped. "I'm not really sorry about that."

He brought it down again, making sure he struck the fleshiest parts of that gorgeous ass. "I'm not either. This isn't punishment. This is reward. You'll find they're kind of one and the same sometimes."

He struck her again, loving how her spine shivered, but she wasn't calling out a safe word.

"That is good to know."

She had more scars on her legs, wispy lines that had once been angry and red. How young had she been when some asshole had hurt her? How much had she suffered?

He couldn't think about that now. She hadn't asked him to heal her freaking soul. He brought the crop down again and again. "I'm going to stop at a count of twenty tonight. Then you're going to stand up, take off that thong, and you'll sit in my lap and thank me for the discipline."

"Yes, Sir. I will, Sir."

He brought the crop down, spreading the pain out over her luscious ass and thighs. He was careful with her. That was the part that made everything interesting for him—to see how controlled he could be, to ensure she got exactly the right amount of pain that would prepare her for pleasure.

He watched as she would shudder and then relax with every strike of the crop. "Tell me how it feels."

"It hurts," she said, her voice breathy and deep. "And then it doesn't. You're quite good at this part."

He'd practiced a lot. He was at eighteen when her head fell forward. Yes, he'd timed that properly.

Or she was excellent at knowing how to play the game.

He brought the crop down again. He wanted to shut down that suspicious voice, but he knew it was for the best. He needed to think of her as a puzzle to solve, one that might end up being a trap in the end.

One more and he was through. Her ass was a pretty pink and she was ready. He could fuck her now and see if that satisfied him.

Her head came up and tears shimmered in her eyes, making them the most gorgeous shade of blue.

He was fucked because that suspicious voice shut down in a heartbeat. He reached for her and knew what happened next would change everything.

Part Six

He helped Charlie to her feet, her hand in his. He briefly thought about tangling their fingers together. He'd held her hand most of the night. At first she'd been awkward, her hand merely cupping his like spoons that didn't quite fit together. At some point in time, that had changed. Her fingers had wound around his and they'd meshed perfectly.

She meshed perfectly with him. Too perfectly. He knew he should fuck her hard and send her on her way. He'd done everything he needed to, but he found himself sinking to the chair and staring at her as she stood in front of him. His dick was hard as a rock, and that wouldn't bother him in any way except there was some piece of him that was softening.

He wasn't even thinking that word. He wasn't some romantic idiot. The woman in front of him was hot as fuck, and that was the end of it.

Her hands went to the only piece of clothing she had left. She pushed the tiny thong off her hips with an endearing klutziness. She nearly tripped and fell over as her right foot caught on the lacy thing. He jumped up to catch her, but she managed to stay on her feet.

Her face went pink, and she balanced against his upper arms. "Not as sexy as I wanted it to be, but there you go, Master Ian. One thong."

That hadn't been the only thing he'd asked of her. He sank back down and patted his lap.

Charlie stared at him for a moment. "Master Ian, if I sit on your lap, you're going to have to get those leathers cleaned."

Because her pussy was wet, ripe and ready.

He let his eyes narrow, focused his will on her. He hadn't asked her to take care of his clothes.

She said not one more word before planting herself right on his lap. Her arm went around his shoulders and her head found the crook of his neck. "Thank you for the discipline."

It was what he'd asked her to do. He'd set this particular scenario up with a dozen subs. It was his go-to move to end a disciplinary session and begin the sex. He would ask the sub to sit on his lap and thank him for the discipline. Then he would have the sub ride his cock. He would thank the sub for the sex and move on.

He did not shove his face into the sub's hair and breathe her in. He did not hug the sub tightly against him and revel in how warm she was, how smooth her skin was against him. He definitely did not hold the sub for long moments, cradling her to his body.

Damn but he wanted more from her. A single night with this woman and he knew the rest of his experiences had been somewhat hollow. He'd sought out physical pleasure, but this felt like something more.

This felt like connection.

"I like this, Master Ian," she said. "I like being close to you."

He liked being close to her far too much, but he couldn't find the will to push her away. He could find the will to tip her head up and bring his mouth to hers. He kissed her long and deep, their tongues playing intimately.

He didn't kiss often. It was too much, too intimate, but he couldn't help himself with this one. Her lips were lush, but that wasn't why he couldn't resist her. There was something about this woman, something infinitely warm and yet complex. Like an excellent Scotch. Somehow he knew she would burn down his throat and then settle in, filling him with her warmth.

He let his hands roam, stroking every inch of her skin, from the velvety fragility of her neck to her silky legs. He took his time because she'd never had a lover who took care of her before, who put her pleasure before his. She'd never had a Dom who lived to take care of her, who based his whole world around her.

Then again, he'd never been that Dom either, but the need was rising with every moment he spent with Charlie.

He hesitated, knowing that if he took this woman, things would change, and he wasn't sure that was what he wanted. His life was comfortable. Not in any kind of physical sense. His life sucked when it came to that. There was no nice home to go to at night. There was no real home at all. He went where his boss sent him. There was no real future beyond the next op. He would end up like John Bishop. One day he wouldn't be quite fast enough. All it took was one bad day and he would be done, leaving nothing behind.

"Master Ian?" Charlie's hands came up, cupping his cheeks. The expression on her face was soft, understanding. "Ian, it's okay if you've changed your mind. It's okay. I don't want to take more than you want to give. You've given me so much already. This has been the best night of my life."

Her soft words cut through him, and he wasn't sure why he said what he said next except that she'd knocked him on his ass. "Do you ever think about what it would be like to be normal?"

She shifted on his lap, the movement easy and comfortable, like they'd been lovers for a long time. Her eyes met his, clear and blue, open with honesty. "Every minute of the day. I wonder what it would be like to not be afraid, to trust the people around me. I wonder what it would be like to love a man, a good man, and to build something with him. It won't happen. I have too many responsibilities, but I dream about it. Do you?"

"I think about having my own club." But he'd been alone in all those dreams, the king of his palace.

Damn, but she would make a magnificent queen.

The dreamiest smile came over her face. "It would be beautiful."

She was beautiful.

The song that drifted up from the floor below changed from a deep throbbing R&B song to a familiar, bittersweet guitar wail.

Sweet Child o' Mine.

Her eyes drifted closed. "I love this song."

He loved it, too, though he hadn't understood parts of it until this moment. If he stared too long…

He kissed her again, letting the song and the words and the woman herself take him away.

He let go of his normal bullshit, all the posturing he did even in his head, and allowed himself to simply be with her. He kissed her again and again, their mouths melding even as his body longed to merge with hers.

Somewhere in the back of his head alarm bells were going off, as though that hard core of himself felt his walls shaking, but he ignored them all. It was so much nicer to ease her back in the big bed, to kick his boots off, shove his leathers down.

"You're so beautiful, Master Ian." Charlie was staring at him, her body taut and waiting.

She was the beautiful one. It was odd. No one had ever used that word to describe him before. He wasn't beautiful. He was bloody and battered, and sometimes he was more tired than he ever wanted to admit. But that look on her face made him feel stupid and young and hopeful.

He grabbed the condom, managed to get it on his cock. He meant to stand at the end of the bed and spread her legs, shove his cock in and let himself fly.

But her arms were open, and he couldn't resist the call.

He laid himself out, covering her with his body, not holding an ounce off her. She could take it. She could take him.

She wound her legs around his body, staring up at him. They were so close. He could feel her breath, her heartbeat.

"Please, Ian. I want this. I want you more than I could have imagined. Show me," Charlie was whispering in his ear.

He could show her what it meant to want. The idea that no man before had shown this woman the extent of her sexuality, her power. He could do that for her. He could be necessary to her.

He lifted himself up slightly, hating even that small distance between them, but it was necessary because he couldn't wait a second longer. He stared down into her eyes as he took her, slowly working his cock inside. She was tight around him, the feeling so exquisite.

"Tell me it's too much." He could be a lot to take.

She shook her head. "It feels so good, Master."

It felt more than good. It was sheer perfection. Her body was silky and slick, and fit him like a glove.

The song continued and he found a rhythm, connecting to it and to her.

There wasn't an ounce of pain in her eyes as he thrust up in her. There was wonder and joy, awakening in her eyes.

He felt that same awakening. This was new. This was something he'd never had before. This wasn't something that took him out of himself. This was something that made him more. She made him something more.

Her nails bit into the flesh of his back, but he welcomed the tiny pain. It reminded him that she was with him.

Her whole body tensed and her face contorted as she clamped down on him. Her mouth opened and she cried out his name.

He kissed her, drinking down the sweet moans that accompanied her pleasure. And then it was his turn. He wasn't ready for how hard the orgasm hit him. He was always in control, but this was a flash fire he couldn't contain. It rolled over him and he clutched her, his cock pounding inside, not wanting the moment to end.

He finally fell on top of her, their bodies slick with sweat, but he didn't care. He liked being stuck to her. It felt right.

Her arms were still around him, and he could feel her kissing his shoulder and neck. "Thank you, Master. It was wonderful."

There was nothing in her voice or actions that told him she was angling for anything beyond his affection. She was happy. He could feel it. He'd made her happy, and that did something for him.

He reluctantly shifted off her.

She rolled to her side and stared down at him as though memorizing his face. "I guess I should go."

Yes. That was exactly what should happen, but it wasn't going to. He was going with his instinct on this one. He wanted something for himself, and she was it. "Stay with me."

She stilled but didn't move away. "Do you mean it? You want me to stay for the night?"

"I want you to stay with me while we're in Paris." He wouldn't think beyond that. But for a few weeks, perhaps they could find a bit of the normalcy they both craved.

Well, in between assassinations and espionage. Normal was a

relative word.

"I will stay with you as long as I can, Ian."

He didn't correct her because this wasn't about a Master and a sub. It was about Ian and Charlie.

She settled in against him.

As long as she could? That was all he could ask for.

2

Sweet Child o' Mine

Sweet Child o' Mine takes place between You Only Love Twice and Luscious.

Chapter One

Ian Taggart frowned as he looked at his childhood friend. Sullivan Roarke had grown up with Ian, Alex, and Sean. As a teen, Sully worked the same shitty jobs Ian and Alex had worked for the same shitty pay. He'd given Ian some of that pay when Ian had a hard time keeping a roof over his and Sean's head. Sully had never asked for payback.

Until today.

"So what you're telling me is this douchebag lets you film his life and people watch it? Like actual living people who breathe and shit."

Alex, who was sitting beside Sully, groaned. "Ian hasn't developed tact in the decade or so since you last saw him."

Sully sat back with a wry smile on his face. "I wouldn't expect him to. And we don't call Hoover the douchebag. We like to call him the talent."

"Which only proves you have no understanding of the word." Tact was useless in Ian's mind.

"Perhaps, but I've made a lot of money off *Kendalmire's Way*," Sully replied. "The network recently reupped us for three years. Do you have any idea how unusual that is? I've been in this business for a while now and this show is my goldmine. If I can get six or seven years out of this show, I'll be set for life and I won't have to do reality shows anymore. I'll be able to move into scripted TV, which is where I want to be."

Thank god. He'd worried that Sully had lost his damn mind. "So you don't particularly want to film douchebag rich kids who think they're DJs and their model girlfriends, who shop and prove the American education system has completely failed?"

Sully chuckled. "Not particularly, but then I suspect you've taken on some jobs that weren't agreeable for the sake of money."

Oh, he'd saved a few people who he would rather have strangled. "True."

"So from what I understand you have to run every job by the rest of the team before you take a case?" Sully asked. "Alex explained it to me earlier. I didn't know that or I wouldn't have brought Hoover in today."

Normally, he would present the case to the team and they would decide to take or reject the assignment. The team would figure out who was the best operative to work the case, if they agreed to it. "You didn't just bring Lord Douche. You brought all his douche minions, too."

"The good news is apparently none of them eat because Charlotte offered them cookies and they looked at her like she was crazy," Alex said. "That's in your favor, Sully. If any one of them had touched Ian's cookies, he would have thrown them down an elevator shaft."

They were his freaking cookies. Sean had recently brought in an assistant pastry chef at his restaurant, Top. Ian was a principal investor so he tended to treat Macon Miles like his own personal bakery. Adam's baby bro didn't seem to mind. He'd kept Ian supplied with sweets. Ian needed them because he was caught in a never-ending cycle of pain. He got nervous about Charlie giving birth and he ate. He got worried that he was going to end up as big as Charlie and with no actual babies coming out of him, so he worked out. He then worried he was working out too much and neglecting Charlie and he reached for the cookies again.

He was going to be so freaking happy when the demons were all born and life could get back to...

Yeah, he wasn't sure what normal was anymore.

He really wanted one of those cookies followed by a couple of rounds of punching the shit out of someone in the ring he'd set up at the new Sanctum facility. Or he could punch Hoover Kendalmire. That would be fun, too.

"We're taking the case," Alex assured Sully.

They were. Because he owed Sully for all those precious ten dollar bills he would slip to Sean for school lunches and for showing up with pizza right about the time Ian's paycheck would run out. "How many times has he been assaulted?"

"Yesterday makes three. It was a really close call. Someone took a shot at him. We have it on camera," Sully explained.

Ian had already looked over the footage. Hoover and his model girlfriend, Brie, had been filming their high-end picnic when someone had taken a shot at Hoover with a high-powered rifle. Unfortunately, they'd only managed to hit the bottle of Cristal that had then splattered all over Brie's overpriced shirt and she'd thrown a fit. She hadn't been pissed someone had nearly taken off her boyfriend's head, but damn she wanted to hurt whoever had ruined her designer wear.

Ian wished whoever had tried to kill the fucker had been better at their job. He sighed and leaned forward. "Why don't you go and join your crazies in the conference room. Alex and I will be right out. I want to take one more look at that footage before we talk to…god, I hate even saying his name…Hoover."

Sully stood. "Yeah, his parents had more money than sense. I often think they named him after the vacuum cleaner, which is oddly appropriate since he sucks the intelligence out of any room he enters. But damn that kid's got a million-watt smile. And if you can solve this case without Hoover dying, I can use all of this as a storyline for next season. If the kid dies, so does the show. But you aren't going to let that happen. I know you, Ian. You're going to solve this in no time."

Sully was smiling as he left the office. At least someone was happy.

"I say we put Si and Jesse on this case." Alex got straight to the point. "Phoebe and Chelsea won't mind a couple of months in LA. I'll estimate the project at roughly six to eight weeks. We'll need to interview everyone involved and get a feel for what the victim's life is like. I've already been on the phone with LAPD. Derek has a friend in the Threat Management Unit. They're overtasked and apparently Brie and Hoover are difficult to deal with. What a surprise."

Ian touched a button on his computer and looked over the footage again. The shooter had been roughly five hundred feet away, in a cluster of trees. The shot would have taken off Hoover's head if he hadn't caught sight of his reflection in the bottle of champagne. The dumbass actually picked up the bottle and started to admire himself. His narcissism saved his life.

The cops had found the spot where the shooter had likely stood, but they couldn't determine much. The spot was a hiker paradise. There had been too many footprints to make any kind of guess.

"I'll talk to them. Maybe we should send one of the new guys, too." He'd recently set up a close-cover bodyguard unit within McKay-Taggart. His operatives were almost all family men, and that didn't seem to go well with twenty-four seven close cover. "Do you find any of the new bodyguards annoying? Because I want to set someone annoying on this guy. Jesse and Si will be too nice. Hey, maybe Chelsea can do some of that rat bastard stuff she used to do to me."

Like putting him on a no-fly list and subjecting him to body cavity searches every time he flew. It had been a complete dick move and one he respected. He didn't fuck with his sister-in-law much anymore. She was mean and he could understand that.

Charlie could be mean, too, but when she was he would spank her sweet ass and show her who was boss. Well, *she* was boss and he damn well knew it, but in the bedroom there was no question who topped who.

God, he wanted to top her. Lately, he was too worried to. He looked at that big belly of hers and worried things were going to change again.

"Stop."

Alex's words had Ian looking up. "What?"

"You've got your 'worried dad' face on."

Ian frowned. "I do not have one of those."

"You do," Alex countered. "It's a little like your 'I'm going to murder someone' face but slightly less happy. You're going to be fine."

He hated this. Hated all this touchy-feely shit. Still… Alex was kind of his go-to guy. If he couldn't talk to Alex, he couldn't talk to anyone. "I have no idea how to raise girls. Why couldn't they have had penises? I know what to do with a boy. Shove 'em out in the backyard and let them free range for a few years. They'll build their own cabins and become self-sufficient. I don't think I can do that with girls. Speaking of complaints. Why two? One I could maybe handle, but it's going to be a freaking girl gang at my house. Do you think they're pulling a fast one on dear old Dad? Maybe they're hiding their penises and laughing their asses off in utero."

Alex laughed, the sound lightening the mood. "This has been a fun nine months for me, brother. I can't wait for the rest because there are no penises and that gang of girls is going to be so much fun for me to watch when they get to be teens."

Ian shuddered. He didn't want to think about teens.

Alex leaned forward, that sensitive "I'm about to give you words of wisdom because I watched a lot of Oprah in my time" look on his face. "You're going to be fine, Ian. I know you think because your dad walked out that you won't know what to do, but Sean would disagree. Sean would tell you you've already been a great dad. There's only one rule."

"Don't kill the children. Charlie already made me promise." He didn't like the fact that Alex was right. Or that the idea of Sean thinking he was going to be good at the father thing made him a little soft on the inside.

Alex rolled his eyes. "God, you're a pain in the ass."

"What?" He wanted to know. "What's the one rule?"

"Be there," Alex said. "And let me tell you, Ian Taggart's got that one down. So relax. You're going to be a pro at this in no time. And I think you're going to look good in the pink sling Eve bought you."

"Oh, that was so not Eve, asshole." The baby shower had been a revelation. So much fucking pink.

Alex gave him a shit-eating grin. "I laughed the whole time I was buying it. I tried to find a place that would bedazzle the fucker, but Eve wouldn't let me."

Ian stood. "You know what, I'm going to make that shit manly. You think I won't wear a pink sling? I will rock that motherfucker."

"If anyone can, it's you," Alex conceded. He grabbed his laptop. Alex would deal with setting up the project files and all the administrative stuff that came with a new case. He'd backed off of active duty since he and Eve had adopted a baby boy named Cooper.

Who would one day likely turn that innocent gaze of his on Ian's daughters.

"You tell your boy to keep his hands to himself."

Alex groaned. "Oh god. I hadn't even thought about that. You're going to be that dad. You know the one who thinks his girls are perfect angels and all the boys around them are the devil? Can we wait until they're born before you accuse Coop of trying something with them?"

Ian kind of thought Cooper eyed Charlie's baby bump as though he knew something good was going to come out of there. "You're wrong. I know my girls won't be angels, and that's why I intend to keep an eye on them at all times. And they're going to look like Charlie so they'll be gorgeous. No doubt about it. Those girls are going to be trouble."

He followed Alex out into the hallway. It was so weird to walk this hallway now. At one point the floor had been damn near empty. In the beginning, they'd only needed reception, the main conference room, and seven offices, though when they'd first begun, Ian had claimed they only really needed six because Adam was so far up Jake's butt they should share one.

He still loved giving Adam shit. It was one of the constants in his life.

When McKay-Taggart first opened, they'd closed off half the floor and now he was thinking about buying the floor below him if he could convince those damn lawyers to move out. The back conference room had been turned into a daycare center. Charlie now occupied a corner office where she helped Alex with the administrative stuff and was the chief liaison with clients and the outside world. They'd lost Sean to the culinary arts and the world was a better place for it, but somewhere along the way they'd picked up Simon, Jesse, Phoebe, Erin, and now even damn Tennessee Smith had an office, though he'd put Ten in the back next to the babies so he didn't think this was a forever thing.

He was a little scared he was going to end up with all of Ten's former team on the payroll. Since Ten had been disavowed by the CIA for getting too close to a dirty politician, his old team was slowly working their way into the civilian world, and they all ended up at Ian's office with their hands out. He would send the fuckers away but Charlie kept putting them on the payroll.

"Boss, you can't be serious." One of the newbies was marching down the hall, her red hair flying behind her and a look of righteous fury on her face. Yeah, Erin had obviously gotten her new assignment.

"I'm never serious," he replied. God, he loved parts of his job, and fucking with his employees was one of them.

Especially when he fucked with them for their own damn good.

She breathed a sigh of relief. "Thank god. I was hoping it was a joke."

Alex never fucked with anyone. He was practically Captain America. "It's not a joke, Erin. You can pick up your tickets with Grace. You and Theo are set to fly out early Thursday. You have a meeting with the security head of Faith McDonald's clinic on Monday, so rest up. It's a long flight and you've got a half a day's layover in Frankfurt. Grace gave you a nice long layover so you don't miss that flight to Monrovia. Also, since your cover is that you're an ex-military, down-on-her-luck girl looking for work, we put you in coach. I'm really sorry."

Ian snorted. Damn, maybe Alex did fuck with the employees. That flight to Liberia was a killer. "But we made sure Theo's got the seat right beside you. After all, a Master always looks after his precious submissive."

Erin's face went a bright red that could have been anger, but unfortunately her T-shirt was thin and that showed the truth. Poor girl's nipples had gone rock hard, and it wasn't cold in the building.

Really, he should get extra for playing cupid to the clueless.

"Send someone else with me," she said, her shoulders straight and her feet planted like she was standing at attention. You could take the girl out of the Army, but Erin hadn't yet figured out how to get the Army out of the girl. "Send me in with Case or Hutch or Michael Malone. I understand that I'm the only female operative who can handle this mission. Hell, I believe in this mission. I want to take out Senator McDonald as much as anyone, but I don't think Theo is ready."

Was that how she was going? "In what way? Is his SEAL training not sufficient? Was his time as a CIA operative too short for your liking? Or is there something else you would like to tell me? Has he harassed you?"

He hadn't considered that. Theo had been attracted to Erin from the moment he met her. There was obvious sexual chemistry between them, but also his half-brother seemed genuinely fond of her. He tried his damnedest to take care of Erin, though it was obvious she was scared of Theo. But if Theo had been doing something he shouldn't, Ian would shut that shit down, brother or no.

Erin's eyes slid away. "No, Sir. You know he's actually very kind. That's the trouble. I don't know how to handle it. I would be more comfortable with Hutch."

Because Hutch treated her like one of the guys. "Hutch is incapable of looking like he's in love with you and he has zero training in D/s. Faith McDonald has been in the lifestyle for longer than you have."

"Longer than Theo, too." It was obvious Erin wasn't giving up.

"But Theo has been training day and night." Theo seemed to have figured out what Erin needed, and he was trying hard to be able to give it to her. He'd been working with Ten under Ian and Alex's tutelage, and he'd come a long way. His brother was more than ready for this assignment. He was the best man for the job. Ian liked to fuck with his employees, but he took his business seriously. "Theo is perfectly prepared for this mission, and you're the right operative to get close to Faith McDonald. You'll be her personal bodyguard and you can bond over giggling and tea and whatever girls bond over."

Erin flipped him off. It was a good sign. He suspected she had some serious shit in her background having to do with authority figures. Flipping the boss the bird meant she was comfortable he wasn't going to hurt her. Now she simply had to figure out Theo wouldn't either.

"I'll take care of Faith," Erin promised. "I actually kind of admire her. She's smart and seems to be trying to do good in the world."

Unfortunately, her father was an evil fuck who sold out servicemen for a buck and made his fortune off keeping the wars going. Faith McDonald could be Mother Teresa and he would still use her to take down her father. "Don't go into this expecting a lifetime friendship. She's the target. Talk to her. Convince her to come to Dallas with you so she can meet a new Master. She's single right now, but the word is she always indulges during her off time. Get her back here with you and Ten will handle the rest."

"And Theo?"

Did he have to figure out everything? "Don't sleep with him. It's just your cover. Sometimes operatives don't use their covers to get a little something something." Ian scratched his head, trying to think of an example. It was hard. His operatives were the worst when it came to sleeping with their partners—Simon and Chelsea, Jesse and Phoebe, Alex and Eve—or being stupid fucks and falling in love with their targets—Sean and Grace, Li and Avery. Hell, Jake and Adam had married their freaking client. It could be their new slogan. *McKay-Taggart: We Don't Keep It In Our Pants.* Oh, well, there was one he could think of. "Alex and I went undercover once and we did not sleep together."

Alex shrugged. "He tried but I wanted someone a little more tender. Li used to go undercover with Karina, and he's never once slept with her. Then there was that first mission we sent Jesse on at the strip club."

Ian cleared his throat. He was pretty sure Jesse had slept with about ten of those strippers, but that had all been before Phoebe.

Alex shook his head. "JoJo, Eboni, and Misty Rose weren't his partners. Simon was. Si swears up and down they've never cuddled. Not once. So you're safe, Erin."

"You're all jackholes, you know that, right? And Liberia?" Erin was shaking her head as she walked away. "Simon gets to go to Venice. Li's biggest op was in London. I get a tiny clinic in West Africa."

"You're welcome." Ian shook his head as she disappeared around the corner. "They're totally going to do it in Africa."

"Oh, they will so do it, but then that's your plan." Alex started toward the conference room again. "You know she'll probably end up being your sister-in-law. Your girls will call her Auntie Erin and she'll teach them how to make homemade grenades or something."

"Yeah, well, I can't seem to get rid of anyone anyway, so I might as well minimize the damage. God only knows who Theo would drag home if he wasn't all moony over Erin. I'm pretty sure Case is going to show up with some chick he scrapes off the floor of a bar. That boy can drink." He had to smile because the light of his fucking life stepped out of the break room.

Charlie Taggart. The sight of his gorgeous wife made his heart speed up. He knew she was due to deliver their babies in a few weeks, but damn he wanted to fuck her long and hard. She was stunning, a freaking superhot fertility goddess who made his dick stand up and cheer every time he thought about her. She had a grin on her face as she caught sight of him. "Hey, those people from LA are completely insane. They asked for spring water but nothing filtered by modern hands or from any country with a dictator or not approved by Angelina Jolie. They also asked for water without carbs. Seriously. They think water has carbs. We could make so much money off these people."

It would be a miracle if he survived the afternoon. "How does Chelsea feel about heading to LA for a couple of weeks?"

"Months," Alex corrected. "This could take months, and Sully has promised to pay top dollar."

Charlie frowned. "I don't know that I want to be so far away from my sister after the babies are born. I kind of hate that idea."

"I'll figure it out." If Charlie wanted Chelsea, who was the single least maternal woman he'd ever met, around their babies, then Chelsea would be there. "Maybe this once, Jesse can work with Michael."

She went on her toes and kissed him. "Thanks, babe. And have you come up with a name yet?"

"Rocky." It was a joke between them now. "Or Rambo. Hey, maybe you'll name yours Rambo. I think they're perfect names for twins."

She made a vomiting sound and slipped her hand in his as they walked down the hall. "Over my dead body."

"Is he still doing this? What was it last week?" Alex asked.

Ian saw the conference room up ahead. It was full of Sully's "cast." Apparently, it wasn't Kendalmire's way to travel with less than an entourage. "Chuck. Girls can be named Chuck."

"Not if they want to have any kind of a social life. Ian, they'll be here soon. Mine is Kenzie. Her sister needs a name that wasn't plucked from an action movie." Charlie gave him her death stare but it was softened by the hand on her belly. She smoothed it over as though soothing the babies inside. "We can discuss it after the meeting."

He stepped inside, and Sully was talking to his people.

"This is all going to be over soon and it won't disrupt your schedule." Sully spoke in silky tones, like he was calming down an unruly child. "Trust Mr. Taggart. He's got a sixth sense about this kind of thing. We'll have you safe in no time, Hoover."

Hoover Kendalmire stood at the back of the conference room, his likely expensive loafers tapping against the floor. "My life isn't safe, Sully. There's nothing about this life that's safe, and I'm going to put it all into my music, man. You'll see. I'm going to be the new Eminem. Except way more attractive and less angry. Why so angry, dude? But seriously, I'm going to be the Eminem of Malibu."

Sully sighed. "Well, we can get right on that as soon as we get back to California. We'll be out of here soon."

An emaciated blonde flipped her hair back. Ah, the girl who modeled. According to her press kit, Brie Westerhaven was the daughter of a minor rock star from the eighties and a groupie who didn't know how to use birth control. The show chronicled her attempts to make it big on fashion runways while her dunce boy attempted to take on the music business in absolutely the most superficial of ways. They were surrounded by hangers on. Hoover's two brothers, his producer, who looked heavily invested in dental gold if that grill he was wearing was real, two personal assistants, who looked like they really wished they'd finished college and gotten real jobs, and the chick with the crazy eyes.

Maybe they wouldn't need months to solve this case.

Ian looked over at Alex, who shook his head.

"You can't know that," Alex muttered under his breath. "Don't, Ian. We should follow procedure."

"Do you see those eyes?" It was all so clear to him and he'd spent two seconds with these people.

Alex's mouth firmed stubbornly. "It could mean nothing. Let Jesse handle it. He'll follow procedure and we'll actually make money off this."

Brie shook her head as she paced. "God, I hope we get back to Cali soon. This is so boring. I thought Texas was one of those not real places. You know what I mean."

She glanced over at a woman who stood by her side, staring up at the model as if she was the second coming of the Virgin Mary. "I do. You're so smart, Brie. I didn't think Texas was real either. I mean who would? Sully, we should tape this scene. Brie is so funny."

"Dude, anyone who's seen Dallas knows it's real, hello." Hoover waved a hand through the air as though it was all too much for him. "Don't you watch TV and shit? Where do you think J.R. came from? It's a brilliantly ironic television show about global warming."

The pixiesque woman by Brie shot the DJ a look Ian had seen

before.

Damn, Sully had really lost his touch. He used to be good at understanding the people around him. Alex wasn't going to like it, but Ian really couldn't stand the thought of even having these people as an open case halfway across the country. It was time to shut this shit down.

He pointed at the girl because despite the fact that Sully was willing to pay by the hour, if these people didn't get out of his office he was going to launch a grenade at them. "It's Crazy Eyes. She's in love with Dimwitted Blonde, and she tried to kill Douchebag."

Damn, didn't they know it was always the one with the crazy eyes?

His wife turned, about to yell at him—yeah, he knew that look—but Crazy Eyes saved him from the inevitable lecture about giving peace a chance and shit by pulling a forty-five out of her outrageously large handbag.

"You don't deserve her!" Crazy Eyes shouted as she pointed the gun at Hoover.

All hell broke loose, but then it wasn't really a day at the office without a little chaos.

Chapter Two

"Crazy Eyes, I swear to god if you fire that fucking gun in my conference room, I will kill you myself, and you won't like how I do it," Ian swore. His heart was going to beat out of his fucking chest. Charlie was in here. If the bullets started flying, she could get hit. The babies could get hit. Damn it, they were supposed to be safe here.

Brie had a hand over her chest as though protecting herself. "Marcy, what are you doing?"

Sully put out his hands and eased toward Crazy Eyed Marcy with the calm movements of a lion tamer. "Marcy, honey, there's no need for this. Hoover wasn't trying to be mean. You know how he is. Let's calm down and talk about this."

Hoover had ducked behind the dude with the grill and was currently peeing his pants, if the smell was any indication.

Yeah, he was putting a deep clean on the bill.

"Charlie, get out of here." He didn't like how shaky Marcy was. And she'd already proven herself entirely incapable of hitting her target.

"It's fine, Ian." She didn't move, merely watched as the chick with the gun pointed it her way.

"Don't move," Marcy said, her voice thin and reedy.

"God, Marcy, you're such a drama queen." Brie huffed and sat down in one of the chairs and started to look at her nails as though the rest of the action bored her.

"Marcy, honey, why don't you give me the gun?" Sully asked.

"Wait, it was Marcy?" One of Hoover's brothers scratched his head and seemed to be trying to figure the situation out.

"Dude, I thought you slept with her," the other brother whispered in a too loud voice.

Marcy pointed the gun toward Tweedle Dee and Tweedle Dumb. "I only love Brie. I would never sleep with any of you."

Alex leaned toward him. "You get Charlie and I'll take down the girl."

Ian nodded. He had to be careful. Normally he would simply hit Charlie with the force of a steamroller, placing his body over hers so if a bullet came their way it would take him out instead of her. But her body wasn't her own. Her body held their babies. His girls. All three of his girls were in danger. His heart pounded in his chest, adrenaline coursing through his bloodstream. Normally he went ice cold in these situations. Charlie was deadly all on her own. His wife could take care of herself, though he preferred to handle the dangerous stuff. She was competent, but she was almost nine months pregnant. God, if anything happened to his girls…

Charlie had died once. Oh, it had all been a ploy in a spy game they'd been playing, but he'd spent five years in hell mourning her. He couldn't do it again. He couldn't lose her again and god, he couldn't lose their daughters. He had a sudden vision of burying all three of them, and it stopped him in his tracks.

"Ian, are you all right?" Alex whispered.

And that was the moment Charlie chose to make her play. Marcy had backed up, moving away from Sully, who seemed to be putting himself between the gun and his star. Unfortunately, it moved Marcy's back close to Charlie, who had her in a choke hold before Ian could scream. The gun fell out of Marcy's hand, clattering to the floor.

"Oh, my god. Something's kicking me!" Marcy said before her eyes closed and she went limp.

Charlie let her drop to the floor and Alex was kicking the gun away before Ian could move. She grinned his way, her hand on her belly. "Ian, the babies just went crazy. I swear to god they could tell we were taking someone down. They're already helping Mommy take out the bad guys." She frowned. "Babe, are you all right? You are seriously pale."

Ian sat, staring ahead as he tried to get himself under control.

* * * *

"I think you broke him," Eve whispered to Charlie two hours later.

"I can still hear, you know." He hadn't moved in hours. He was replaying the situation over and over in his brain. The sight of Charlie creeping up on a woman with a gun while she was super pregnant wasn't one that would go away easily.

The Dallas Police had shown up and hauled Crazy Eyes off to prison. She was about to find out just how damn real Texas was, complete with a prison system where she could totally find a new girlfriend since Brie wasn't interested. She hadn't been all that interested in Hoover, who had required a change of pants, either. She had been interested when the press had shown up downstairs.

Derek was going to keep McKay-Taggart's name out of it so they didn't become the go-to security firm for douchebag reality stars. Lieutenant Brighton had tried to question Ian, but all he'd managed to say was something about asking Charlie since she was freaking Superwoman and his babies in utero could kick ass.

Jesus. He couldn't breathe.

"Babe, do you want something to eat? I can have Sean bring lunch over." Charlie was using a deeply soothing tone on him as she rubbed his shoulders.

"Not hungry." He might never eat again.

"How about some Scotch?" Charlie asked.

"I know Alex has some eighteen-year-old," Eve offered. "Or we could go back to my office and sit and talk. You've been through something traumatic. You need a safe place to discuss your feelings."

That got him moving. He wasn't going to have a flipping session. "I'm fine."

He stood up and started down the hall but not before he noticed Eve taking a twenty-dollar bill from Charlie, who was shaking her head.

"Told you it would work," Eve said under her breath. "Now you need to go and fix him. That man is in serious denial."

He wasn't in denial. He knew damn well there was absolutely nothing he could do. He strode down the hallway. It was utterly out of his control. He hated this. He wasn't in control of fucking anything anymore.

Adam started to walk out of his office and shrank right back in when he saw the look on Ian's face. At least one person was still afraid of him.

He needed more fear from his employees. He should begin routine beatings. Yes, that would make him feel better. He could randomly beat the shit out of people, and then he would have the illusion of control.

Because it was all an illusion.

He'd just sat down in his chair when she came through the door, closed it quietly, and locked it behind her.

What was that about?

"Ian, I know you're mad."

"I'm not mad." He couldn't be mad. She was ridiculously pregnant and that meant he couldn't get mad. He couldn't take charge. He couldn't do fucking anything. He was supposed to be "supportive" and calm, even when she did stupid things like take down a killer with a choke hold.

"Yes, you are furious, and I don't really understand how you aren't yelling at me. Come on, babe. It would make you feel so much better. Do you want me to get the paddle out? It's been a while since you gave me a good long spanking. We could both use it."

Yes, he could so use a nice session where he took out all of his frustrations on her gorgeous backside. But again, she was pregnant. "I think you're right. I'll have some Scotch and chill out here. It's not a problem, though I'm sure Alex is pissed I didn't draw this out."

She reached out a hand, and when he thought she would lower herself into his lap, her knees found the carpet and she knelt down beside him. "You always have had an instinct for finding crazy eyes."

"Baby, that can't be comfortable. Let me help you up."

She shook her head. "No, I want to be here. You have got to stop treating me like I'm made of glass. I'm fine. You're the one who's fragile right now."

"I am not fragile, Charlie."

A little glint hit her eyes. "Prove it."

Frustration raced through him like a freight train. When she got that light in her eyes, he was usually in for a hell of a time. His Charlie could take as much as he could give. Their kinks matched beautifully. He topped and she loved to be topped.

If he was honest, he would say his kinks changed for her. He'd been hardcore, dominating women for both discipline and sex. His D/s style had been rigid. Now he was a lovingly indulgent top who spanked his wife more because she liked it than for any real disciplinary reasons.

Though today, he'd definitely wanted to smack her ass for pulling that stunt. She could have been killed. She could have lost the babies. Anything could have happened.

"I'm not going to talk you into punishing me, am I?" Charlie asked, her eyes wide and innocent.

He wanted to, but he didn't dare. She was so close to delivery. She might think she was Superwoman, but she was pregnant with twins, and he would be damned if he caused her a single moment's discomfort until she was fully recovered.

Then all bets were off and her ass was his.

And he would still have to deal with the fact that he wasn't in control. Two small girls would prove that to him once and for all. He couldn't control those girls. Kenzie and…

One of his babies didn't have a name yet, and he couldn't come up with one. He'd been joking about Rambo, but he couldn't for the life of him come up with a name. The one thing Charlie had asked him to do.

"Ian, you're going to be good at this. Everything is going to be fine. I know you're scared, and I didn't make that any better by taking down crazy pants by myself. I think you need to relax. You've spent the last several months catering to my every whim, and I really need to pay you back for that." Her hands were close to the fly of his slacks. She was on her knees, that gorgeous mouth of hers trembling. "I need you to top me. I need to know that you still want me. For weeks you've been so sweet and so distant. I know I'm big, but I still need you. I need to be more than the mother of your children. I need to be your wife. God, I miss being your submissive."

And he longed to be her Master. If he was gentle, he wouldn't hurt her.

He twisted a hand in her hair, pulling lightly. He wouldn't be too gentle. Charlie wouldn't like that. He pulled just enough to watch her eyes go soft as she began to submit. "You want to play, brat? You want to play after that stunt you pulled? I need you to understand a few things, Charlie Taggart. Your ass is mine as soon as those two girls who are renting move out."

She bit her bottom lip before running her tongue over it. "What are you going to do to it, Master?"

Fuck. He was going to come before she touched him. He took a tight rein on that unruly and desperate cock of his. She was right. They both needed this. He needed a few moments where he could pretend everything was the same. "I'm going to slap that sweet ass silly. Have you seen some of the new toys I've bought for you, my love? Unzip my slacks and take my cock out. You're going to see to me while I explain how bad it's going to get for you in a few weeks."

He let go of her hair, and she eagerly moved forward, her hands on the fly of his pants in an instant.

It was one of the things he adored about his wife. She didn't hold back or prevaricate. She loved playing with him and she didn't hold back her affection. It was Charlie's honest need for him that had first broken through his defenses and allowed him to love her openly and with a free heart. God, he fucking loved her.

He was also going to torture her.

His cock popped out as she drew back the band of his boxers. He was already hard as a rock and wanting, but he was going to enjoy this, and that meant not shooting off the minute she touched him no matter how much the bastard wanted to. "Lick me. I want you to suck my cock until I tell you to stop, but I swear to god, Charlie, if you're in pain because of the position, you better tell me."

Charlie groaned, and her only real reply to him was a long lick of her tongue over his dick. Her hand disappeared and he groaned as he felt that soft palm cup his balls. She rolled them lightly as she swiped at his cockhead, licking up the cream he was already producing. His dick was always ready to go where she was concerned.

So fucking good. His wife knew exactly how he liked it. She leaned over, her strawberry blonde hair flowing all around, and she sucked at the head of his cock. He shifted his hips, trying to make it easier on her. She settled in and started to suck his cock in long passes. Pure pleasure swamped him, but he hadn't forgotten what he promised her.

He settled back and watched his cock disappear between her plump lips. "Once you're recovered, I'm going to take you to Sanctum. It'll take a few months, but it's going to be perfect. I've stocked it with everything I need to torture you. You won't believe the things I've bought. New plugs to open up your asshole with. Pretty clamps for your nipples."

Her head came up. "It might take a while to get to those, Ian. I plan to breastfeed. You know how sensitive they are now."

They were crazy sensitive now. He could lick one and practically make her come. Her whole body had been sensitive lately. After the initial vomiting period, Charlie had been all about getting a little something something, until the final month when she'd been somewhat miserable because she had two extra humans in her body.

Why did his sperm have to be overachieving? Two babies? Three girls. He was going to be so overwhelmed.

He growled and pushed her back to his cock. "I do not need to talk about lactation right now." Although her breasts were larger. Plump and round. Sexy. He knew the reasons for the change, but he couldn't see her as anything but stunning. And his.

"I built a privacy room that's just for us, baby." He wouldn't have to share it with anyone because there were plenty. He'd built them a suite complete with a massive bathroom. The shower and soaking tub were built for the two of them. The tile was heated because her feet were always cold and the towel racks warmed the big fluffy bath sheets he'd ordered for her. The bed was huge and there would be an armoire stocked with everything he would need to torture his pretty submissive. In that room they wouldn't be husband and wife. They wouldn't be partners. They wouldn't be parents. In that room, they would be lovers, Master and sub. Ian and Charlie.

"I can't wait to see it." She sucked the head of his cock, sending pleasure coursing through his system. Her tongue bathed his dick. Over and over, she laved him with affection.

He was a possessive asshole, but he wasn't going to change. She belonged to him. She'd belonged to him since that moment he'd looked across the dungeon floor in Paris and saw her. Back then she'd had dark hair, but that mischievous grin had been the same.

Lexi Blake

He'd known then and there that he wanted her. It hadn't taken long to figure out he wanted her forever.

Suddenly, he needed more. As she sucked him, he could see it—their life together playing out in sharp scenes in his head. Those first days when he realized what it meant to go crazy over a woman. He'd never wanted anyone the way he had Charlie. It had been refreshing and terrifying all at once. That first time he'd slid into her body, forcing his way in as she clung to him. *Sweet Child o' Mine* had played throughout the club, and they'd taken way longer in the privacy room than he'd signed them up for. He saw her standing there in London as he'd made her his wife and no matter what he did, he would always see her dead. It was always on the edge of his consciousness. He knew what it felt like to lose Charlie.

And to get her back. He could feel himself opening the door the night Alex and Eve had remarried. One moment changed everything. One turn of a doorknob had shifted him into another world—one where Charlie was alive again.

He'd fought her. He'd fought so hard and now he couldn't think of a single reason why. He should have gotten on his knees and thanked the fucking universe for the second chance he'd been given.

There was no one—no other woman in the world—who moved him, who challenged him, who completed him.

He tugged her off his dick. If she went much longer, he would come in her mouth, and that wasn't what he needed. He needed communion. His love for her was sacred and he needed to pray. "No, Charlie. I want to get inside you. I need to be inside you."

He stood, not giving a damn that his slacks slid off. He reached down to draw her up. She was heavier, but that was only because she was carrying their babies. The truth was, she was beautiful always to him. She could gain or lose weight, grow older, change her hair. It wouldn't matter. He would see her one way. He was surprised to find out the Charlie of his dreams wasn't the woman he'd first met. She'd been amazing. She'd haunted his dreams for years, but when he closed his eyes, the Charlie he saw was the one he'd opened the door to. The one who had been smart enough and brave enough to find her way home. The one with strawberry blonde hair. She'd gotten on her knees for him that night, too.

"Charlie Taggart," he said in an authoritative voice as his hands found her hips.

Despite the fact that she was tall for a woman, she had to look up at him. "Yes, Ian?"

He stared at her as though he could imprint his will on her. "Did I ever say thank you?"

Her lips curled up slightly. "You rarely do, but you don't need words to say how you feel. I know."

But she deserved the words. "Thank you for coming back for me."

Her face softened and reached up to touch his, her fingertips sliding along his jaw. "Babe, there was never a question of that. I will always find my way back to you."

"I love you and you should know that if you die on me again, I'll find you. I won't let us be apart again."

"Never again," she promised. "Ian, I'm going to be okay."

She always saw through him. He lowered his mouth to hers. "You better be or there will be hell to pay. I love you."

"Back at you, Taggart."

Her arms went around his neck and he stopped thinking about anything but getting inside her. His tongue plunged deep and met with hers, sliding together. He caressed those sensitive breasts and felt her shudder in his arms. She was right. He'd spent the last few weeks treating her like she was fragile, but his Charlie was strong enough to handle almost anything. He drew her close and circled one of her nipples with his thumb. Even under the cotton shirt and bra she was wearing, he could feel the nipple go rigid, begging for his tongue and mouth. He unbuttoned her blouse and drew the strap of her bra down so he could release one plump breast.

"Please," she murmured as his hand cupped her. "Please touch me everywhere. I miss this so much."

He kissed his way down her neck, her skin so familiar and yet always so exciting to him. This was his true home. This woman. They could be anywhere in the world and as long as he was with her, he was home.

He leaned over and gently captured that pert nipple between his lips. He was careful with her, licking around the areola before sucking it into his mouth. Charlie shook in his arms, her hands finding his hair

69

and fingernails scratching along his scalp. He fucking loved that. He pulled on her clothes until she was bare from the waist up and he got those breasts in his hands. He dropped to his knees and began to drag the voluminous cotton skirt she wore over her big belly.

"You're sure it's not horrible?" She stared down at him.

She might still get a spanking. He dragged on the skirt until it hit the floor and then ran his hands over the outrageous curve of her stomach, smiling when something kicked back at him. His girls. They weren't calm or patient. They wriggled around as though anxious to get this life going. He kissed her belly. "You are the most beautiful woman in the world, and for that I'm putting you on the human hamster wheel. No talking shit about my property."

She was his and no one talked shit about his queen. Not even his queen.

He gently eased her back on his desk, his hand running down between her legs. He could already smell her arousal. Sweetest damn smell in the world. His fingers found her, parting her and playing through her labia. So hot. She was already wet for him.

Charlie spread her legs for him. She was supported by his desk, her palms flat behind her so she leaned back to where she could get comfy. Yeah, he could work with this position. He circled her clit.

"Hamster wheel?" Her voice came out in a breathy pant. "You can't be serious."

Oh, he was serious. "Top of the line. And after you're through breast feeding, I'll trade out the little water bottle for vodka."

She threw her head back and laughed, the sound sweet to his ears. Like everything his wife did, she laughed with great enthusiasm. She moaned as she tilted her pelvis up. "That feels so good. And you're insane if you think I'm running on a hamster wheel. Hey, maybe we should get one for the girls. If they're anything like their cousin, they'll be rambunctious. Carys is a little ball of energy. We can let them run on the hamster wheel for a couple of hours a day and then they'll sleep."

And she matched him for deviousness. "Done, baby. I knew Sean was too easy on that kid. He lets her play with Aidan and Tristan. He's asking for her to get involved in some weird ménage thing."

"Yes, right there. Oh, right there." Her head dropped back. "And you have to go easy on the boys. They're infants. They're not trying anything."

He wasn't so sure, but he would keep his own counsel on that one. And he was definitely watching the boys in his daughters' playgroup. He might even have a little man to baby talk with all of them so those boys knew the lay of the land. Charlie had liberal ideas about how girls should be raised. He was thinking about going old school and locking them in a very nice cloister for the first forty years or so.

She was close, but Ian liked to tease. He withdrew his hand.

His wife's head came up, those gorgeous eyes flaring. "Ian!"

He was ahead of her. He lined his cock up and started to work his way in. He spread her wide but kept the penetration shallow. In another two months or so he would take her hard and plunge deep, but he was careful now. "I'll give you what you need, baby."

He found her clit again and pressed down as he thrust inside her.

Something kicked him hard, a sure sign that those girls were going to make his sex life very difficult. Luckily, he didn't let anything get to him when he was fucking. They could kick all they liked. This was his time.

Charlie tightened around him, but he was ready. She responded so easily to him, as though she was always primed to take pleasure from him. He set a steady rhythm and watched as her breasts bounced as she moved against him, trying to force him in deeper. It wouldn't work. He controlled this, but he liked to watch her fight for her orgasm. He pressed hard again, the pad of his thumb tight to her clit, and she flushed. Charlie's body tightened and her eyes went soft. She called out his name and squeezed him tight.

This was what he'd needed. Connection. When he was inside her, everything was right with the world. The rest of it—the worry and fear—it fell away until there was only her and pleasure.

He felt his balls draw up and thrust faster, getting just a bit deeper. It wasn't all he wanted. He wanted to be balls deep, but he would take her any way he could get her. He was addicted to this woman. He craved her.

He let go and his orgasm flooded his system with pure joy. The world seemed softer than before, his troubles further away. He pumped into her, giving her everything he had.

He sighed and reached for her, pulling her close. Her belly was between them, and the girls seemed more active. He chuckled as he kissed her nose. He even loved her damn nose with its light dusting of freckles. "That didn't make them happy."

Charlie laid her head on his shoulder. "It made me happy." She draped herself around him. "I swear they're fighting for dominance in there."

He ran a hand over her flesh. "They're Taggarts. What else would they be doing?" He suddenly wanted to stay this way, alone with her, naked with her. "Baby, why don't you get dressed and I'll take you home. We'll take the rest of the week off. Hell, let's take vacation and we'll wait for the babies."

She turned her head up, a frown on her face. "I really am fine."

She wasn't because she obviously didn't understand him. "I wasn't concerned about your health." Though he really always was. "I want to be alone with you. In a few days, there won't be much alone time. I want some peace before the demons show up."

She laughed and lightly slapped him across the chest. "Stop calling our daughters demons, Ian Taggart. They are going to be sweet little ladies."

"So you cheated on me with the UPS guy?" Because his daughters likely wouldn't be very ladylike. Not if they took after their dad.

She hugged him again and then pushed away, getting to her feet. He kept his hands on her, making sure she didn't fall. She looked him up and down. "You are the only man in the world who can have his junk hanging out like that and I still find attractive. Naked is so much hotter." She proved it by turning around and walking toward the bathroom conveniently located a few feet away.

"You didn't let me get undressed, baby. You were too hot for that." He bent over and dragged his slacks up, tucking his shirt back in. His body was humming and the sight of his gorgeous wife walking across the room made him wonder if they shouldn't take a nice long shower before they went home.

She disappeared behind the door.

Why not take the next few weeks off? Alex could handle the administrative crap and Simon could deal with clients and operative questions. They didn't have too much on the docket. Sully had written him a hefty check despite the fact that it hadn't taken him more than a few moments to solve the case.

He could easily spend a couple of weeks nesting with his wife, and he could start by washing that lovely body of hers off in the shower he'd had installed a few years back. Back then that bathroom had been all about function. He often slept at the office in the early days. Now it was definitely helpful for those times when he and the missus decided to get their freak on.

And he suspected Sean sometimes hauled Grace in here just for kicks. It would serve him right since he'd screwed Charlie on Sean's desk at Top a couple of months before.

The heart wanted what the heart wanted…and his dick definitely wanted her.

He was almost to the door when it opened and Charlie stood there, her eyes wide.

"Ian," she said in a breathless voice.

His heart nearly seized. "What?"

"My water broke."

How the hell did water break…shit.

Normal was over.

Chapter Three

"Do you think they can tell?" Charlie asked when the doctor left.

"Yes," Ian replied. "They can tell you're pregnant, baby. They are really good doctors and they know a pregnant lady when they see one."

She'd lost her damn mind, but he was going to be supportive.

Her eyes rolled and she shook her head as she maneuvered her way to sitting on the hospital bed. "No. I'm talking about sex. Do you think they can tell that we had sex?"

He gave her belly a pointed stare. "Yeah."

She sighed. "I meant recently. I meant like two hours ago. That kid was all down there looking at my lady bits and I was wondering if he could tell you'd been up in that today."

"Not at all." Probably, but he wasn't about to tell her that. "All they can see is the centimeter thing."

Charlie's whole body stiffened and she reached for him. He moved as quickly as he could, giving her a hand to hold on to as the pain took her. It seemed to last forever, but he knew it wasn't more than a few seconds. His wife was in pain and he couldn't do a damn thing about it. Well, he could.

"Take the epidural."

"I will if it gets to be too much," she agreed. "But right now it would only slow down the labor."

He needed everything to slow down. He needed it to stop. From the moment she'd told him the babies were coming to now seemed like both forever and the blink of an eye.

The door opened and Chelsea strode in. "Hey, sis. Looks like my nieces are eager to get here."

Ian took that as a sign that he could step out for a moment. He kissed his wife and left her with her sister. Dr. Bates couldn't have gotten too far. He had a few questions he didn't want to ask around his wife.

He walked out the door and jogged to catch the OB who was standing at the nurses' station. Melinda Bates was a lifestyle friendly doctor. There was a small network of them. Dr. Bates had grown up with a mom and dad who were full-on 24/7, and she understood. It made Ian infinitely more comfortable to have her watching out for Charlie. She wouldn't look at them sideways if Charlie forgot and called out for her Master.

"Doc," Ian began.

"Yes, Mr. Taggart? Is Charlotte all right?" Dr. Bates asked.

"For now. Shouldn't we be doing a C-section? And isn't it early? The babies are going to be premature. Shouldn't we have things set up to take care of them?" They would be small. So fucking small. They would be fragile, and if anything happened to them it would be Ian's fault. This was his family. His girls.

"Ian, it's going to be fine." She put a hand on his shoulder, obviously tossing aside formality. "If she hadn't gone into labor this week, I likely would have pushed to induce her soon. The babies are at a good weight, and from what I can tell they're already obedient little girls. They're both in a heads down position and ready to be born. Charlotte's placenta isn't obstructing her cervix. This is a textbook case for delivering twins vaginally. Everything is going perfectly."

"And if something goes wrong?" He didn't even want to think about it. He would almost rather just get it all over with.

"Then we do an emergency C and she's still fine. Look, nothing I say is going to make you feel better. You're out of control and I can't give it back to you. This is woman's work and it always will be. There isn't a man in the world who's watched his beloved labor to bring their child into the world and not felt helpless," Dr. Bates said with a sympathetic smile. "But Charlotte is strong and your daughters are strong. Let them do their work. For now, all you can do is let them know how much you love them."

He nodded, but her words didn't really help. All he could see was

Charlie looking pale in that hospital gown she'd had to change into.

So many things could go wrong. He could lose them all.

"Ian?"

He turned and Sean stood there. He was still in his chef whites, as though he'd walked out in the middle of prep for tonight's dinner. Which given the time was the most likely scenario. "You didn't have to come up here. It's probably going to be hours."

Sean simply walked up to him. "I wouldn't be anywhere else. My sous-chef can handle Top for the night. I'm staying here with you. Grace and Li stayed behind to close up McKay-Taggart, but they should be here soon. I think you'll find everyone else is here. They've kind of taken over the waiting room. We are going to be hell on the volunteers."

God, he hadn't expected that. "Tell them to go home. Like I said, it's going to be hours."

Sean put a hand on his shoulder. "Walk with me. Chelsea's got Charlotte covered for the moment. I want to talk to you."

He stepped back, wary. "I don't need touchy-feely shit."

"Sometimes I wonder why we put up with you," Sean said under his breath. "Fine. I'll go to plan *B*. Ian, I've got lemon cookies Macon made in the waiting room."

"Oh, I will take those." As long as he wasn't about to get some lecture about the step he was about to take. He didn't want to hear about that. He kind of didn't want to think about that. Sometimes it was best to simply let things happen.

He started to follow Sean down the hall.

"Do you remember the moment you decided you wanted kids?" Sean asked.

Touchy-feely territory. Yep. His brother was trying to get him there, but Ian was good at avoiding the land mines. Usually he would simply walk away, but he wanted those cookies so a little deflection was necessary. "Nope. I do remember the day Charlie said she was no longer on birth control and what was I going to do about it. Here's a hint. I did not get snipped, which was the only option she gave me besides rolling the dice."

"Seriously, that's what you're going to tell those girls?"

He shook his head. "Nah. Charlie really wanted kids. You've seen her with Carys. Besides, Carys deserves family. After you and Grace made the decision to keep her a single, it kind of fell to me and Charlie to give her cousins."

"You make it sound like we did it to spite you," Sean groused. "The doctors told Grace another pregnancy could be very difficult. She wanted to try. I said no. Carys needs her mother more than she does more siblings."

This was the way it was with him and his brother. They worked out their issues through sarcasm. They didn't need the therapy crap other people did. "Well, I think she needs cousins. I will say if I'd known about Case and Theo at the time, I totally would have shoved this duty off on them."

"Don't even say that," Case said, walking up to them.

Theo was at his side with a big grin on his face. "I'm up to the challenge, big brother. Well, maybe not the actual babymaking challenge, but I'm willing to practice."

Case rolled his familiar blue eyes. "He thinks he's getting some in Africa. He's absolutely certain Erin is going to fall into his bed while they're fighting Ebola and stuff."

Theo didn't back down. "I'm optimistic. I'm getting her alone and I'm pleading my case."

"Yeah, she's going to respond by shoving her foot up your ass, little brother," Case explained.

Ian kind of figured that Erin would try to shove her boot up Theo's ass, but he also thought she might not fight him too hard. "Any way I can convince you to go to Africa and just get the job done?"

He'd often found that the people around him did exactly the opposite of what he asked them to, so he employed reverse psychology to get his way. In this case, it wasn't exactly his way. It was Theo's way, but Theo was going to waste a ton of time if he didn't go after that girl and take her down. She wouldn't respond to roses. She responded to a man strong enough to take her shit and protect her from whatever the hell she was afraid of.

Theo frowned. "I'll try, but I gotta be honest. I'm probably not going to try very hard. Something about that woman does it for me. I can't help it."

Case groaned. "I swear I'm going to beat him to death if he bursts into song."

Ian sympathized. "It's disgusting, isn't it? I had to put up with Sean singing about Grace for weeks."

"I did not sing, asshole," Sean shot back.

They continued down the hall. "I distinctly remember you singing and weeping and playing really bad guitar."

"I did none of that," Sean clarified.

"I'm pretty sure Theo's been writing poetry." Case fell in step with Ian.

Theo shook his head. "Never once in my life have I written poetry."

Sean and Theo walked alongside but there was zero way to miss the similarities. Case and Theo might be twins separated by mere minutes, but they were he and Sean all over again.

Before they got to the lobby, Case put out a hand and held Ian back.

Shit. Was Case about to ask him not to send Theo to Africa? Case could be super protective of his younger brother. Another thing they had in common.

"What?"

Case frowned. "I just wanted to say something. I know I was kind of an asshole when we first met."

"You can't help it. It's your personality." He knew what Case was talking about. Case had always resisted acknowledging their connection as anything past a coincidental biological link. He was wrong, of course, but Ian didn't bother to point it out.

Charlie, on the other hand, had been pretty specific with his brothers. They were family and therefore her responsibility, and she didn't care if Case agreed. A while back, Case had broken his leg, and without bothering to ask the boy what he thought, she'd simply moved Case into the spare bedroom and taken care of him while Theo was off on assignment in Dubai.

"Yeah, well, it's yours, too," Case shot back. "Look, this is hard for me. Could you please shut the fuck up and listen? I'm sorry I was an asshole. I worried you would come in and Theo would look up to you."

Ian felt for the kid. He remembered what it felt like to only have his brother. "I was never going to take Theo away from you."

"I know, but I think you should also know that I wish it had been different."

Ian could only imagine. "I'll get Charlie to back off. It was never my intention to run roughshod over you, Case. I just wanted to get to know you."

"That wasn't what I meant. I didn't mean I wish we hadn't met. I mean I wish you'd been my big brother, too. All those years…I wish it had been you and Sean and me and Theo."

The Taggart brothers. The very thought…he had to shut this down and fast. "You understand I'm going to beat the shit out of you."

"Jesus, man. Is that a tear?" Case looked properly horrified.

"It's manly hug time." He caught his brother and gave him a good pounding on his back. "And now we're done."

Case's mouth turned up. "Thank god because Theo would have drawn that shit out."

Sean popped back out of the waiting room. "What's going on?"

"Absolutely nothing," Ian lied because Sean would drag that shit out, too, and the last thing he needed was a bunch of crying dudes hanging on him.

"Not a thing, brother." Case gave him a nod and joined the rest.

Sean stared at him suspiciously. "Yeah, I believe that." He sighed. "You know you're going to be good at this, right?"

"I'm good at everything." But not this. Maybe he would be awful. He was sarcastic and didn't particularly believe in showing his emotions to anyone but Charlie. He worried that he was going to resent the kids for taking time away from her, and didn't that make him a complete asshole?

"Joke all you like, but in this I'm the leader, brother," Sean pointed out. "I know what this feels like. I know how awful it feels to watch your wife do something you can't help her with. You can't take this burden from her."

Ian shrugged. "Charlie's tough."

"And I also know what it feels like to worry that your whole world is about to change," Sean said, ignoring him completely. "And guess what—it is. Nothing you've gone through prepares you. A lot of people will tell you you've already been a parent to me, and in some ways you were. You took care of me. I know what you sacrificed, but Ian, I wasn't your kid. You have no idea how you're going to feel when they put that first baby girl in your hands, and nothing I say will prepare you for it. But I am going to say this."

"Do you have to? You know I think those dudes back in the sixties had it right. We should go and sit in a bar somewhere and a nurse will call us and tell us the baby's here."

Sean put a hand on his shoulder. "Wasn't that the life? Sorry. Come in the waiting room with me. I know you say you're not afraid, but I'm going to do this anyway."

He led Ian through the doors of the waiting room, and Ian was shocked at how they'd taken up all the space.

Li and Avery sat with Jake and Adam and Serena. They'd set up a small playpen and the boys were sitting in it while Carys held court between them. Grace was talking to Eve while Alex was pacing the floor, his cell phone against his ear.

"Yes, Damon. I'll be sure to call when they're born," Alex was saying. "Yeah, I know. Two girls. They're going to drive him absolutely insane. Say hello to Penny for us."

Simon was sitting with Jesse and Phoebe, and at least half of the members of Sanctum were here, too.

Sean put a hand on his shoulder. "I know one thing in this world and that's the fact that Ian Taggart knows how to create a family. None of us would be here without you, you sarcastic asshole brother of mine. So go and help your wife make our family a little bigger."

Ian did just that because the last thing he wanted any of them to see was the way his eyes had watered.

They'd come together because they'd all been defeated one way or another. They'd all been broken—by death or loss or failure. Ian hadn't wanted to lose them. He hadn't wanted to lose himself, so he'd started McKay-Taggart in order to give them all something to do.

How had they become more than friends? More than colleagues? Those people had become his family.

And his family was about to welcome another two of their own.

He slipped into Charlie's room, ready to face the future.

* * * *

Ten hours later, he was fairly certain his hand was going to break.

"One more big push and the first one will be out, Charlotte," Dr. Bates said. "You're doing great. I wish all my twin deliveries went like this."

Charlie grunted and squeezed his hand and seemed to put all her willpower into her task. Then again, she was trying to push two whole human beings out of her vagina. She glanced up at him. "You could say something helpful."

"Nope." He really couldn't. He'd spent hours watching her in pain and not being able to do or say anything that could make it better. He hated this. He hated every part of it. They were never doing this again. These two girls better like each other because they weren't getting siblings. No way. No how. For the first time he actually thought about getting snipped so she would never have to deal with this kind of pain again.

"Wimp." Somehow Charlie managed a smile right before she screamed again. And then with a long sigh, she laid back.

"Oh, hello pretty girl," Dr. Bates said. "Ian, do you want to cut the cord?"

He wasn't getting anywhere near that. He didn't even like the symbolism. "I'll pass."

He needed to stay with Charlie. He needed to make sure she was all right.

"You are lucky, Charlotte," the nurse said. "Any longer and you would have been giving birth to two toddlers. The first twin is five and a half pounds. She's perfect."

"Go and see her," Charlie said.

"I'm fine. I can wait until the other one is out."

The nurse was holding a tiny bundle in her arms that looked absolutely nothing like a toddler. Toddlers were resilient, if Carys was any indication. The kid could bump around all day and not really come to any harm. But whatever was in that little pink blanket, that was a fragile thing.

He was far more used to killing than nurturing.

"Show her to your wife," the nurse urged.

Ian shook his head. "Charlie should hold her."

81

Dr. Bates looked up from between his wife's splayed legs. Yeah, it was that kind of a day. "No. I think this one is close. Charlotte needs to push again."

Charlie nodded. "I can feel it. This one isn't going to wait. Let me see her, Ian."

Deep breath. He could do this. It was just one tiny baby that had recently been expelled from his wife's body. He could handle one small female. Hell, he was the Dom of Doms. He was the ultimate authority figure.

The nurse placed the bundle in his arms and Ian looked down.

The baby looked up. Not *the* baby. His baby. His daughter. She had Charlie's eyes and the sweetest cap of strawberry blonde hair. There wasn't much of it, but it was there. She had a little bow mouth and a tiny nose. And a totally misshapen head.

"She looks like an alien." An alien version of a baby Charlie. A gorgeous baby girl with a cone for a head.

"If you don't show me that baby right now, Ian Taggart, I am going to pull your balls off," Charlie growled.

He knew when to obey. Even the baby's eyes had popped open, as though she knew the sound of her mother in a killing rage. "I think this is the one who tried to take out Crazy Eyes. I'm naming this one."

He lowered his daughter down and watched in wonder as Charlie's eyes softened and she reached to touch her daughter for the first time.

And then her body seemed to seize. "Oh, here comes your sister."

He cradled baby number one in his right arm and held Charlie's hand with his left. He kept switching his gaze between his girls. The baby in his arms was yawning as though the whole event had been tiring but no big deal.

Her sister was born three minutes later, and ten minutes after that he found himself following his daughters down to the nursery. He stood outside, watching through the glass as the pediatrician began checking the babies over. Baby number one was wrapped in her pink blanket and number two was in yellow. It was a good thing because he couldn't tell them apart by looking at them. He wouldn't let them out of his sight and explained in no uncertain terms that his daughters wouldn't be left there overnight. Charlie had been very specific about it. She was keeping them in the room with her unless they needed to be checked out, and then Ian would be watching. At the time, he'd thought she was being unreasonable. She was surely going to need sleep. He'd been planning on quietly letting the girls go to the nursery.

Never. Not even once was he letting those babies out of his sight. They were his.

This was what Sean had meant. When they'd put baby number two in his arms and he lowered them both down to Charlie, he'd finally understood. He'd protected Sean, but Sean hadn't been his.

These two small things were his and Charlie's. They were proof beyond all doubt that they loved each other. Those girls were immortality, a way for his love for his wife to always live on. In that one moment, he understood what it meant. His love for his wife could be selfish. He wanted things from her. Love. Affection. Sex. Submission.

He wanted nothing from these girls except the right to love them, the right to protect and teach them.

Loving Charlie had made him a man, but these girls made him a father, and that was so much more.

"Look at that," Sean said, coming to stand beside him. The rest had gone with promises to come by in the morning, but his brothers had stayed. Oh, Case and Theo had both fallen asleep in the waiting room, but they were here.

Ian and Sean watched the babies through the glass as the pediatrician checked them out. Kenzie, daughter number two, was lying peacefully while his firstborn had already kicked out of her swaddling and was currently giving the doctor hell. Baby girl didn't like the eyedrops. She didn't like the shot. She didn't like being poked and prodded, and now the whole hospital knew it.

"That one's going to kick a little ass, Sean." He smiled as his daughter screamed her head off. He could already tell that scream wasn't about pain. She was pissed.

And then her sister tuned up with her, as though crying in sympathy.

Damn but they could make a racket.

"Any idea of what you're going to name her?" Sean asked.

"Yeah. I think I got that all figured out," he said with a smile.

Some time later...

"Kala? Isn't that like the goddess of chaos in Hindu mythology?" Adam stared at Ian like he knew something was going on. Adam followed him out on the porch, away from the rest of the team who were now getting ready to sit down to Charlie's welcome back dinner.

She'd only been in the hospital for two days, but Ian had made them wait two weeks before getting together in a big group. Charlie needed peace and quiet, but now she was ready to show the babies off to their family.

Naturally, Kenzie had gone to sleep right after her feeding and Kala had fussed, so Daddy was holding her close, cuddling her so she could rest. His Kenzie and his Kala.

Adam was always far too perceptive. It was precisely why Ian loved to give him shit. "That's Kali. Kala is a perfect name for a precious baby girl. In Sanskrit it means virtue."

Adam's eyes narrowed. "You looked it up?"

Maybe he shouldn't have mentioned that part. At the time it seemed like a really good way to throw people off the scent. Charlie had accepted his explanation of Kala without blinking an eye. She'd told him she loved it and that it was perfect.

If only she knew how perfect it was...

"I can look things up, Adam. It's my daughter's name. It's important."

Adam took a drink off the coffee he was holding. This dinner party was booze free since Charlie was breastfeeding. Sean and his sous-chef had made a grand Italian dinner for the group. The smell made Ian's stomach rumble. "I don't believe you. You're the man who wanted to name them Bruce and Arnold."

Ian shrugged, patting his daughter's back. She seemed to like to sleep on his shoulder for some reason. Kenzie preferred being cradled, but Kala always wanted to be up high. "I have a deep affection for 80's cinema. What can I say?"

Adam frowned. "I'll figure it out in the end. Hey, Charlotte. Did the other little princess wake up?"

His wife stepped out onto the back porch with Kenzie in her arms. "She never sleeps for long if Kala isn't close. We tried to force them to sleep in separate beds, but they cried until we put them together."

He loved to watch them sleep. Honestly, he kind of loved to watch them do everything. He'd never understood until he looked down at a baby that was equal parts him and the woman he loved more than life. He would sit there like an idiot and watch those babies sleep, cuddling together like they had in the womb.

"I'll go see if I can help with the prep work, but I meant what I said, Tag. I'll figure it out and I'll find some way to use it." Adam grinned as he walked back in the house.

It would likely be fitting if Adam was the one who took him down. He gave Adam more crap than all the others, but he was fairly sure his friend wouldn't figure it out.

God, he hoped Charlie never figured out he'd named their daughter an acronym for Kick A Little Ass.

"What was he talking about?" Charlie said, suspicion in her voice.

Ian gave her his most innocent look. "No idea, baby. You know how he likes to torment me."

Charlie laughed and sank into one of the two rockers on the back porch. "Yeah, Adam torments you. That's one world view. Sit down for a minute. Sean will come and get us when dinner's ready."

He sank down beside her. "Too many people? I can throw them all out."

She shook her head. "Don't you dare. That's our family in there, but I wanted a couple of minutes where it's just us."

Us had been him and Charlie, and now that one word meant something more. *Us* meant two sweet girls who would likely drive their father utterly mad.

He reached for her with his free hand. He always wanted the connection with her. "Think you'll ever want more?"

Charlie's eyes widened. "Eventually, yes. I thought I would have to fight you on it."

He shook his head. "No. I get it. I think I thought if we had kids, I would have to share you and I do, but I also thought somewhere in the back of my head that I wouldn't be me anymore. I'm just a different me. I like this me, Charlie. Best thing I ever did was to open that door and welcome you home."

Her jaw dropped. "You are such a liar, Ian Taggart. You gave me hell."

Sometimes it was good to be him. "Not how I remember it." He was good with his revisionist history. When she started to argue with him, he hushed her. "You'll wake the babies."

The gorgeous gleam in her eyes promised retribution. And he would take it. He would take everything he could get from her and give her back all of himself.

He held her hand and rocked while inside his family waited.

A man couldn't ask for anything more.

3

Adam Tells All

Adam Tells all takes place between Master No and Just One Taste.

Ian moved through the office, his mind on one thought and one thought only. It was the most important thought in his brain. He had to concentrate, had to focus because if he didn't, he lost out and the world would flip. This was the most important truth in the world.

There was only one lemon tart left.

He should have picked it up earlier, but he'd been a dumbass. He was going to buy that damn mini fridge he'd had his eye on. That way he could hide the treats Macon Miles sent up to McKay-Taggart.

There were technically three Miles brothers. Some douchebag twit, Adam, and the Pie Maker. Douchebag Twit and Adam had been false starts in the Miles DNA chain. Sure Adam had his uses, but the dude didn't provide him with pie. All Adam provided was sarcasm, and he had enough of that in his daily life. Macon was the prize. He was the man who could take something as humble as the simple lemon and turn it into a symphony for the taste buds.

Thinking about the Miles brothers made his brain go to the honest to god truth. To the real place his every thought went to. He'd lost his brother. He'd failed and now there were three Taggarts where once there had been four.

He stopped in the middle of the hall, the truth once again nearly sending him to his knees. It had been weeks since they'd lost Theo and every time it hit him like a fucking freight train from nowhere. His first impulse was to go to his knees and howl out his pain.

His daughters wouldn't know their uncle. They wouldn't have his unique presence in their life. He wouldn't know his brother as fully as he should have.

Erin had lost her love, her should-have-been husband.

It was on him. He'd been in charge. He'd overridden Ten, who thought Erin should have been second. He'd put Theo there because he'd played to his instincts. He'd let logic go in favor of affection. He'd wanted Theo to get what he'd longed for, and it had cost Theo his life.

His youngest brother.

"Ian!"

That shout saved him from hitting his knees and screaming.

He looked up and felt his eyes widen as Adam strode down the hall, his left arm pointing Ian's way.

Thank god. Something else to focus on.

"I figured it out, you son of a bitch!" Adam had the most triumphant look in his eyes.

He let out a long breath and silently blessed Adam's cantankerous nature. "Figured out what?"

Adam stopped, his eyes softening for a moment as though he knew what Ian was thinking. As if Adam knew about the war going on inside his head.

"Don't," Ian warned. He couldn't take a moment's sympathy. "Don't you fucking dare. Finish what you started."

Adam pointed a finger his way. "Oh, brother, I'm not doing this in private. Break room. Right now."

He shot Adam the finger, but he was fairly certain Adam understood that he'd saved him from a moment's weakness.

He couldn't cry. That was only for Charlie. She got his softest self, that place no one else could touch.

"Oh. I'm coming, you bastard." He followed Adam. He might as well have thanked the fucker.

His brothers always knew what he needed.

He hit the break room with a smile on his face. Adam had done his job as the resident drama king. Everyone had gathered.

He looked across the break room and saw his wife standing there, talking to Eve and Phoebe, a mug in her hand. Red and blonde hair swept over her shoulder, her lips curling up in a way that got his dick hard.

Of course, all Charlie had to do was walk in a room to get his dick hard.

Gorgeous. She was the most gorgeous woman who had walked the face of the earth and she'd given him two beautiful baby girls. His girls. Charlie and Kenzie and Kala. When he thought about Theo, he held his girls close and promised he wouldn't make the same mistakes with them.

And then he called his brothers and made sure they were all right.

Ian was fairly sure Sean and Case and Alex, Liam and Adam and Jake, Simon and Jesse and Ten wanted to strangle him. He'd turned into a worried old woman.

"Hey, babe." Charlie grinned his way. "What did you do?"

"Not sure." It had to be good though, the way Adam was smiling like he knew something everyone else didn't know.

"What's going on?" Li asked as he entered the break room. "Adam told us he had an announcement, but we had to meet in here because Ten and Faith are using the conference room."

Ten was meeting his father for the first time. He was getting a piece of himself back. At least something good had come out of that clusterfuck of a mission.

Alex and Kai joined them, along with Eve and Grace. Jesse and Phoebe entered, holding hands as they talked to Simon.

He noticed Erin wasn't here. She would be in her office, writing reports or plotting ways to get back into the field. She wanted something to take her mind off of Theo. He would send her out in a heartbeat if he didn't suspect what he did...

"All right, that's your 'I know something you don't know' grin," Jake said, sliding his partner a long look.

Adam stood in the center of the room and yes, he was definitely flashing a shit-eating grin. "I know something Charlotte doesn't know."

Ian went through a massive mental list of shit he didn't want his wife to know. Some things Adam had been involved in—like the time the guys set up a ramp across the creek that ran through Ian's property because Case had sworn he could jump it on an ATV. Yeah, they'd explained the destruction of that ATV as an accident. The same way they'd explained Case's concussion. It had been a beautiful train wreck. But one Adam wouldn't want Serena to know about either. The women didn't understand a male's deep need to watch his brothers make jackasses of themselves. It fed the soul.

Maybe Adam had found out that his preferred method of changing

91

diapers when Charlie wasn't around involved hosing down his daughters' butts. They didn't seem to mind, and he'd totally stayed away from the power washer. He wasn't stupid.

So what the hell did Adam know that was making him grin like an asshole?

Charlie had gone still next to him. "Is this about the ATV? Because I never bought that deer coming out of nowhere story. Also, you didn't hide that ramp very well."

Maybe he wasn't as good as he thought he was. Or Charlie was simply his natural match. "Baby, I can explain that."

She put a hand up. Yeah, he'd spank her for that later. "I do not need to hear about the desperate male need to watch people fall on their asses."

"It's better than that, Charlotte," Adam promised.

Ian was kind of interested now. Had he figured out the Sharpie trick he used to tell the girls apart? He'd tried to hide that from Charlie, too. Right until he caught her looking for the pink mark before she called Kala by name. "Let's hear it, buddy. It better be damn good."

"It is. Charlotte, Ian didn't name Kala because in Sanskrit it means virtue. Like he even knew what Sanskrit was," Adam said.

Oh, shit. Yeah, it was actually the one thing that might set his gorgeous wife off. "Baby, I can explain."

Adam moved on. "It's an acronym for Kick A Little Ass."

There was a collective gasp before Li's laughter boomed through the room. They all started laughing, with the singular exception of his Charlie. She'd gone totally still.

He was going to kill Adam. He'd read about a fish in the Amazon. It liked to burrow its way up the slit of a man's penis and settle in for a nice long stay. He could James Bond that motherfucker. He saw the scene play out in his head. He'd have a big tank brought in and he'd lower a bound and gagged Adam down slowly while he monologued the entire time. Adam would be able to see the fucker, but he wouldn't be able to do anything about it. Ian would explain that the eel-like fish's body was barbed, so the only way to fix it was to cut Adam's dick off. Oh, look, here's a handy machete.

"Ian?" Charlie was looking up at him, tears in her gorgeous eyes.

Or he could simply beat the shit out of Adam.

"Baby," he began.

"It's perfect." She nodded and threw herself into his arms. "It's so perfect. It's the most beautiful name in the world."

He pulled her close, his rate tripling the minute she was in his arms. "I thought you'd be pissed."

Charlie shook her head. "I totally lied. I told you Kenzie was a family name. I named her after a character on a sci fi TV show. She was beautiful and always had great shoes."

He grinned and chuckled. "Like you, baby."

"I want to fuck you right now. Do you have any idea how hot you are?" Charlie whispered.

A collective groan went through the room. Ian did not care that he'd likely fucked his wife more times at the office than anyone could count. It was his damn office and she was his wife, and he would take care of her wherever he wanted to.

He put his hands on her glorious ass and hauled her up. Her legs went around his waist and squeezed. "You're the hot one."

He kissed her long and hard, his body already ready.

"Get a room, guys," Jesse called out.

Luckily, he had a room. His office was the perfect place to spend an afternoon. His wife was the only person he wanted to spend it with. The girls were tucked away in the day care center and he could forget for a little while. He could forget everything but her.

He shot Adam the finger as he moved toward the fridge. He hadn't forgotten. A man needed fuel to properly take care of his sub. "Alex, could you pass me that tart?"

Alex shook his head as he gave Ian the small bag from Top.

"Damn it," Adam said. "One of these days, Ian."

He grinned at his brother. "Not today."

Today he would get what he needed. A little sugar. A little tart. A whole lot of love.

4

Make Lemonade

*Make Lemonade takes place between Submission is Not Enough and
Perfectly Paired.*

"I smell something good."

Ian looked over from the stove as his gorgeous wife waddled in. There was no other way to describe it. Charlie waddled like a cute penguin, if said penguin had swallowed what looked like a ten-pound basketball. Not that he would tell her that. He was a man who had learned how to handle his woman. If she asked, he could barely tell she was pregnant. He had to remind himself sometimes, he would tell her.

Of course, he could tell her the truth. She was stunningly beautiful when she was pregnant. He loved her every curve and the way her breasts looked when she was carrying his child.

But he'd discovered that depending on the amount of hormones flowing through her, that could go either way, so he stuck with the "can't even tell" plan.

"I thought you might like breakfast in bed," he said before flipping the pancake over the way Sean had taught him.

What he thought was that she should stay in bed and rest, but he wasn't going to mention that either. Charlie was two weeks away from delivery, and she got weepy at almost everything. He just wanted to make her smile.

This pregnancy had been harder on her than the twins. She'd breezed through Kenzie and Kala, but she'd struggled with serious morning sickness this time around. It lasted far longer than the first time around. She blamed it on all men, since according to all the sonograms, she was carrying his son.

Charlie made her way to the two highchairs that sat side by side. His girls were sitting together, happily munching on their pancakes. Kala was using her fork and carefully picking up the small squares he'd made of the pancakes. Kenzie's fork was on the floor, but it didn't matter to his baby girl. She shoved that food in after mashing it with her delicate fingers.

Kala was careful. Kenzie was vibrant and bright. He wasn't sure how they'd managed it, but somehow the twins had mirrored their parents' personalities.

One day Kala would be a deadly assassin. Kenzie likely would be, too, but she would do it all with a sunny smile on her face.

"I wanted to walk a bit," Charlie said as she leaned over to kiss Kala's head. "My lower back is tight."

This was the part he hated. He loved her being pregnant, adored putting his hand on her belly and feeling their child moving underneath. He loved the way she would cuddle against him, and that amazing second trimester when she couldn't get enough sex.

He hated the part where she was in pain and he couldn't take it for her.

"After breakfast, I'll rub it for you. I've got a bit of time before I have to be at the office." He would wait on her hand and foot for the next several weeks. This was his last week at the office for a while. He'd cleared his schedule at work so he could take a few weeks paternity leave. He would clean and cook and take care of the girls so Charlie could focus on their son and bonding and healing.

She smiled, her lips curling up in a saucy grin. "I bet I know exactly what you'll rub it with."

"Daddy, berry." Kala pointed toward the bowl of blueberries he'd washed.

Kenzie nodded her head, syrup clinging to her cheek. "Berry! Berry!"

Yeah, they loved to tag team Dad. He grabbed the bowl and poured some onto each of their plates. Kala started spearing them one by one. Kenzie grabbed them up in her grubby paw and shoved a bunch in her mouth. She grinned at him, drooling blueberry down her chin. He grabbed the wipes Charlie left everywhere and quickly mopped Kenzie up. Not that it mattered since she quickly replaced the blueberry drool with syrup.

He looked back up at his wife. "I'll take anything you're in the mood to give, baby. You want some of me, it's yours."

In the past, he would have told her if she wanted a little cock, he could give it to her. Though not in the little way. She would have to take a big cock if she wanted his.

Then his daughters had said the word cock over and over again at day care and he'd started to be a bit more subtle.

Charlie ran her hand over Kenzie's head. "Hey, it worked the last time. Maybe we should. Why don't you call up Sean and Grace and see if we can get some alone time? I'm ready to bust this baby boy out of womb prison."

The last time they'd had sex when she was this pregnant, she'd given birth roughly twelve hours later.

He loved his girls, wanted his son more than anything, but nothing on earth scared him more than Charlie in labor.

"You've got two more weeks." He knew she wanted to give birth, but he also knew she wanted to give their son the best chance he could have. It was his worst fear. Losing Charlie. Losing their baby. He dreamed about it at night and woke up in a cold sweat. "And Sean's out of town for a few days. He's filming in LA, and Grace went with him. Case is in Austin with Mia. That leaves Theo. I'm worried Theo still doesn't remember he's human, much less how to handle a couple of baby girls."

He plated her pancakes and used tongs to grab a few pieces of bacon for her. It was odd. He found cooking soothing. He would never have guessed it, never had any interest in it before his Charlie had come back from the dead, but now he enjoyed it. Shortly after they'd gotten back together and his house had felt like a home, he'd asked Sean for a few lessons. Nothing major. He just wanted to know how to make her some meals. Charlie took such good care of him. She'd learned all his favorite foods and made sure he was satisfied. He wanted to take some of the burden off her. She still handled most of their meals, but he could step in when he needed to.

His family. He needed to be able to take care of them, and not just in a financial way. Charlie should know if she was tired, he would step up. His girls should see their father always supporting and loving them.

Maybe it would make them less likely to end up with some asswipe he would have to assassinate. He already had contingency plans for that scenario. They involved a lot of blood loss for the other man.

Charlie took the plate and hoisted herself up to the barstool at the breakfast bar. "I love the fact that I can turn on the TV and see Sean cooking. It's really fun. Can I get some decaf?"

He turned to the single cup maker and started her selection. His brother was becoming a real star in the culinary world. It made him damn proud. Sean had followed his dream. He'd only found the real strength and courage to do that when he'd met Grace Hawthorne all those years ago. At the time he'd thought she was bad for him. Now he would do absolutely anything for his sister-in-law. She'd supported Sean while he'd studied, given him everything he needed to make his dreams come true.

He grabbed the coffee and placed it in front of Charlie. "I want you to rest today. I'll take the girls into work with me. You stay here and watch some TV or something. I could call Chelsea."

Charlie's eyes rolled. "She's a horrible bed rest companion. She only wants to watch the news, and she makes fun of them for being wrong about political stuff. She makes all kinds of snarky comments, but then she won't tell me what she means by it because it's classified or some bullshit. It's awful. And don't bring in Phoebe. I've seen *Harry Potter* twenty times. Eve feels the need to psychoanalyze every single character in my shows. We had a violent argument about Cookie Lyon. She's a goddamn saint, I tell you. Erin fidgets too much, and Serena barely looks up from her computer. I need Grace. She'll watch all my shows and talk about them."

"I can stay home." The thought of watching a long run of *Empire* or *Grey's Anatomy* kind of made him want to vomit, but he could handle it. Somehow. Maybe he could sneak some Scotch in.

Charlie laughed as she picked up the coffee mug. "Oh, you're the worst to watch TV with. Never, mister. You only ever want to watch sports or war movies, and you criticize the shit out of the latter."

Kenzie looked up at him, her blue eyes gleaming. "Shit."

He sighed. "No, baby. That's a Mommy and Daddy word."

"Daddy shit," Kala said with one of her infrequent grins.

He glared at his wife. "I'm not taking the blame for this one. This one is all you. You know that, right?"

"Because I'm the only one with a potty mouth? They're fixated on

Daddy, not Mommy." Charlie was sending him a righteous smile. She took a sip of her coffee and sat back, her food untouched.

She was so stunning. He leaned over the bar, reaching for her hand. "You're the one with bad taste in lovers. You decided to toss out that birth control. I think those two hooligans are your fault. After all, I'm the clean-cut former Green Beret and you're the Russian mobster."

She flushed a delicate pink. "You know how to hit a girl where it hurts, Taggart."

He moved around the island. "Hey, I happen to find bad girls incredibly sexy."

She glanced up at him. "I don't feel like a bad girl right now. I feel like a bloated whale."

He slid a hand over her belly. "You look good enough to eat." He leaned over because the last thing he needed was his baby girls learning how to dirty talk. "You want me to eat you up? Because I can be late."

Work could wait. He would spend the whole day worried about her if he went into the office. He wouldn't get a thing done. Liam could handle the office. It was quiet right now anyway. Simon and Jesse were on an assignment in New York. Alex was on paternity leave of his own. He and Eve had recently adopted their second child. Jake and Adam were working up the nerve to tell him they would be leaving soon.

Like he hadn't figured that out already.

Charlie winced and set her mug down. "Help me up. I swear this kid weighs more than his sisters. If I give birth to a twelve-pound baby, we're having such a talk. Hey, Bud. Has Daddy already taken you out this morning?"

He sighed at the massive mutt currently occupying his hallway. He wasn't sure what it was. Part St. Bernard and part horse, maybe. It had been hoisted off on him six months before when Charlie had insisted that a sweet puppy would be good for the girls. They'd toured a shelter and Charlie had been given the sob story about a poor puppy who would have to be put down soon if no one wanted him. He was such a tiny guy. The runt of the litter. She'd come home with the tiny guy cradled in one hand.

Six months later the fucker weighed sixty-five pounds and the girls could ride him. And he wasn't finished growing.

He fit his name. Big Ugly Dog.

The trouble was he was a sweet mutt and the girls adored him.

"Bud!" Kala grinned as the dog approached.

Kenzie held out a hand. A grubby, food-caked hand.

Yeah, that was when Bud started to lick her. Kenzie giggled, and he barely managed to catch her before she put that hand right back in her mouth.

There weren't enough wipes in the world to clean that mutt's bacteria.

"I promise I'll take the hell hound out before I leave." He stared down at the dog, whose tongue lolled out as he watched with completely worshipful, vacant eyes. "If you piss on my shoes again, dog, we're going to have a serious problem. And we have to talk about why you vomit in front of my damn chair."

Charlie moved to Bud's side. "You know that's actually a way of showing his affection."

"It doesn't feel affectionate, Charlie. That damn dog doesn't know when to stop."

Bud's tail thumped.

Kala looked up and said, "Piss."

Ian closed his eyes, seeking out something he'd never had to before. Patience. In the past, if something annoyed him, he tended to murder it. Oh, maybe not in a literal sense, but he certainly could make said annoyance's life hell. Now he loved the people who annoyed him.

Except for the dog.

"Baby, stop mimicking your daddy," Charlie said with a smile. "You're going to end up scaring off all the boys. Ian, he really needs to go."

Maybe it wasn't such a bad idea. He definitely liked the idea of scaring off all the dudes who couldn't handle a strong female presence.

Ian went to grab the dog's leash. Bud started up his pee-pee dance, his massive body twisting and turning as he ran after Ian. His big paws thudded against the brand new hardwood he would never have spent that godawful amount of money on had he realized a dog would pee on it.

He looked back Charlie's way. "You know there's a whole forest out back for him to go in. He should be a free-range dog. Aren't we taking away his dogness by putting him on a leash?"

Charlie frowned his way as she refilled Kenzie's cup. "Yes, he's the mighty wolf dog, Ian. I watched him run away from a bunny the other day."

He grabbed the leash. "See, if he had to go out and hunt, he wouldn't be such a shitty guard dog. Don't even say it, you two. Say good words. Not Daddy words."

Charlie put a hand to her belly. "I swear this one will come out giving the world the finger and cursing."

Bud whined, running back and forth in front of the door. Ian sighed and attached the leash. He stepped outside and Bud took off, barking and jumping against the leash until he managed to drag Ian out onto the lawn where he immediately squatted in the middle of Charlie's azaleas and started to take a crap.

Yep. This was his life. Watching the dog crap. He was so building a fence. "You know you were supposed to be a guard dog. You were supposed to be a raging, feral beast who would take out anything in your way."

Sort of like Ian had been at one time.

He'd been the bane of intelligence agencies. He'd been Dr. Death, raining down justice and protecting America.

Now he was a dumbass with a mortgage, a dog who seemed to be a bit constipated, two tiny chaotic things, and another on the way. No one even let him kill people anymore.

It was a never-ending cycle of waking up in the morning and seeing their faces, taking care of them, going to work, coming home, and going to bed with his wife.

It was kind of fucking awesome.

Sure, his younger self would likely tell him he'd sold out and he was a pathetic version of himself, but his younger self had been stupid as shit. His younger self thought a great time was following a known terrorist around for three weeks so he could find the cell he worked for. His younger self had needed a freaking shower, some decent food, and a comfy bed.

And a dog who didn't take his time with the poop.

"Come on, Bud. Pinch off, man. We've got shit to do today." Well, he did anyway. He was sure Bud would have a full day of licking his private parts and waiting for the girls to drop food. Bud seemed forever optimistic that one of these days the girls or Charlie was going to drop a ham in front of him.

A butterfly landed on the bush next to Bud and that was when he went into protective mode. He barked, the deep sound threatening to anyone who didn't know what a wuss he was, and he pulled hard at his leash.

Hard enough to make Ian stumble and damn near break his toe on the garden gnome Alex had left as a joke. Hard enough to send Ian crashing down to his knee, pain flaring and making him curse.

Bud twisted again, and Ian tripped over the riding ladybug thing Kala liked to push around the yard. He landed flat on his back, looking up at the sky.

Taken down by a freaking ladybug. And his back was spasming. The pain flared through him and he could feel his lower back seizing like a motherfucker.

Bud suddenly blocked out the sky, his big doggie face staring down.

"Don't you dare."

It was too late. Bud licked his face and Ian realized he shouldn't have gotten up that morning. Nope. He should have stayed in bed and then he would be warm and happy and not having his face licked by a gargantuan mass of body odor and a tongue that licked its own ass from time to time.

God, if he didn't die from breaking his spine he was going to catch some dog disease and waste away. Right here. Because he wasn't sure he could move. "Bud, I need you to go get Charlie. Go on. Run and get her." He let the leash drop. Bud simply sat down beside him. "Go get Charlie, boy. I think she's got a ham for you. Go on."

Bud laid his big head down on Ian's chest.

Now he had a sleeping mutt and a garden gnome that was practically up his ass. He could feel the pointy cap thing attempting to violate him.

"Ian? Ian, I need you."

Thank god. His wife would laugh her ass off, but at least she would be able to maybe help him up.

"Ian, I think the baby's coming."

Yep. It was that kind of day.

* * * *

"I wish you would let me call the ambulance." He pulled out the small suitcase Charlie had told him would serve to carry everything she would need for her stay. One week later and it would have been packed and ready to go, but no. Baby boy didn't want to wait for Mommy to be ready or Daddy to be able to move without agonizing back pain.

He must have slipped a disc or something. Damn he was getting old, but he was still Ian Taggart. He was the man who'd taken two bullets in Kabul and still managed to rescue his unit, gather the needed intel, and perform admirably when he needed to seduce his way out of a prison hospital. He wasn't going to let a few muscle spasms hold him back.

Charlie shook her head. "It's quicker to drive. You know how long they'll take, and they won't go to the right hospital. I want Presbyterian and I want Dr. Bates. The contractions are still nine minutes apart. We have time. My water hasn't even broken yet. Don't you dare forget to pack a couple of bras, Ian Taggart. This is not the club and I need those bras."

He personally thought she looked better without them, but he knew that tone in her voice.

He shoved a couple of bras in and zipped the case. He bit back a groan as he stood up. He had other problems and they mostly had to do with the fact that his family was almost all out of town or at the office, and he'd chosen a house outside the city. He loved the peace and quiet of having his own small slice of the country, but it meant there was next to no one out here who could take care of the girls.

His wife wasn't going to like the only option he'd found, but then if she didn't want to take it, she shouldn't have gone into labor. She should have waited for Sean to get back.

Charlie paced, her hand on her lower back. She'd been perfectly calm the whole time. She'd gotten the girls' stuff together. That had been easy since all she'd had to do was add an extra pair of clothes to their day care bags. She'd put up her hair and rounded up her purse, but the suitcase had been stuffed in the upper reaches of the closet. Otherwise she likely would have packed for herself and not bothered to come find his injured ass until she needed him to drive.

That's what he got for marrying a warrior woman.

"Are you sure you're okay?" Charlie asked. "I've got some liniment I could rub into your back. Poor Bud seems a little freaked out by the experience."

"Poor Bud? That big-ass ball of chaos is why I've blown at least two discs."

Charlie leaned over and patted the dog. "Poor baby. Daddy scared you."

Daddy was going to scare him. Damn it. She was so calm and he was a freaking wreck. He'd been through whole wars and not worried as much as he did about getting one woman to the hospital.

He leaned over and hauled one of the twins up and into his arms. He had to do this carefully. He grabbed the other baby and both girls started squirming and trying to crawl all over him like he was the best jungle gym ever. He leaned over and got Charlie's suitcase. He could do this.

Kala started blowing bubbles against his face while Kenzie tried to poke out his eye while singing Daddy over and over.

And his back spasmed again.

They wanted another kid, why?

"I can get the suitcase," Charlie said as she started to follow him. She stopped and breathed in long and deep as her stomach clenched.

How much time did they have? What if she was wrong and they ended up being that couple who stopped in the middle of the freeway because his kid's head was coming out, and the local news caught his wife's hoohaw from the helicopters circling above.

He'd just had his truck detailed.

"Baby, I think we should call an ambulance."

His wife's eyes opened and Hell was in them. Yep, his baby knew exactly how to show him with a single stare what she was going to do to him if he didn't behave.

When they were in the dungeon he gave out those looks, but when it came to birthing babies, she kind of took the lead.

He would have held his hands up, but they were full of wriggling babies. "Okay, let's get this show on the road. We have to make a quick stop."

She followed behind. "Where? Are we going to the office to drop the girls off? Or are we meeting someone?"

Getting to the office at this time of the morning would be an hour-long drive. No way, no how. That way led to his son's place of birth being listed as a Ford F-150. "There's only one person who lives close enough. He can take the girls into the office, and then I've already called Case and he and Mia are on their way back from Austin. They'll take the girls tonight."

She stopped in the middle of the hallway. "Are you talking about who I think you're talking about?"

He grimaced. "Baby, there's no more time."

"Oh, I wasn't complaining. I just thought the day wasn't going to be fun. Now I know differently." She walked by him, picking up the keys to his truck. "Come on, Bud. We're going for a ride."

"We can't take the dog."

"Sure we can. After all, we can't leave him behind. Remember the heart attack you nearly had when you saw how much the floors cost?"

He groaned as Kenzie head butted him and immediately started wailing. That got her sister to sympathy cry and both the twins' laments made Bud howl, his head thrown back as he made a sound like a dying water buffalo.

If he survived the day, it would be a miracle.

* * * *

He watched as Charlie made her way up to the small house on the outskirts of Dallas. They were only a few miles from her preferred hospital, but somehow Remy Guidry had managed to find the one house that looked like it belonged in the middle of a gator-infested swamp. Guidry's big truck was parked alongside one of those tiny toy cars some women liked to drive these days.

"I've changed my mind. I'll just carry the girls." And check to make sure that big Cajun bodyguard he'd hired wasn't making meth on the side.

Charlie waved him off as she walked toward the ramshackle house. "He's fine. He can certainly be trusted with driving the girls to the office, and he'll take care of Bud. There's no room for him in Case and

Mia's apartment. Besides, this is going to be so much fun. Stay back a little. This works best if it's just me."

What the hell was she doing? "Baby, I didn't call him because I didn't want to give him a chance to run."

"Oh, he won't be the one running." Charlie marched to the door and banged her fist against it. "Remy! Remy Guidry, you son of a bitch, get the hell out here."

There was a long pause. The girls went still in his arms, as though they knew their momma was about to put on a show.

The door opened and Remy stepped out wearing nothing but a pair of what looked like hastily put on jeans. The top button wasn't even done. "Such a manwhore move. Don't ever fall for that, girls. That's man cleavage right there. Dude walks out in low-riding jeans and he's basically tempting you to look down below. Don't you do it. It means he's a douchebag. Tell him to put on some damn clothes."

Remy smiled broadly when he realized it was Charlie on his doorstep. "Hey, pretty momma. How are you doing today?"

That was when he saw her. A blonde with sex hair and what looked like a shirt that didn't belong to her pulled back the drapes to spy on her partner for the night.

"Your mother is the single meanest woman on the face of the planet." He was getting a little teary. And so hot. Damn, but that was a woman. She was having contractions and she still thought of a way to mess with a man. "Goddamn I love her."

"Do you have another woman here?" Charlie asked.

The Cajun's eyes went wide. "I do. Her name is Sharla. Or Darla. Why? Is something wrong at the office? Look, Charlotte, I picked her up at a bar last night. I didn't talk about business at all. I know Big Tag can be paranoid…"

"I'm not paranoid." Bud sank down beside him, showing no interest in leaving the girls to explore the world around him.

Damn that dog was somewhat like Ian. He knew a good thing when he saw it, and he wasn't about to let it get away.

Kala patted his face. "Para…dada…paranod."

"It's only paranoia if the world isn't out to get you, baby girl." He had evidence that it was.

"How dare you have a woman here when I'm about to give birth to our child!" Charlie put a hand to her belly and pointed at the window. "Damn straight, I'm talking to you. Yes, you, woman. Did he get you pregnant, too?"

The face in the window disappeared but not before it had turned a bright shade of perfectly indignant red.

Remy's eyes had gone wide. "Charlotte, have you lost your damn mind? Sharla, baby, she's joking. She's my boss's wife. She's got a sick sense of humor."

"You keep right on lying, Remy. You know this baby is the product of our love." Charlie grimaced, but she soldiered on. "How dare you deny it?"

Sharla, Darla stomped out, her walk of shame turning into a march of female anger. "You bastard."

"Now, Sharla," Remy began.

The blonde reared back and slapped him full-on across the face. "I'm Megan. Sharla is my sister, you asshole."

Remy nodded, as though finally remembering. "Oh, yeah. You tell her hi for me now."

Megan shot him the finger as she stalked toward her hamster-wheel car. She glanced over at Ian. "Did you have his babies, too?"

Ian nodded solemnly. "He wasn't even a tender lover."

She shook her head. "You're all weird." Her voice shot up. "And I was faking it. Sharla was right. You're bad in bed."

Remy put a hand to his heart. "I'm wounded, *chère*." He leaned toward Charlie. "And that wasn't what she was saying last night. Now, it appears to me you've actually done me a favor, Mrs. Taggart. Have I mentioned how stunningly beautiful you are today?"

He reached for her hand.

"Hey, none of that hand-kissing stuff. That hand belongs to me." Ian started up the walk, his back aching. It was all right. Bud was there to ensure that every single step had to be made with the absolute greatest of care since the dog seemed determined to walk underneath him.

Charlie paced the porch as she talked. "I thought you might find that fun. The gossip mill had it that you went home with a crazy blonde last night. You know I live vicariously right now."

"Any time you want me to talk about my amorous dealings, I will.

Only for you though, *chère*." He glanced over Ian's way, looking deeply amused. "What can I do for you, boss? Since it appears the lady boss has done me a great kindness. Sharl…whichever one that was woke me up talking about going out for breakfast and fixing up my house. I saw visions of a ring running through that girl's head."

It was good he considered it a favor because Ian needed one of his own. "I have a bodyguard gig for you. It's a VIP gig, and I need you to take it seriously."

Remy stood straight, his whole persona becoming competent in a heartbeat. Remy was good at his job, hence Ian putting up with his douchebag himbo private persona. "Absolutely, boss. Who's the client?"

He held up Kala, shifting the girl into Remy's arms before he could protest. "Kala, meet your bodyguard. And this is Kenzie."

Remy went a lovely shade of white. His jaw dropped as he found himself with two arms full of Taggart princesses. They immediately started exploring the new guy, patting his face and pulling on hair that was way too long to be serious guy hair. "What's happening? Why? Ian, I'm not…why?"

He dumped the car seats and two diaper bags on his doorstep. "Charlie and I are going on vacation. We'll be back in two weeks. Don't let the girls die and feed the dog. Bye."

He reached for Charlie's hand. He didn't care what she'd said earlier. Those contractions were getting shorter and shorter, and the freeway birth was rapidly becoming a real option. They would have to name the baby I-75 if they didn't get a move on.

Charlie grimaced and her body went still for a moment. Yep, they were getting longer and longer. "Remy, I'm in labor and I don't think I have time to get to the office and back to the hospital. All you have to do is drive the girls to the office and Li will be waiting to take them up to day care. Case will pick them up this afternoon."

"What do I do with these seats?" For the first time since he'd hired the six-foot-four-inch muscular ex-soldier, he looked scared.

"Strap 'em in, buddy." Ian started hauling Charlie toward the truck.

Bud whined and tried to follow after them.

Ian stopped, looking down at the dog and giving him his best alpha badass voice. "You go back and you protect those girls. If the dumbass manwhore does something that might hurt them, you kill. Am I understood? You kill anyone who tries to hurt them and then raise them as your own. Go."

Bud barked and then went back to the porch, where the girls were attempting to climb up the new guy's head.

"I'll work overtime with no pay," Remy offered.

"They're just little girls. Play princess with them and they'll love you for life. But watch Kala. I think she's already into starting fires," Ian shouted back. "And Kenzie will put her fingers into light sockets. She thinks it's fun."

"Call Li." Charlie seemed to have some sympathy for the man. "He'll walk you through setting up the car seats. I would stay and let Ian do it, but I'm afraid my water just broke and we need to go."

Her water broke? He looked down and sure enough, there was a wet spot on her pants. Her water. The stuff that was keeping his son alive and safe. Amniotic fluid.

He'd seen so much blood in his life, but the sight of that small spot made him woozy.

"Ian? Babe?" Charlie was staring at him.

They were wasting time. He started to turn. "We need to go."

Pure panic threatened to overtake him. His son couldn't be born here on Remy's lawn. There was likely some kind of STD in the grass. Their baby needed to be born in the safety of a damn hospital with his whole family surrounding him. He should have called the ambulance. He shouldn't have given in. He'd gotten soft, and it looked like it could cost them all.

He turned, ready to drag her to the truck. And that was when his foot hit the beer bottle someone had left just lying around, and for the second time that day he found himself upended and falling.

"Ian!" Charlie was yelling and he heard the dog bark.

His back hit the ground and he felt a nasty pain go through his skull.

And everything went black.

* * * *

"Mr. Taggart? Mr. Taggart, can you open your eyes for me?"

Pain flashed through his brainpan and nausea rolled through him. Some asshole was flashing a light into his eyes while he was trying to sleep.

"Whoa, brother. Theo, help me with him," a familiar voice was saying.

"And I thought I was bad. Bad Taggart. Down."

He felt arms holding him and the sound of his younger brothers arguing about the best way to deal with him.

"Are you sure we can't tranq his ass?" Theo asked.

"His ass isn't what I'm worried about," a masculine voice said. It was familiar, too, but this wasn't one of his brothers. "His brain took a beating. Come on, you big bastard. Open your eyes so I can make sure you're not brain-dead in there. Do you know how many people are waiting to see if they can pull your plug?"

Yes, he knew that voice. Will Daley. He was a Dom at Sanctum. He was also a doctor of some kind.

What the hell had happened? Had an op gone bad?

He remembered something dirty and smelly. Something had been touching him. Jeez, had he been violated by Big Foot?

Nope. Bud. It had been that mangy mutt his daughters loved.

His daughters. His wife. Ian forced his eyes open. "Charlie. Where's my wife? Where's Charlie?"

What had happened? Charlie had been in labor and then there had been water.

"I'm over here, babe." Her voice washed over him like a calming wave. "Welcome back. You were totally right. We needed that ambulance. That happened way faster than I thought it would. It was about twenty minutes from the time my water broke to giving birth."

She was somewhere to his right. He tried to turn, but Will got in his way.

The neurosurgeon looked down at him. "Ian, you took a nice fall. You were in and out of consciousness and managed to scare some of the ER nurses. You have no idea how hard they are to scare. Your CT scan came back as nothing more than a mild concussion, and you likely pulled a couple of muscles in your back. Let me look you over and I'll let you see your babies."

He wanted that more than anything. He tried to relax as Will examined him by shining a way-too-bright light in his eyes. That was when the words he'd said actually penetrated.

"Babies? I thought the girls were going to day care. Did they come with us in the ambulance? By the way, I'm charging Remy for that. None of this would have happen if that asshole cleaned up his yard and was way less a redneck."

"He took the girls to day care," Charlie explained. "Li says they're perfectly fine and Remy's agreed to watch Bud until we get home. He says Bud is whining for the girls but he likes burgers."

Oh, good luck with that. Bud liked to eat. And vomit. And eat again. And vomit. Maybe he would have his revenge on Remy after all. His vision came back into focus. He could see his two younger brothers standing at his bedside.

Bedside. He was in a hospital, a damn IV in his arm. What the hell had happened? The last thing he could remember was falling.

Babies?

"Charlie, please tell me you didn't have twin boys," he practically pleaded. They would be outnumbered. Hopelessly outnumbered, and he was pretty sure Bud would side with the children. Maybe if he gave the dog that ham he always promised...

"It wasn't twin boys, silly," she said. "The sonogram was completely wrong."

"But the CT wasn't," Will said. "I think you're going to be fine, but we'll keep you overnight so you can get some rest and help Charlotte out. Her birth was smooth and easy. No problems at all except the fact that you were unconscious and unable to see your new baby girls born."

He sat up. He thought he'd been afraid before. "The doc said it was a boy."

"Nope." Charlie smiled his way. "Two more girls."

He reached out and grabbed Will's coat. "I'm going to need drugs. Lots of drugs because you're wrong. There's something fucked up in my brain."

Theo and Case started laughing and he knew he'd been had. Even Will couldn't help a smile.

The doc looked back at Charlie. "Sorry, that was too funny. I'll

113

send the rest of them in. Make sure you both take it easy. I'll be back in a few hours to check on him."

"Charlie?" He was well aware of the amount of pleading in his voice.

Charlie was sitting up in bed, a bundle in her arms. She looked tired, her hair pulled back and her skin a bit pale. She was the most gorgeous woman on the planet. "Sorry, babe. I couldn't help myself. Do you want to meet Seth? Just Seth. He was a good boy and didn't multiply in the womb but damn, Taggart. He's nine pounds. He's going to outweigh his sisters in no time at all."

Case moved to the side of her bed, picking up the baby and crossing the space between them.

Ian forced himself to sit up. Charlie was all right. His son was here. His girls were safely stashed away with a whole office of people who loved them.

His boy. He looked down and no matter what Charlie said, he was so damn small. So precious.

How the hell had his father walked out? How did any man walk away from this? He'd been around the world, been powerful in ways most men couldn't imagine, but this…this was everything.

Seth Jason Taggart yawned as though the whole birthing experience had been a bore. Then his eyes opened and he grinned a little.

And Ian fell in love all over again. In love with his family. In love with the life he'd built.

"He's beautiful, Charlie."

"Well," she said, "he does take after his dad."

The door opened and they were inundated with family.

* * * *

Long after everyone had been shooed out by doctors and nurses, Ian sat up in bed. His IV had been declared no longer needed and he was only staying overnight because Will Daley was a man who knew how to take advantage of a situation.

Sean and Grace had flown home and they'd come by a few hours earlier, bearing gifts from Top. The Piemaker had heard about Ian's no good, shitty, horrible, backbreaking best day ever and sent along a plate of lemon squares.

Ian glanced down at the card that had come with it.

When life hands you lemons, I'll make you some kick-ass lemonade bars.

"Hey, don't eat them all," Charlie said, her eyes coming open. She'd been napping, but now seemed like the perfect time to invade her space.

"I'll save some for you, baby." His back hurt, but it didn't matter. Seth was fussing and Ian lifted him from his crib, holding him close as he climbed into Charlie's bed.

Into their bed. It didn't matter that they were miles from the house they called home. Her body, her soul—they were home to him. He crawled in next to her and they cuddled close, their son in between.

He looked at the woman who meant more than life itself to him. "Hey, babe. How was your day? Mine was a little up and down."

The smile that crossed her face lit up his world. "I don't know. I thought it was memorable." She looked down at their son, wonder in her eyes. "Welcome to the world, Seth Taggart."

He cuddled his wife close. "Welcome home, Seth."

5

Rough Night

Rough Night takes place between At Your Service and Nobody Does It Better.

"Are you sure this is a good idea?" Charlotte Taggart stared at her husband and then back at the man he'd brought in to handle the night's responsibilities.

Michael looked scared. Michael Malone was a former Navy SEAL/CIA team member who had worked many dangerous missions with a sure and steady hand. He'd grown up on a cattle ranch and spent much of his time on oil rigs. This was not a man who typically looked like he was going to faint.

"I don't know," her husband said in that tone he tended to reserve for the dumbasses in his life. Unfortunately, according to Ian Taggart, there were a lot of dumbasses in his life. "Malone, you think this is a good idea?"

Malone's jaw squared. "I think I need to stop betting against Hutch."

Yep, sometimes her husband was right about being surrounded by dumbasses. Although she'd discovered that even the most intelligent of men could be turned into a dumbass when they gathered in large groups and someone—usually Ian—came up with a fun game. His fun games in the past had included using an ATV to jump over the creek at the back of their property, sending exploding glitter dicks to his rivals, and his favorite, pitting his men against each other in the stupidest of contests. She was worried what they'd come up with now. "What did you make Hutch do?"

Ian shrugged one big shoulder. "It was just a little bet. Hutch and another guy were talking some smack about who could eat more tacos. It was taco Tuesday, so I only spent like fifty bucks on a hundred tacos, and I won us this sweet, sweet babysitting gig."

She should have wondered why there had been cheering and groans of defeat coming from the break room a few days before. She'd been told by Phoebe that if she wanted to keep her belief that their crew had any sense whatsoever, she should avoid that room. Charlie had taken her advice. Now she knew why Hutch had been downing antacids for days. "Who was he up against?"

Malone's eyes went wide. "Boomer."

Shit. She shouldn't have missed that. Boomer was really just a walking gut who also happened to be one of the world's best snipers. She'd seen Boomer eat quantities of food that would have killed most human beings. "How the hell did Hutch beat Boomer?"

Malone sighed. "I didn't know Boomer had already been to an all-you-can-eat breakfast buffet. But I suspect your husband did."

Ian managed to look as innocent as a rat-fink gorgeous bastard could. "The dude asked for pancakes. What was I supposed to do? And don't play that game with me, Malone. I know you and Case spiked Hutch's coffee with bulk fiber, you assholes."

And that explained why poor Hutch had been in the bathroom for days.

"So Ian bet a night of babysitting and Michael bet what? Also, what did Hutch and Boomer stand to get from this besides heart disease?"

Michael put up a hand. "First off, all Big Tag said was I would owe him one. And all I wanted from him if I won was his Sunday Cowboys tickets."

"I figured if I lost, I would give my seat to Malone and you could have Sunday to go and have a spa day or something," Ian said. "It was kind of a win/win for me. I either got to spend time with you tonight or I got to make sure you had a day off on Sunday."

That man. He was sneaky and manipulative, and no one should bet against him. She turned back to Malone, pointing his way. "He wins. He always wins, Michael. And everyone knows what owing him one means."

Malone managed to pale as he looked back at the two girls playing quietly in the living room. "I kind of hoped it would be something like embedding myself in a crazy scientist's clutches for months or joining a drug cartel so we could gather intel. You know, something like that. I

120

could do that."

Coward. Her sweet baby girls weren't…no. She couldn't even pretend in her brain. Those girls were trouble with a capital T, but it was only an hour and a half away from their bedtime. Seth was already down for the night.

And it would be fun to go out for a little while. It would be nice to play. Ian had announced that he was taking her out after they'd finished a lovely dinner of honey soy pot roast that likely would have lasted for days with a normal family, but her husband knew a thing or two about putting food away, too. Eric Vail was having a play party and they were attending. Between work and kids and all their various projects, they hadn't had a lot of time to play lately. It had been weeks since they'd even been to Sanctum.

A big hand cupped her shoulder. "Come on, Charlie baby. It's one night out and he was a Navy SEAL. He can handle a sleeping infant, two tiny girls, and the mutt from hell."

There was a chime from her phone that let her know someone was on the property. A minute later, Ian was ushering in Boomer. Where Kenzie and Kala had mostly ignored Malone, they lit up when Boomer walked in.

The big guy's face brightened, and he suddenly had his burly arms filled with tiny girls. "Hey, boss. Mike said since I failed the taco test, I have to come and help him. Are we babysitting? I thought it would be something bad. Can we watch *Moana*? I love that movie. Especially the chicken. The chicken is hilarious. Hey, do you think we could order some chicken, Mike? I'm a little hungry."

Ian shook his head Michael's way. "Touché, Mike. Well played. He'll eat us out of house and home, but I'm not backing down because Macon is at the play party and he's made lemon tarts. And Charlie can buy some more groceries. She does it all the time."

Charlie sighed. Boys. All of them.

Boomer dropped to the ground and let the girls climb all over him like a jungle gym while Ian explained to Malone what would happen if his precious babies didn't survive the night.

Honestly, she was a little more worried about the men surviving…

* * * *

An hour and a half later and Charlie was definitely seeing the plus side to her husband's plotting. Sometimes his manipulative side produced awesome results. Though she was a bit worried about the chair.

"Are you sure this thing is sturdy? I don't want to break Eric's chair."

She sat in Ian's lap in Eric Vail's beautifully decorated kitchen, waiting for the fun to start. Relaxed. How long had it been since she'd felt so relaxed? Since she'd been able to simply hang with her hubby and not worry about anything more than how long dessert was taking.

They were watching Macon Miles as he put the finishing touches on the dozen or so small lemon tarts he'd made especially for Ian. She always found it fascinating to watch the massive ex-soldier use his huge hands to create delicate treats.

"The chair is fine. Perfectly sturdy enough to hold us both. Come on, baby. Relax. Tell me this isn't fun," Ian growled against her cheek.

"You know I can't." Sitting in her husband's lap, one hand on his chest, was kind of the bomb. She was wearing her favorite corset and a tiny little thong that didn't cover anything at all. She liked it though. After her Master tortured her for a while, he would slide that ridiculous thong off and fuck her silly.

She needed that so very badly.

It was like Ian knew what she needed and had found a ridiculously manipulative way to give it to her. And yeah, that did something for her, too. Her Master was a ruthless bastard who would plot and plan and find a way to have her no matter what it took.

Her cell phone buzzed.

She glanced down. It was a text from Malone.

Okay to make the girls some S'mores? We're having a pretend campout in the living room.

So maybe the billionaire oilman's son wasn't so bad at entertaining the kiddos. She texted a smiley face and a thumbs up and looked back at her Master. Here, that's what he was—the dominant manly Master and she the sweetly bratty sub.

It felt so good to be his submissive for a bit.

A single brow arched over Ian's icy blue eyes. They could go super cold when he wanted them to, and like blue flames when he was hot with desire. "You brought your cell phone?"

She wasn't making any apologies for that, though she had hidden it in the left side of her corset. It fit in right under her arm. She and some of the other moms/subs had sewn in a little patch of matching material to hold their phones in. A little like a holster, but for information and communication, not a gun. Ian could carry the guns. She'd had enough of that for a lifetime. Besides, she knew that sometimes information was way more dangerous than bullets. "Normally I wouldn't, Master, but we're not at Sanctum and our babies aren't with their usual sitter. I trust Malone and Boomer, but the girls…not so much. If they can cause chaos, they will, and they'll giggle the whole time."

She slipped the phone back into her corset.

"Well, I tried Serena but apparently she's busy having a mental breakdown and went to nekkidville, which is somewhere in Southern Colorado. At least that's what Jake said when I called earlier. He and Adam are taking a late flight so they can meet her there. I had to think fast so we didn't get stuck with two more kids and no more sex. They managed to get Jesse and Phoebe to take them, but that meant they couldn't take on ours, too."

Charlie gasped a little. She'd looked at the calendar earlier in the week and sent them a nice card. She tried to keep all the important dates on her calendar. "But Ian, it's their anniversary today."

"I think they forgot, and it is so not my place to remind them. Look at it this way, now they have two more little ones to celebrate with," he said with the smooth smile of a predator who knew he'd gotten away with something. "It wasn't like they were going to do anything special. They would probably watch *Harry Potter* or something. They can totally do that with the kids."

"That was mean."

"Well, I didn't remember it was their anniversary," he admitted. "If they forget, how am I supposed to remember? Damn, you smell good."

"I'm pretty sure I still smell like pot roast." She should have insisted on a shower, but the minute she'd acquiesced, he'd bundled her into his truck and started for Fort Worth. She'd found out how carefully he'd planned everything because his kit had already been in the cab along with the bag she usually carried with her to Sanctum.

He ran his nose over her neck, breathing her in. "Yeah, you do smell good enough to eat. I'm going to eat you up later on. I'm going to get you tied down and once everyone is watching because my sub is so beautiful, that's when I'll show them how good you are at taking a cock."

She shivered at the thought because he would take his time and do it all right. He would spank her and warm her up and play with all her parts until she couldn't handle it a second longer.

Charlie couldn't wait.

But she would have to because Macon was holding out the one thing in the world Ian would want to devour even faster than her pussy.

Ian had been on a low carb diet for weeks. His blood work had come back and she'd made him eat better to bring down his cholesterol. Healthy diets made her Master crabby. They had agreed he could break his sugar fast and have a little dessert at the play party.

"Here you go, Big Tag." Macon handed the plate to Charlie and tipped his head. "I'm going to find my wife and tie her up for a while. You two have a blast."

"Thanks, Macon," she said, balancing the tray against her thigh. "You're a lifesaver."

Ian was already staring at the small tarts. "You're the best, Pie Maker. I love you."

She wasn't sure if the last words had been said to Macon or the pies themselves. He'd kind of whispered the words, so she rather thought he was talking to those tarts. She picked one up. Two could play at this game. He would take very good care of her later on. She could make him happy now.

The door to the kitchen came open, but that didn't bother Charlie at all. She was completely looking forward to some crazy exhibitionist sex.

She hadn't known she was an exhibitionist until Ian Taggart had shown her. She could still remember him walking into The Velvet Collar. He'd been the target that night, a young, arrogant CIA operative she needed to distract in order to save her sister.

"God, Ian, you still look the same to me all these years later." The words seemed to slip out of her mouth.

His lips curled up. So often he smirked and she found it sexy, but

124

when that man truly smiled he could light up the world. "That's because I put shit in your coffee to make your sight bad."

She rolled her eyes.

His arms tightened and he got serious. "You're still the same glorious woman, Charlie. You walked into that dungeon and my world flipped. I took one look at you and knew I'd do anything to get a collar around your neck. You took my breath away. You still do. You will until the day I die and that day, I'll still see you standing there in the dungeon waiting for me."

Her eyes clouded. She had been waiting for him. "I didn't realize what I was waiting for until the first time I saw you. I knew. I knew I wouldn't ever want another man. Come here, baby. You didn't get dessert."

She kind of realized they weren't alone, but again, it didn't matter. When she was with Ian, soft and submissive in his lap, it was easy to shut the world out.

It was Javier and the new girl. Juliana, she thought, but she went by Julie or Jules. They were standing in the middle of the kitchen, staring at the stove. It was a nice stove, but then she wasn't a crazed foodie chef so maybe she didn't get the sexy.

To each his own.

Ian's hands came up, brushing against her cheeks. "No dessert because I knew what was coming. And by coming, I mean you. You're going to be coming, my love. Over and over and over again. You're going to come until I can't stand, until my dick stops working. Take the first bite."

They were practically having intercourse over a lemon tart and she was fine with that. She brought the tart in her hand to her lips. "It smells so good."

"Nothing like how you smell, baby. You smell like sex and mine."

Mine? Oh, yeah, she was his. She didn't want to be anything in the world but his. She licked the tart, knowing full well that he was watching her every move. Hell, she could feel his dick swell under her butt. He didn't try to hide it. That was hers, too. He shifted his pelvis as though trying to make himself more comfortable, but she knew he was really rubbing that massive erection against her. In these moments, he was a horny predatory tiger, rubbing himself against her leg to relieve the tension.

Charlie brought the tart to her lips and slowly took a bite, her eyes never leaving her husband's. They were locked together, bodies touching as she savored the light, tart taste of Macon's finest work. He was a master at turning lemons into perfectly prepared bites of heaven. Charlie licked her lips and then turned the treat her Master's way.

"Only you, baby," Big Tag whispered back.

Charlie loved the look in his eyes as she offered him the tart. She loved watching him enjoy it, knowing all the while that wouldn't be the last treat he would enjoy that evening. Soon she would be the one he was enjoying, her legs splayed and her body at his mercy.

Right before she was sure he would take the tart, he pulled her down instead. His mouth took hers, tongue dominating in a bold move that chased the breath right out of her lungs. She relaxed against him, giving him the power in that instant and letting him know she was his to do with as he wished.

Which only worked because she loved him, trusted him, knew he would never do a thing to hurt her.

As he kissed her senseless, she wondered where she would be if she hadn't met Ian Taggart. It was funny how in her most desperate moment, her salvation had come in the form of a man who should have been her enemy.

"You taste better than any pie, my Charlie," he whispered against her lips. His hands tightened on her and she felt one of those big palms stroke her thigh. "Why don't you straddle me and let's see what happens?"

She knew what would happen. She placed the tray of treats on the table beside them and gingerly shifted, twisting so she straddled her Master's lap. Yes, there it was. His cock was right against her pussy. All she had to do was…

Ian groaned as she rolled her pelvis. "That's right, baby. Now give me some of that sweet, sweet lemony goodness. Ride me and feed me. That's what I want. Let me watch you come."

"And if I can make you come?" It was a fun little game. She would try to see if she could get that big dick of his to go off before she did.

"Then I'll walk around for the rest of the night a bit on the uncomfortable side," he replied, his hands finding her hips. He shifted and she found herself with her clitoris in the perfect position. "But that's not going to happen. I know exactly how to make you moan, Charlie baby."

She felt her phone vibrate. Charlie winced. "It's another text."

He pumped his hips up against hers. "Answer it. If it's anyone except Malone telling us one of the children is missing, I'm texting them a dick pic and asking them to leave us alone. Let's see if you can text while I do this."

His erection slid over the perfect place and Charlie could feel the orgasm starting to build. How could he still do this to her? All he had to do was start touching her, using that deep Dom voice on her, and her whole body was ready to comply to his any and every whim.

Did she have to answer? It probably wasn't anything important. Was anything in the world as important as the way this man made her feel?

"Give me a taste of that tart, baby. Or better yet, pull those pretty nipples out and let me taste them. Let me lick and suck and bite on those sweet nipples."

Her vision was going soft as he hauled her close. And her phone vibrated again.

"Ian," she started.

"Do what you need to," he replied as he licked her collarbone. "I'll do what I have to."

She was going to kill whoever was texting her. It was probably Malone, trying to figure out where the damn marshmallows were.

She bit back a groan and reached for her phone. It better be so good because she was getting close, and the minute Ian started sucking on her breasts she wouldn't be able to hold...

Do you have a fire extinguisher?

"What?" Charlie shifted, trying to get a better grip on the phone. And the chair under Ian kind of exploded.

Charlie hit the floor, her knees knocking on the tile. Ian had gone backward but he'd managed to twist his body so he landed on his shoulder instead of knocking the back of his head against the windowsill.

Panic flooded Charlie's veins. She scrambled to find her phone. "Ian?"

"I'm fine," he groaned. "Call him. Damn it. Can't we have one fucking night out without the world coming to an end? Ah, yeah, this is going to hurt."

Had he thrown out his back again? She couldn't stop and find out. Sarah Stevens was here somewhere and she was a nurse. Surely she could help.

Charlie grabbed the phone from the midst of the now fallen lemon tarts. The tray had turned over, but there were still several that had landed on the table. She would have to shove those in her purse if they were about to flee home. With shaking fingers she dialed the number for Michael.

"Hey, Charlotte, I think I got the fire out. Boomer stopped, dropped, and rolled on it. That did the trick. The girls thought it was hilarious, but we've got another problem now," Michael was saying.

"There was a fire?" She practically screamed the question.

"Tell Boomer to sit on it," Ian said from the floor. "Put him on speaker."

She didn't need his sarcasm, but he had the right to listen in. She clicked to go to speaker. "Where was the fire, Michael?"

"Well, you see when I told the girls we could have a campout in the living room, I kind of thought we would build a fort made out of sheets, you know what I'm talking about," Michael continued, his Texas drawl slow and steady. "Damn, Charlotte. I didn't think the girls would take it so literally."

Her girls took everything literally. "The girls tried to start a fire? In my living room?"

"It was minor," Michael promised. "Mostly because they couldn't take apart the furniture to burn. That was their plan. Apparently Ian taught them how to use whatever's around to stay warm in case they find themselves out in the woods at night. I saved the sofa, but they did manage to get that wicker basket of yours to burn. Kala said she had to use it because she couldn't get to the hatchet."

Charlie turned to her husband. "Why would our daughters know how to use a hatchet?"

He was a nice shade of pale, and his shoulder seemed weirdly out of place. "You told me to teach them some life skills."

She was going to kill everyone. Charlie turned her focus back to the man on the phone. "So the fire is out now?"

"Mostly, but there's a problem with a crossbow," Malone admitted. "Basically, Kenzie thought she should provide meat for the fire her sister started. Uhm, long story short, she shot Boomer. It's okay. He gets shot a lot. He's used to it, but I need to know if you have some tarp or something because when I pull this arrow out it's going to get bloody. Should we do it in the garage? And where does Ian keep the first aid kit? Damn it, Kala. Don't play with the arrow!"

"Don't you take that arrow out." She didn't even know where the hell the arrow had lodged. It could be holding one of his arteries closed and when they pulled it out—bam, dead Boomer on her floor.

"You tell him I will kill him if this incident scars my baby girl for life," Ian swore from his place on the floor. "Charlie, baby, my shoulder's out of socket. Could you help me out?"

This was all his fault. He thought it was fun to teach the girls where the freaking crossbow was. And his shoulder came out of socket all the time. It was an old wound. He sometimes jerked it from the socket just to freak people out. Charlie grabbed one of the unspoiled tarts and shoved it in his mouth. "Happy now? I told you that chair wouldn't hold us both, and it's the babysitter who got shot. Boomer might die on our living room floor." She was back on the phone. "I'm so sorry. We're on our way right now. Seriously, don't take that arrow out."

She glanced around. They weren't alone. Javier and Jules had walked back in from the backyard and Macon and Ally ran in from the living room. This was not the exhibitionism she'd wanted tonight.

Ian popped up, his arm hanging limp at his side. It didn't stop him from grabbing another tart with his good hand. "Macon! Buddy, I'm going to need these to go. Date night's fucked up again. Javi, some help here?"

Javier shook his head and put out an arm, bracing himself. "Has anyone ever told you you're completely insane?"

Big Tag grinned and used Javier's straight arm to shove his shoulder back into socket with an audible crack. "Never heard that one before. Use condoms. Like three of 'em."

"Call 911," Charlie said into the phone.

"I think I can get the arrow out, Charlotte," Malone drawled.

"Especially if the girls kind of help me hold him down. Now that I think about it, we could tie him down."

She heard one of the girls squeal in delight. That was so not happening. "911. Right now."

"How about I call Theo? He and Erin are both pretty decent medics," Malone argued. "Have you thought about the CPS visit that will inevitably come after we call the cops?"

Holy shit. She was going to lose her babies. Tears blurred her eyes.

"It doesn't really hurt," Boomer shouted over the line. "I'm totally stable and everything. Hey, could you pick up some Taco Bell on your way? I'm kind of hungry."

"There's some leftovers in the fridge. Where is he hit?" She was well aware she was walking through a play party. She tried to keep her voice down.

"It was just his leg," Malone said. "No real problem. Not even much blood yet. It went through the meaty part of his calf. And if you're talking about that chicken, yeah, he already found that and ate it. He also ate all your breakfast cereal and four ham sandwiches."

"Damn it," Ian cursed behind her. "Where the hell does he put it?"

Malone continued. "And do you know why the dog keeps whining? I tried to let him out, but he wouldn't go."

Boomer had eaten an entire chicken? And a whole lot of cereal, and then he'd moved on to the deli portion of her kitchen? She might have to let that go. She made it back to the master bedroom and grabbed her purse and her clothes. Those would have to go on in the truck because she didn't have time. "Bud's terrified of coyotes. There's probably one in the back somewhere."

"I can take care of it, Momma!" a delicate feminine voice yelled.

"Don't you dare," she growled into the phone. "I swear whichever one of you little demons tries to go outside and murder the local wildlife will find themselves in a corner for the rest of your life. Do I make myself clear?"

"Dang, Charlotte. She's crying. You made her cry." Malone managed to make it sound like the worst thing that had happened all night long.

"Could you order some pizza?" Boomer yelled. "Don't cry, little girl. I'm okay. Just hungry."

Charlie took a deep breath and looked back at Ian, who was following along.

Yep, she'd been right. Totally bad idea.

* * * *

"Charlie, baby, you have to see the humor in the situation," he said after roughly twenty minutes of chilly silence. "I mean the girls are barely five and they've got two Special Forces dudes on the ropes. There's some humor there."

This time the chill had come entirely from her direction.

She kept her eyes on the road. She was driving because Ian's shoulder had popped back out of place when he'd twisted the wrong way trying to get to the box of leftover lemon tarts.

"Did you or did you not teach our baby girls, who aren't even in kindergarten yet, how to build a fire?" She knew the answer to the question, but she wanted to hear it from his damn lips.

He turned to her. "How are they supposed to go to kindergarten if they don't know how to build a fire? There are basic skills that are required to live, and I won't apologize for that. They also know how to pitch a decent tent."

Always with the sarcasm. Well, he wasn't the one who had to deal with the public. He wasn't the one everyone judged. "Do you know what they said to their preschool teacher the other day? You're not the one who got called in. I am. I'm the one who has to deal with the teachers."

"What did they do?" Ian asked.

She hadn't mentioned it to him because she didn't want to get mad. There was no way to avoid it now. He should know what his influence was doing. "The teacher told them it was time to come in from the playground and Kala said she didn't want to."

He sighed. "Baby, she's stubborn. You know she didn't just get that from me."

He didn't understand the half of it. "She got the other kids together and explained to them that they didn't have to go in because there were fourteen of them and only one of the teacher."

Ian snorted.

"She talked about how they could flank the teacher and take her out. She made plans in the dirt with a stick. She showed the others how they could overrun the teacher's defenses and take back the playground. I'm not joking, Ian. Miss Mayberry was terrified."

Ian winced as he turned in his seat. "Next time I'll go and talk to the teacher."

That would so put that sanctimonious teacher at ease. Shouldn't a preschool teacher be tougher than that? "And that's going to go so well. You think those girls can do no wrong. Do you know what they did to me at the grocery store?"

His eyes seemed to glaze over. "Well, yes, baby. They decided it would be funny if they played hide and seek with Mommy. You yelled about it for three days. I totally know."

But she was going to tell him again. "They decided it would be funny to hide from Mommy and they pulled out the cereal boxes and hid behind them."

"You called 911," he said, proving he definitely knew the story.

"I called 911."

"You thought our babies were dead."

"I thought our babies were dead somewhere." She still hadn't gotten over the panic. They'd taken years off her life with that stunt. "And what did you do about it, Ian Taggart?"

He held up his working hand as though trying to placate her. "In my defense, I knew they weren't dead. They were right in front of me."

"You laughed, Ian. You high-fived them."

He grimaced. "And that was wrong. I'm sorry, baby. I'm new to this whole parenting thing."

"And I'm not?"

"No, you are not. You've been raising kids since you were a kid. I sometimes feel like a dipshit compared to you."

He did? And honestly, it was rather clever. They'd managed to perfectly conceal themselves and stay off the security camera. They were only five but they'd considered the security cams. She turned on to the freeway that would take them home. "You raised a kid, too."

"Nah, I raised a Sean. He wasn't any trouble. He ate like a horse and he couldn't comprehend algebra to save his life, but he was a good kid. Ours are rotten. Like Chelsea was."

But it was said with a grin.

She would give him that because her sister still called him Satan from time to time. Chelsea hadn't been easy. She'd been hard. She'd been stubborn and obnoxious. It had taken everything Charlie had to keep her sister alive.

Because they'd loved each other. They'd loved each other as fiercely as her twins did. Even at this young an age, Kenzie and Kala had each other's backs. They watched out for each other in a way few children did. Bonded. They were fiercely bonded.

"Oh, god. It's my fault." Her hands tightened on the wheel as the truth rolled over her. "They're not like you. They're like me."

"Well, I did manage to support my sibling in a legal fashion," Ian said quietly. "I worked as a bagger and cleaned up at a fast food joint. You managed to become a teenaged assassin and then built one of the world's most notorious information brokerages. And I find you endlessly fascinating, too. I know it makes you crazy that I love it when the twins do bonkers shit, but it's all because when they do it, I am reminded of just how much I love their mother. Their mother is a crazy bitch who rocks my world every single time she enters a room. Their mother is the best woman I've ever met and I want my kids—the girls and the boys—to be every bit as smart and savvy and badass as their mama."

Damn. Now she wanted to pull off on the side of the road and mount him at the first possible opportunity. Mount that man and ride him hard because he was hers and she was his. Because they made badass babies who might bring about the apocalypse and burn the world down, but they were going to be such amazing women someday. Women who could fight for what they believed in. Women who pushed the world forward.

Their daughters.

"You know Miss Mayberry never once mentioned that Kala already has amazing math skills," Charlie said. "That teacher just talked about the bad stuff. How many kids know what it means to set up an army in a flanking position? From what I could tell between the teacher's sobs, Kala's battle plans were nearly perfect."

"Damn straight they were. And I'll give you a better one. That crossbow was locked up in the safe. They figured out my damn password."

A thrill of terror went through her. "Holy shit. I thought one of them was watching me. I took out the Ruger to go with Erin and Phoebe to the shooting range the other day and Kenzie kept making up excuses to stay close. They've been planning this. I shouldn't have let them watch *Brave*. They've been obsessed with bows and arrows since then."

"I…I don't think it was *Brave*." His face was tense in that way that let her know she wouldn't like what he said next.

"What did you do?"

"I thought *The Hunger Games* was about food. You know how much they like watching food talk," he spit out. "It came on cable and I might have fallen asleep. It was right after Seth was born and then they totally blackmailed me so they could watch the second one, but I found out what happened in the third and I got dirt on them so we had mutually assured destruction and they haven't seen *Mockingjay*. No way. No how."

Her babies had blackmailed their father.

She'd blackmailed her dad. Oh, sure, he'd been a horrible Russian mobster who she'd eventually maneuvered into a position where she'd had him killed to save her and her sister's lives, but…like mother like daughter.

"Charlie, baby, I know they make you crazy but they are the best things in the whole fucking world. I love my nieces and nephews— both blood and found—but damn, they're sheep compared to our little psychopaths. Seth is my boy. He's going to be dumb and strong, and he's going to need his big sisters to show him who to beat the shit out of. They're going to run the Agency, baby. I know it. I've already seen Fain looking them over. He's not a weird pervert so I'm pretty sure he's sizing them up as potential operatives. I'll be happy if we can just keep them out of the business through college."

They were super smart. A little ruthless for baby girls. And so much her and Ian.

"And they're marrying Americans. Now that Damon has a boy I have to worry about foreigners," Ian pronounced. "I'm instituting an arranged marriage thing in our family. Americans only. No Brits and dear god, no Canadians allowed."

She groaned. He was so obnoxious. "Just because you don't like their bacon doesn't mean Canadians can't make good partners."

Almost home. She got off the freeway. Was that a glow in the distance? Had Malone lied and the fire was still raging? Was their house in flames? Had they gotten the kids and Bud out? Had someone pulled the arrow out of Boomer's leg and he'd bled out on her living room floor and they would have to deal with his poor, sad, likely still hungry dead body.

"A civilization's bacon says something about them, and you will never convince me otherwise," Ian replied. "The only thing that could be worse is if one of my precious babies marries a vegan. What the fuck is almond milk, Charlie? Nuts don't have breasts. They don't have breasts."

The truck shuddered and went still, rolling along but without any life.

Oh, shit. She glanced down at the display.

"We're out of gas. We have to walk." How could she have forgotten about the gas? Ian had mentioned that they would need some on their way back, but he'd been eager to get to the party. Hell, he'd probably wanted to get there to ensure no one else got a lemon tart.

Her cell phone vibrated. She glanced down.

Please Charlotte. Please. I'll do anything. I can't handle it. It's too horrible.

Her heart sank and she passed the phone to Ian.

He paled. "Park the truck."

She shoved the F-150 into park. She was still in her corset. She'd shimmied into yoga pants but she didn't have her sneakers on. There hadn't been time, and who the hell could put on sneakers while wearing a fucking corset? No one. Not even Dita Von freaking Teese could manage it.

They were blocks from home. They lived in the country. She couldn't walk without shoes. She would have to get out of the corset, and Ian only had one working arm.

The world was bleak. Her babies…her precious babies.

Ian came around to her door, opening it and holding out his good hand. "Come on, baby. I'm going to Emmitt Smith this motherfucker."

"What?"

"Emmitt Smith. Dallas Cowboys running back. 1992. It's the last game of the season and the Cowboys need to beat the Giants in order to win a first round bye and home field advantage for the playoffs, but their best player, Emmitt Smith, severely separates his shoulder before the end of the first half. He's got two choices—go to the hospital or suck it up and win. I'm going to suck it up and win, like Emmitt. I'm going to do it for our girls. And our son. Not the dog. He smells."

She gasped as Ian leaned over and put his good shoulder in her midsection, lifting her into a fireman's hold. "Ian!"

"I'll get us home. I'll save our babies from dumbasses and themselves. I'll do it for us, Charlie."

"Emmitt Smith was only holding a football," she pointed out.

"His most precious possession." Ian broke into a jog. "You're mine, baby, and I won't ever fail you. I'm leaving the lemon tarts behind. Be safe, little ones."

He ran, sprinting in a way no man with a separated shoulder who didn't play for the Dallas Cowboys in their heyday should run. His feet pounded the concrete, bringing them ever closer to their home and their devil children who might or might not have murdered Boomer this evening.

"I don't smell smoke," he said as he turned down their street.

It was a good thing. They might still have a house. Three more blocks and they would be home.

"Have I told you, you have the sexiest ass I've ever seen." It was right there, his well-toned glutes working in time with his muscular legs. "I love you, Ian. If our children weren't currently attempting to kill their babysitters, I would fuck you right here."

He should know. He should never question where her desires lay.

He was her hero.

"And if I didn't think my baby girls were currently attempting to burn down our house and accidently kill their infant brother, I would fuck you right here, too." He never stopped running. "Yeah, Linkmans, I would fuck my gorgeous wife on your perfect lawn that always gets TP'd because you suck! Go get 'em, whoever you are. Get 'em good."

She looked up and sure enough, there was a kid with a bulk pack of toilet paper standing at the edge of the Linkmans' yard. Was that Johnny Kellerman? It didn't matter because Ian was still running.

He ran past a minivan parked on the street. She was almost certain she knew that van. And it was rocking slightly. Whoever was in that van was having a nice night.

"Who are you?" TP boy asked, his voice hushed. "Is that Mr. Tag?"

"I am motherfucking Emmitt Smith!" Ian screamed and picked up the pace.

She held on as her husband heroically took them home.

She knew they were there when she heard Bud's barking. The door came open and Bud nearly ran them over.

"Thank god!" Malone ran out into the yard.

Ian set her on her feet and she took a moment to reorient.

Malone had Seth in his hands, holding him under his little armpits and as far from his body as he could. "I'm pretty sure the toilet is overflowing because the girls were waterboarding their Ken doll. Boomer is alive but really hungry. The dog vomited on the rug. Five times. It's okay though because four times he totally ate it again. Only the last one stuck. And this one...god, he smells so bad. So bad. What do I do? How do you live like this?"

"Seth? That last frantic text was about Seth?" Charlie stared at him, her hands on her hips. "You were calm when the girls tried to set fire to the house and nearly killed one of your best friends, but you flip out over a baby's poop? He pooped, Malone. It can be taken care of with a box of wipes and a clean diaper."

"I'm used to terrible things happening. I can handle fires and Boomer getting shot. Been there, done that," Malone admitted. "But not that smell. God, not that smell."

Ian fell to the ground and didn't even whine when Bud started licking him.

Charlie took her baby boy and cuddled him close.

"Situation normal, baby," Ian managed to say.

Yep. All fucked up.

* * * *

Two hours later, Charlie closed the door and the house was blissfully silent.

Date night had gone to hell, but the damage seemed fairly minimal. The house was still standing. Everyone seemed to be alive, though Malone had complained that his sense of smell had been forever damaged.

Boomer had survived. Theo had come over and stitched the big guy up as he'd enjoyed not one but two large pepperoni pizzas. Theo had some medic training and his wife, Erin, had helped out because… Well, she really liked blood.

The night was over and everything was quiet.

What a fucking day.

She locked the door and moved back into the house. What the hell had happened? Her girls. That's what had happened.

So tired and yet she felt the need to check in on her babies.

She made sure the alarm was on and then headed to the room Kenzie and Kala shared.

No one there. Her heart skipped a beat. Why? Why did she do this? She should have taken the money from all the info brokering and lived a happy, designer clothes-filled life where her children never tried to burn down the house or murder people with arrows or…

She stopped in front of her own bedroom door. Ian was in the middle of their bed, his left arm taped up but still holding on to a baby girl. His eyes were closed, his head on the pillow, his arms filled with babies. Kenzie was on one side, Kala the other, and Seth was happily asleep on his father's bare chest, his diapered rump in the air.

Yeah, that was why she did it. This ridiculous, overwhelming feeling of love was why she went home every night, looking for these amazing people who made up her family.

One eye opened, looking her way. "You coming to bed, baby? Sorry I left you with Theo. The girls were tired."

She flicked the light off. "World domination is tiring."

Even in the low light she could see the way he smiled. "Yeah, it is. It's a Taggart world. My baby girls are princesses, but there's only one queen, Charlie."

Her. This was her house and she was the queen. She settled onto the mattress and cuddled close, one of their twins in between them. All of the warmth of her family encompassed her. They were here. Maybe they were whole or maybe there were even more Taggart demons to come.

Bring 'em on.

She was ready.

Charlie Taggart felt her husband's fingers tangle with hers.

"It was a pretty good night," he said.

She bit back a laugh. "Yes, it was, baby. Yes, it was."

6

Stuck at the Office

Stuck at the Office takes place between Long Lost and Charmed.

Ian Taggart put the code into the security system and heard the locks click. He kept the phone to his ear as he opened the door and let his little monsters into a place they knew all too well.

The office.

"We're here, and I managed to not lose a single one," he said to his wife on the other end of the line. "No matter how hard I tried. Those girls can keep up. I'm so sorry, baby. I'll try harder on our way back."

A throaty chuckle came over the line. "I'm sure you will, but those two are true Taggarts. You need to make sure they don't destroy the office. How is our baby boy doing?"

"He's the truest Taggart of all." He shifted his son, who was asleep on his shoulder, his small body completely deadweight. "He ate a sandwich, belched like a man, and promptly fell asleep. He's out like a light."

One of these days that would be his life. He would have raised all his demonlings and passed the company on to them, and then he would be the one eating all the sandwiches and taking all the naps. It was going to be a good life.

Not that this one was bad. It was simply way more chaotic than he'd thought his life would be, but then he hadn't thought he would actually be alive at this age, so he was going to take it all as a win.

He heard a giggle as the twins ran past the cubicle where his admin, Genny, worked.

He knew what was going to kill him now. Those two. His daughters. Kenzie and Kala would definitely be the reason for his heart attack.

"Put him down in the crib in the nursery, but remember he's gotten

143

really good at climbing," Charlie reminded him.

He needed no reminder. Seth Taggart was an expert at climbing out of his crib. Good at climbing, bad at landing. "I'll take one of the monitors with me and sprint when I hear him waking up."

It was good for his heart. Gave it a little shock. Maybe all those little shocks would make it stronger and he could survive the twins' teen years and make it to his sandwich/napping days.

The doors closed behind him, and he touched the pad to lock it all down again. It was a Saturday, so he wasn't truly worried about anyone coming into the office uninvited, but the girls had been known to play some pretty hardcore hide and seek, and he'd caught Kala trying to learn how to pick locks. The last thing he needed was to have the girls decide to break into one of the other businesses in the building.

Although letting them into Adam's office might be fun. It could be interesting to see if Adam's virtual assistant could deal with his baby girls.

Kenzie was getting pretty good with a computer, though. She might take over TESS and start World War III.

He was definitely going to have that heart attack.

"Have I told you thank you for taking the kids with you to the office?" Charlie asked.

That hadn't been the plan. His original plan had been to come up and do as much paperwork as he could so he didn't leave Alex and Liam a huge mess while he was on paternity leave. He might joke about that term and vomit in his mouth a little, but there was zero chance he was leaving his wife home alone with a newborn and three small demons. He liked his marriage, and he knew when to sacrifice for it.

Besides, he kind of liked those early days when they closed themselves off from the world and got to simply be a family for a few weeks.

"No need, baby. You take the afternoon and enjoy the quiet. It's the last you'll have for a while," he replied.

Because next week their final kiddo was due. Another boy. Two boys. Two girls. All the trouble two adults could possibly handle.

He'd meant for this to be his alone time, but Charlie had looked so weary he hadn't been able to walk out the door without taking the burden with him.

It was good no one was scheduled to be here because he'd made a huge show of how he was going to come up here alone on a Saturday. He'd talked about how important it was to get his work done before he left them alone while he took some time off.

He would likely get some ribbing over bringing his kids up.

"Bud and I will enjoy some quiet time," she replied. "I'll see you in a couple of hours."

"Love you, baby." He hung up and slid the phone into his pocket.

It was a good thing he was doing. Charlie needed peace and quiet, and honestly, how bad could it get?

There was a terrible crashing sound and then silence.

But only for a second because Seth's eyes opened.

"We're okay," a feminine voice yelled.

"Mostly," came the other one.

Seth started crying, and Ian took a deep breath. It was going to be a long day.

Two hours later Ian stared at his screen, trying to read through the latest report from Deke and Bear. They were in Kansas City on a corporate case and thought they were almost ready to wrap it up. They knew who was embezzling funds, but they needed a bit more evidence in case the client decided to pursue criminal charges. They likely wouldn't. Corporations seldom prosecuted, but he liked to give the client the option.

There was a little huffing sound from the baby monitor that let him know Seth was still asleep. It was the soft sound of him turning, and Ian knew for certain if he walked into the nursery, his son's butt would be up in the air while he sucked on a dream pacifier. Or probably one of his momma's boobs.

He'd almost gotten those boobs back. So close.

Where were his monsters? A prickle of awareness went up his spine. It was a little spark that he got usually right before someone tried to kill him.

He glanced over to the sitting area of his office. Charlie had furnished it with a comfortable couch and two chairs, a coffee table between them. It was where they often sat with Alex and Eve and had lunch. That couch had also been the site of many a good time between he and his wife. It was precisely why the couch was leather. Easy to clean. Didn't end up smelling like sex. Not that he minded the smell of sex when it came from his Charlie, but otherwise it was off-putting to clients.

Of course now the space was covered with tiny ponies and tons of crayons and colored pencils and paper he'd stolen from the copy machine.

He stood and walked over. He'd given the girls two dollars to go and raid the vending machine. It wasn't something he would normally do, but a dad did what he needed to when he was leaving voice mails for four-star generals and didn't want giggling girls in the background. They'd been playing with the multicolored ponies, who had some serious drama going on given they were plastic toys.

How long had they been gone?

He'd blocked off access to the floor downstairs, right? The security system would have beeped if they'd managed to get into the stairwell.

Kenzie had been showing off her art skills by drawing some rainbows and smiley faces. Then there was the drawing of a kid being hit by lightning. He was pretty sure it was a kid named Henderson and the artist was his little psycho, Kala. In her kindergarten class they kept a jar of marbles that they earned through being good. When the jar was full, they would get a pizza party. The teacher was mean—something she would need to be in order to survive Kala—and she took one out when one of the kids fucked up. Henderson apparently fucked up a lot, and Kala took exception.

She was either going into the Agency one day or she would be in jail. He had to figure out how to avoid either possibility because he didn't want that for her.

Being a parent sucked sometimes. He often wondered if Charlie was playing the odds, if she wanted a bunch of kids because some of them had to become sensible human beings and not supervillains.

It wouldn't be Kala, and Kenz might turn out to be that superpredator who smiled a lot right before she ate her victims.

Maybe that's just what happened when a grizzled ex-Agency dude hooked up with a superhot assassin chick. It was inevitable that they would have little demons.

He should probably tell that Henderson kid to chill out.

It was definitely too quiet.

The door to his office came open, and Kala stood there. She was dressed in a pink T-shirt with some anime character on it and jeans, her strawberry hair in a high ponytail he'd had to learn to perfect because she was picky about her hair. "Daddy, I need some butter."

Oh, he didn't like the sound of that. "I thought you were grabbing a bag of chips. Why would you need butter?"

Kala shrugged. "I like butter with my chips."

He would give it to her. She was a cool customer. "Where is your sister?"

Her little mouth firmed. "She's in the break room waiting on me to come back with some butter."

"But the butter would be in the refrigerator, and that's in the break room," he pointed out.

Her brow furrowed. "Okay. I'll look there."

She turned and ran back.

And he followed because he knew damn straight when something was going on with his girls. He followed his daughter through the main office and its banks of cubicles. She wove her way through like she could lose him in his own office. He would give her credit for sheer arrogance.

She slipped into the break room, and he could hear them talking.

"Did you get it?" Kenzie asked.

"No, but Dad said it would be in the fridge," Kala replied. "There's a lot of yogurt in here. Eww. And some gross stuff. Ah, there it is."

"Uh, I think we should talk to Dad." Kenzie was the reasonable one. "I think it might be gross."

Oh, they were not going to do some weird science experiment in the break room. He strode toward the door. "Guys, I said you could get one bag of chips and something sweet to share."

Kenzie was on the floor, her little arm all the way inside the vending machine. "It got stuck."

"So did Kenz," Kala admitted, holding up a stick of butter. He was fairly certain it was the butter Erin used on her toast every morning.

"But I'm going to grease her up and get her out."

That was the moment Seth chose to start crying.

Yep, just another day at the office.

* * * *

Charlotte tried to stretch her lower back. It had been aching all morning, but then she was only a week away from her due date and something always ached. The baby in her womb kicked like he was trying out for a professional soccer team.

Travis. They'd already decided on Travis. Her last baby because Ian hadn't believed her whole "I never want to be pregnant again" line and done the one thing he'd sworn he wouldn't do. He'd gotten a vasectomy. He'd whined and complained, and she'd had to hold a bag of frozen peas to his ball sack, but she knew why he'd done it. It was far easier for him to have it done than her.

The phone rang, and she gave serious consideration to letting it go because it was all the way across the room and sitting seemed so nice.

But then she remembered that Ian had all three kids, and while it meant she had a quiet house, it could also mean disaster for her husband.

Bud's head had come up. He'd been napping at her feet as she'd sat and gone through file after file of papers her cousin had sent to her. Not that he didn't nap most of the time. The dog she'd convinced Ian they needed had started out as an adorable, energetic ball of fluff and had grown into an adorable, lazy ball of fluff. She often caught Bud and Ian napping together.

"You want to go grab my cell for me, buddy?"

Bud's tail thumped but he did not move. Yep. When he wasn't trying to herd the girls away from potential danger, the big mutt was storing up energy so he could later hoover up all the food they dropped.

Charlotte yawned and pushed her chair back. There was nothing for it. She was going to have to answer. It wasn't like she was getting anywhere. Every single lead she got seemed to direct her to a dead end.

Dead. Damn it. That was the one word she hadn't wanted to associate with her investigation, but it was the only piece of information she'd managed to find.

148

She picked up her cell, recognized the name of the caller, and swiped across the screen. "Hey, Chels."

"Hey," her sister said. "I was calling to see if you needed me to come by. I saw Michael this morning and he told me Ian made a big-ass deal out of saying he was going into the office to finish up all his paperwork before he goes on leave because that's what good employees do. Apparently Erin flipped him off. She couldn't help going into labor early."

Ian was good at pissing people off, but then she happened to know Erin had told everyone she could have the baby and never look up from her paperwork. "He took the kiddos with him. I'm good. It's the first time this house has been quiet in...forever."

She stretched, trying to get her back to release. She was pretty sure Travis would end up being her biggest baby. Oh, the doc tried to tell her he was only seven pounds, but she swore there was a toddler in there.

"Ian's got three kids with him up at the office?" Chelsea laughed. "Well, we'll see how that goes."

It would likely go south at some point, and Ian would clean it up and never tell her the tale. He would tell the girls "don't tell Mom" and actually believe they could keep a secret. She knew everything. She knew about the time Ian had rushed and gotten the booster seat in wrong and Kala had ended up climbing over the seats in the middle of the freeway, causing her man to dump his morning coffee everywhere.

"How are you feeling?" Charlotte moved toward the kitchen, hoping there was still some ham left. She could eat.

"I'm good. I'm still bummed about the whole breast feeding thing," her sister began. "I mean, my boobs are huge. Why don't they make enough milk?"

Chelsea had a three-month-old and had a terrible time breastfeeding. After Chelsea's third bout of mastitis had landed her in the hospital, Charlie and Simon had convinced her it was okay to give the baby a bottle. "Hey, you can't blame yourself for that, and you need to know that fed is best. Always. However you need to feed her is the best way for you to feed her."

"Says the woman who is already leaking." But her sister said it with a chuckle. "I know. I just wish it had worked. I think she's my

149

only kid. I think we're going to be okay with one."

She would give her sister no pushback on that. "And however big you want your family to be is fine, too."

It had taken Chelsea a long time to decide she wanted a baby at all. Their childhood had been rough, to say the least, and losing their mom the way they had affected Chelsea. But after a few years enjoying married life, she'd surprised them all by announcing she would add to the world's overpopulation with her very own demonling.

Sophy was a dream baby, and with the exception of her breastfeeding problems, Chelsea's transition to motherhood seemed to have gone off without a hitch.

It hadn't hurt that she'd had tons of help. Simon's parents had stayed with them for a few weeks, lavishing affection and help on the new parents. No one should have a say in whether or not a couple had a kid, but she was happy Chelsea had.

"Are you done?" Chelsea asked.

"Giving birth to kids? After this one, yes." Three pregnancies. Four kids. She was good with pushing no more babies out of her vagina.

"But you're not done with kids." Chelsea sighed. "I wanted to talk to you about Sasha's daughter."

This was the project she was working on, and Chelsea was helping her. Ever since they'd figured out the man they'd known as Sasha had a daughter, they'd been searching for her and her mother. She'd managed to find Sasha's real name, and that had led her to Moscow and a woman named Marta who'd been killed in what the reports called a robbery, but Charlie recognized as a hit.

Sasha had angered his SVR bosses. From what Charlie had discovered, he'd likely been ready to blow the whistle on corruption in his department when the men he'd worked for had sold him to Dr. Hope McDonald. Sasha had been born Oleg Federov and he'd "died" according to the records. His wife hadn't been willing to let it go, and she'd actually been killed. Now his daughter was an orphan. At least Charlie hoped the girl was still alive.

"I've hit a brick wall," she admitted. "I called Dusan."

Her cousin was the head of an infamous syndicate in Russia. If anyone could cut through red tape, it was Dusan. And they were family.

He wouldn't put the usual strings on her. For a mobster, her cousin had an oddly soft heart. Especially when it came to kids. He knew what it was like to grow up in a harsh environment.

"Good, because I'm at a loss, too. I can't find enough information about Oleg Federov, and what I can find I have to question because I think Russian intelligence erased what they didn't want anyone to know," Chelsea said with a sigh. "But that's not what I wanted to talk about. We're going to find her. I promise you that, but what do we do *when* we find her?"

She knew what she was going to do. "We give her a home."

"I knew you would say that," Chelsea replied. "Have you thought about this?"

Of course she'd thought about it and come to one conclusion. "She needs to come home with us. Unless she's happy with a good family somewhere, we need to bring her to the States, and you and I are the best candidates. And it's going to be me."

Chelsea sighed. "That's what I thought you might say. I've been talking to Si. You're about to have four kids. We only have Sophy."

She opened the fridge. Rat-fink bastard had eaten her ham. Ice cream it was then. Ian knew better than to touch her ice cream. "In this case, I think more is better. I know I've got a ton of kids, but Kala and Kenzie speak her language. Seth is already babbling in a mix of English and Russian. Ian and I speak…"

"You speak Russian. Ian speaks some weird version I can halfway understand," Chelsea countered.

He wasn't that bad. He just missed some of the nuances because he didn't speak it every day. "I could say the same thing about Simon's English. Sophy is going to grow up calling the trunk of her car a boot."

It wasn't exactly the same, but she felt the need to defend her husband. She was sure his Russian had been excellent once. They really needed to start speaking it more often. She spoke to the kids in Russian much of the day, but tended to switch back to English at night.

"Sure, that's going to be her main problem," Chelsea said with a snort. "I just think we should all sit down and talk about this as a family."

Charlotte set the ice cream down, and suddenly there were tears in her eyes because her heart felt so full. How far her sister had come.

151

"Yes, we'll sit down as a family. How about you bring Si and Sophy over tomorrow?"

"And we'll also bring food because you don't need to cook. I'll have something catered in," Chelsea said.

Her sister had become a kind, thoughtful woman. For years Charlie had been the one to take care of her little sister. Now Chelsea always tried to take care of her. "All right. That sounds like a plan. Now I am going to take a break and eat a bunch of ice cream and read a hot romance. Or maybe I'll watch TV that isn't a cartoon."

It had been a while. Her afternoon was wide open, and she should take advantage of that. She went for a spoon and...

Fuck. Why were her thighs suddenly wet?

Damn it. She was dripping. Not some wild gush the way it was in the movies, but enough to let her know what had happened.

"Hey, you okay?" Chelsea asked.

Nope. She wasn't okay.

Bud looked down at the floor and then back up at her as though to say "when I do that you get mad."

"I'm having the baby. Like right now." Her belly seized, and she realized she was a dumbass because she'd been in labor all morning long.

* * * *

"Butter is not going to help, and now I'm a little worried I should call the fire department because I have no idea how you got stuck in there." Panic was starting to well inside Ian, and he was not the guy who panicked. He was the dude who kept his cool even while taking enemy fire. When the bombs started dropping, Ian Taggart chilled and dealt with the situation.

"I think the butter might work." Twenty minutes later Kala was still holding that stick of butter and he was still alone, despite the fact that he'd called all three of his brothers and Alex.

He'd gotten voice mails from everyone. Every single one of the fuckers was apparently doing something so fucking important he couldn't answer the phone.

"Didn't it work on Winnie the Pooh?" Kenzie was the calm one.

She just sat there while her dad thought about how Charlie would divorce him if she lost an arm in a vending machine on his watch.

She never paid attention. "No, sweetie. They had to starve Pooh Bear to get him out of the hole."

Now Kenzie's eyes went wide and tears formed. "I don't want to starve. I'm already hungry. I really want some chips."

Okay. He had to go about this logically. He'd unplugged the machine. He'd tried to gently ease her arm out. He'd even maneuvered her bodily, but that sucker was stuck.

Seth was still wailing.

"So it's okay for me to eat the candy bar?" Kala asked. "I mean, I don't need to starve, right?"

"Go and comfort your brother." He wasn't going to yell. No. He was keeping his cool. He'd taken out an entire unit of enemy soldiers on his own with too little ordnance and very little cover. He could handle one vending machine without losing his shit.

Seth had been wailing for a while now and it was starting to grate, but he wasn't sure what the best dad in the world should do in this particular situation. Should he leave his trapped daughter to change his son's pants or fill his never-ending gut?

If he smashed the vending machine open, could he take it apart without slicing his baby's arm off? Maybe she wanted a bionic arm.

Alex was better with tools than he was. Theo was good with his hands, too. Maybe he could figure out a way to take the machine apart. Or he could call the vending machine company. Did they have a help desk? Frequently answered questions?

Charlie was going to have his head.

His cell buzzed in his pocket. He slipped it out, praying it was Alex.

It was Charlie. How long could he duck this call?

He looked down at his daughter. "Do not move."

Kala had obviously gotten to Seth because he quieted down.

Kenzie was crying. "I don't want to starve."

"I'm not going to let you starve." But she might grow up here. He would make it comfortable for her. He could put in a cot, and she would have lots of company because Hutch used this sucker three times a day.

Fuck. He took a deep breath and slid his finger across the screen. "Hey, baby. How's the relaxation going?"

He would tell her. One day. But she was resting today. She didn't need to worry about their daughter being attached to a vending machine for the rest of her life.

"Ian, I need you to come home. I'm in labor. I think I've got enough time for you to get back here and take me to the hospital," she said.

"I'm sorry, what?"

"Baby. Coming. Soon."

His heart was going to stop. The baby wasn't supposed to be here for another week. How could this be happening? He had to deal with it. "I want you to call 911."

"I don't think I need to," she replied. "I think I'm okay. I would rather wait for you."

"Don't tell Mom," Kenzie whispered.

He sent his daughter a stern look and stepped away. "How far apart are the contractions?"

He would call until he got someone on the phone. He would send someone over to hold her hand, and he would get the fire department out here to smash the fucking vending machine. That was a plan.

"I don't know. My water broke," she admitted.

It was time to take control. "Charlie, I'm calling 911 if you don't. The traffic shouldn't be too bad on a Saturday. I'm twenty minutes away if I leave right now, and I can't."

"Don't call 911. I was on the phone with my sister when it happened. Chelsea's already on her way. Why can't you leave?"

There were times when he couldn't hide shit from his wife. "Kenzie's arm is caught in the vending machine."

"What?" The question came out on a screech.

"Baby, I will deal with it. I need you to get to the hospital. I will meet you there. I promise you this is fine." He moved back into the break room and held the phone out. "Kenz, tell your mother you're fine."

"I'm fine. But Daddy told us we had to share our snacks and Kala picked the candy bar, and I think she's going to eat all of it," Kenzie began. "And that is not fair, Mom."

154

He put the phone back to his ear. "See, she's fine."

"Okay. My contractions are still eight minutes apart. I've got time, but if Chelsea hits traffic she could be thirty minutes out. I'm calling Faith. She's in town so she's nearby. If I call Faith, would you be okay with she and Ten driving me?"

Faith was a doctor, and he trusted her. Ten had been his friend for years. He would do what he needed to do. "All right. Text me when they're on their way. I mean it, Charlie."

"Okay. I'm calling now. I love you." She hung up.

"Hey, what's going on?" Erin Taggart walked into the break room, a couple of bags in her hand. "Is there a reason Kala and Seth are in the nursery? I don't know that he should be eating chocolate in the crib. It's getting messy."

"She gave my half of the candy bar to Seth?" Kenzie started crying again. "That's not fair! She doesn't get any of my chips."

"Why are you stuck in the vending machine?" Erin's green eyes were wide as she looked back at Ian. "I brought some lunch because you were supposed to be working today. I need to write up the Grate investigation, and Theo's got the kids for the day. I thought it would be quiet up here."

"Yeah, well you thought wrong, sister. I'm calling in the damn fire department because I can't get her out and Charlie's in labor. I tried getting Theo on the line but his ass won't answer," Ian complained as he started to dial 911.

"Kenzie, let go of the chips," Erin ordered.

What? "She's not holding onto the chips. She's stuck."

Erin shook her head. "She's totally holding onto the chips. Do you honestly believe this is the first time some dumbass got their arm stuck? I managed to ease Boomer's out and his arm is thicker than Kenzie's whole body. If she's stuck, it's because she won't let go of the chips."

For fuck's sake. He stared at his daughter.

She started crying again. "I'm really hungry and Kala got the candy bar she wanted. And I didn't even like the candy bar she picked and then she gave my half to Seth."

Erin stepped in front of him, putting her hands on his shoulders and obviously trying not to laugh. "Go to Charlotte. I will handle the

155

mob. I'll call Theo and he'll start the phone chain. Go. I can handle them."

He let out a long breath. "Thank you, sister."

He ran out the door even as Erin started in on a lecture about how life wasn't always fair and that didn't mean she had to give up an arm.

Kenzie was in good hands. All his kids were.

And it was time to welcome another one.

* * * *

Charlie felt the morning light on her face and kept her eyes closed, letting the warmth caress her skin. Her first full day with Travis Alexander Taggart. He'd been born at 10:14 p.m., giving his father plenty of time to get to the hospital and hold her hand the whole way. And late enough that they hadn't had visitors yet. That would happen the minute visiting hours started, but for now, it was the three of them.

She opened her eyes and sure enough, there they were. Ian was sitting in a rocking chair next to her bed, his shirt off and Travis on his chest. A blanket covered them, but Travis's little head was resting on his dad's broad shoulder.

She loved this, loved seeing her husband with their babies. She could remember how dangerous he'd been in the beginning. He'd been a gorgeous lion who might eat her up, and she'd thought he was sexy as hell.

And somehow he was sexier now with a few more lines around his eyes, a little gray at his temples.

He was precious. This life they'd built was precious.

"Hey, you in pain, baby?" His eyes had come open, and a worried look crossed that face she loved. "I can call the nurse."

She'd needed a stupid episiotomy because Travis was eight and a half pounds, with a big old head she'd barely managed to shove out of her hoohaw. "I'm fine."

"You're crying," he countered and then nodded. "This is one of those times when you thank the universe for how easy I was to land, right?"

He made her smile. "Something like that, babe. How's he doing?"

Ian shifted and stood up, expertly holding their baby boy. "He's

156

strong. I'm pretty sure the kid gave me a couple of hickeys already. You want to hold him?"

She nodded, and then she had her arms full. Her last baby. She kissed his forehead. The kid was a true Taggart, with a mop of blonde hair and big blue eyes. He yawned and immediately started rooting.

She placed the baby to her breast, and he was a champ.

Ian settled the blanket around them and reached for his shirt. "You sure you trust me with the kids? I was not the one who got Kenz out of the vending machine."

"Hey, it takes a village," she pointed out. "Or a really big extended family."

It had been Chelsea who'd calmed her down, Faith and Ten who'd picked her up and gotten her safely to the hospital, Erin and Theo who'd taken their other kids in.

She could remember when it had only been her and Chelsea, and the world had seemed so cold. Then she'd walked into a dungeon on a mission and found the other half of her soul waiting for her.

Ian's expression was soft as he brushed a tear from her cheek. "He's perfect, and so are you. I love you, baby."

They were the only words she needed. "I love you, too."

There was a knock on the door and the nurse came in. "I hope you're ready for some visitors."

Her girls rushed in and started cooing over the new baby while Theo handed over Seth to Ian.

Her world was full.

But there might be room for one more.

7

Homecoming

Homecoming takes place around the time of part one of No Love Lost.

Ian Taggart's cell phone rang and he glanced down at the number. He didn't recognize it, but hey, if it was someone offering him a car warranty extension, he could always hang up. Sometimes his employees called from burner phones, and if he didn't answer, someone got left in the middle of a firefight with no backup.

He was getting too old for this shit.

"This is Taggart."

"Mr. Taggart, my name is Kelsey Owens. I'm a private investigator your wife hired," the voice said over the line.

That made him stop. "My wife hired a private investigator? Is there something I should know?"

He couldn't think of why she would hire an investigator when they literally employed like fifteen of them. If Charlie thought he was cheating, she wouldn't hire someone to follow him. She would take him out on her own and hard. It would not be a pretty death. It would be ugly and likely involve his entrails.

God, he loved that woman.

"She doesn't know it yet, but yes. Though I won't be sending her a bill because I was told I couldn't. Which is rude when you think about it. Anyway, I couldn't get her on the line so I tried you."

Now he was intrigued. This was probably a play to get a job, but it was a new one. And he could use more estrogen in the office. He also liked a bold move, and this was definitely bold. "I think you should explain yourself, Ms. Owens."

"I get that a lot, but I'm kind of a no-explanations chick," the woman on the other end of the line explained in a flat, no-nonsense tone. "So I found the girl you're looking for. I can do one of two things. I can sit back and let you figure this out on your own, because your wife is good and she probably will. She's on the right track, but probably still a couple of months away from cutting through all the red tape. Or I can send you the information and you can get that child out of the orphanage."

He sat up straighter because now he thought he knew what she was saying. "Are we talking about Natasha Federova?"

Natasha Federova. Oleg Federov's daughter, the one he'd been taken from when his intelligence agency sold him to Hope McDonald and her memory experiments. She'd renamed the man Sasha and tortured him until he became one of her supersoldiers. He'd forgotten his former life, but before he'd died he'd held one memory, one thing she couldn't take. He'd been able to see a child in his hands, a baby he'd thought was a girl.

Sasha had died saving one of his "brothers," and the whole group was dedicated to finding that child, to making sure she had everything she needed. They'd hoped she was with her mother, but Charlie had information that Sasha's wife was likely dead.

"Yes, I've tracked her down," Kelsey explained. "Now I have some questions before I send you the information."

He had some questions, too. "How did you get this number? And what do you know about the girl?"

"I know she's alone in the world," Kelsey said quietly. "I know that SVR killed her parents and shipped her off, and if no one helps her, she'll grow up in a system that will eat her up and spit her out."

His gut clenched because one word the woman on the other line had said washed over him. "She's in an orphanage? I was hoping there was family who could take her in."

"I haven't found any family for the girl beyond Mom and Dad. Mom's been gone for a while now. She went looking for the dad, and apparently no one in the KGB wanted him found. From what I can tell, he was looking into corruption in his department. They didn't take kindly to that and he was sent to…" There was the sound of paper rustling, as though the woman was shuffling through her notes. "Some chick named Hope McDonald. She's dead, too."

"Yeah, I was there." Now his hackles were up. "All of this

information is classified, so I would like very much to know who you are."

"I represent an interested party. My client would like to ensure Natasha Federova finds a new home. Am I wrong in assuming we're on the same page, Mr. Taggart? Are you looking for her out of mere curiosity?"

"No. I'm going to find her and protect her." In the beginning, he'd meant to find her and offer her mother assistance. When they'd learned Marta was gone, too, he'd hoped he would find Natasha safe in a grandparent or an aunt or uncle's home. The idea that the child had been alone in the world made his heart ache. The whole family had been destroyed because Sasha had tried to do the right thing.

He could still remember how tortured the man had been, how dark he'd seemed. At one point, Ian had thought Sasha might be violent enough that he had to be dealt with, but then the man had laid his life down.

And Tag owed him. They all did. The only way to honor Sasha's sacrifice was to take care of his only child.

"Are you going to adopt her? You would be the best family for her. You or your sister-in-law. She needs someone who speaks Russian," Kelsey said.

"I don't know. I thought we would bring her and her mother either to the States or England. I thought we would be moving them somewhere safe. When we found out Marta was dead, I thought I would do the same with whoever was taking care of her," Ian explained. "I need to talk to my group about it, but you should understand she will have a family at the end of this."

They wouldn't leave her alone. They would likely fight over who got to keep her.

"Good. Then I came to the right man," Kelsey said. "She needs a safe place, and having someone who speaks her language should make things far easier for her."

His fear had softened a bit because the woman was pushing for the right things. "Did Sasha have more family than we've discovered? Is that who you're representing? Why is she in an orphanage if she's got family?"

"No, there is no more blood family. He has people who care for him," Kelsey replied. "Cared for him. He was a good man, and he would want his daughter taken care of. He thinks...he would have thought yours would be the best family for her."

He wondered how close this woman had been to Oleg Federov's family that she still stumbled when she thought about him being dead. Sasha had been missing for a long time. The fact that this woman not only knew who he was, but seemed to believe she understood what he would have wanted, was interesting. He softened his tone. She was trying to help, and the truth was Charlie had run into some problems hunting down the information they needed. "I will talk to my wife about it. Now I've said more than I should have. I would like very much to know about you and this client of yours."

"The info is in the email I sent. That's all you need to know."

No matter how well-meaning this woman was, he didn't like not knowing who this mysterious client was. "How can I trust that intel if you won't tell me who you are?"

"I did tell you. I'm Kelsey Owens, though good luck finding me. And the fact that you call it intel makes you a douchebag. It's information, dude. We have the same aims, and that's getting that girl out of the orphanage."

"I'm not a douche for calling it intel. It's what it is...." Why was he arguing with this woman? He hopped on his laptop and sent a quick text to Hutch, who better fucking be at his desk and not hanging around the vending machine waiting for a girl to walk by.

Trace the call to my cell and find out who Kelsey Owens is.

"Oh, it's douchey," Kelsey was saying with a sigh. "It's meant to be all military and shit, like the rest of us never fought a war. When you think about it, it's totally elitist. Until you've taken down a couple of demons all on your own, don't talk to me about..." There was a muffled sound, and then he heard Kelsey sigh. "Sorry. Apparently I'm getting off topic. Look, I'm sending you the information. Do with it what you want. I'm out of it now."

He needed her to stay on the line a little while longer. "I still have questions."

"I'm sure you do. You seem like a curious guy, but I've got a full day ahead of me," Kelsey replied. "And I haven't even gotten a nap in yet."

He could already tell she was done. He wouldn't get her to talk. But he might get her to answer the most important question of all. "Whoever your client is…I need to know if your client is going to show up on our doorstep one day."

Would he bring Natasha here only to have her life upended again?

"Only if you need him. The world my client lives in…it's not suitable for her." Kelsey was quiet for a moment. "Good-bye, Mr. Taggart."

The line went dead and the door opened. Hutch stood there, looking down at his phone.

"Hey, you know we don't trace cell calls the same way we would a landline, right?" The kid who served as the head of his cybersecurity arm looked even younger than his twenty-something years.

Ian sat back with a sigh. "Yeah, well, I don't think we would have found her anyway. Get me everything you can on Kelsey Owens."

"Do you have any other information on her? I know it seems like there should be only one of them in the world, and every person is unique and shit, but lots of people probably have that name," Hutch said. Ian sent him a stare, and Hutch stood up straighter. "I'll find them all then. Awesome."

It was good to know he could still scare someone. He obviously wasn't intimidating to that Kelsey chick. He pulled up his email and sure enough, there was one marked *Information not Intel*.

Well, at least she spoke his language.

Ian opened the file. The records were all in Russian, and he wondered if Kelsey was connected in some way. She'd mentioned a client, but she wouldn't talk about him or her. Had Sasha had mafia ties? Or did someone feel guilty for what happened to him? Guilt could be a good motivator. And living in a world of either spies or mobsters would qualify as unsuitable for children.

It was only one of the reasons he'd gotten out. It also hadn't been good for his soul.

He opened one of the files, and the picture of a young girl popped up. She was thin, with dark hair and big eyes that had seen far too much of the world.

Natasha Smirnova

They'd changed her name. Of course they had. No one wanted her connected to her mother and father—people they'd tossed out like trash. They'd used the most common surname in Russia. Smirnova translated to still or quiet. It could mean meek.

They could change her name, but they couldn't change those eyes. Sasha's eyes. She had the same stubborn set to her jaw.

He quickly went through all the information Kelsey had acquired. None of it had been translated into English, as though she'd wanted to remind him of everything Natasha would have to go through if she didn't have someone who spoke her language.

He had four kids. Four. His youngest wasn't even six weeks old.

Si and Chelsea only had one.

And Simon didn't speak the language. She would have one person to talk to, and no children her age around her. Would his girls make the difference in her having a smooth transition, or would bringing a potentially traumatized child into his family cause pain for all of them?

Did he even have a choice? Those big eyes stared at him.

Simon didn't owe Sasha the way he did. Somehow when Theo had been taken, Ian had ended up feeling responsible for them all. Fucking god complex got him every time.

There was a knock on the door and then Alex was walking through it.

"Hey, I brought lunch." His best friend in the world had two bags in his hand. "Thai. Two different entrees and some spring rolls."

Alex could help. Alex almost always gave him sound advice. Except when it came to pool contractors. The fucker wouldn't even help him bury the asshole's body. And Charlie hadn't let him kill the guy. No one let him have any fun.

"I need to avoid having a fifth child," he stated flatly.

"I thought that was why you had your balls scooped out, buddy." Alex set the bags on the desk and then seemed to understand he was serious. "Shit. Is Charlotte really talking about having another kid? Travis is barely out of the womb. I thought you were done."

He turned the monitor Alex's way. "The question is what do I owe some dude who couldn't stand me when he was alive?"

Alex's jaw dropped. "Shit. You found her. That's Sasha's daughter."

"Kim Solomon sent us some intel that led Charlie to believe

Natasha Federova was taken from Moscow and temporarily put into public care. We were all hoping we would find out a relative had stepped up to give her a home. Until today. Now we know for sure she's alone. Some chick named Kelsey sent this, and now I have a decision to make."

"You have to figure out what to do with her. I'm going to take it she's not safe and happy somewhere," Alex said, his eyes on the screen.

If it were that easy… "They killed her mom, changed her name, and shipped her to an orphanage in fucking Siberia."

"Okay. So we have to get her out," Alex said evenly. "Let's sit down with everyone and decide the best course of action. I know Robert and Ariel talked about taking her in. That might be the best situation for her. Ari's a therapist."

"She doesn't specialize in kids, and she doesn't speak Russian. Tasha's not a baby. She'll need someone to talk to, to play with. She's seven, and she'll be in a foreign country."

A brow rose over Alex's eyes. "Do you want me to talk you out of this? Or into it?"

He groaned. "I don't know. I need to think. I need to talk to Charlie. I want to say this isn't my problem. I want to shrug and not deal with it because I've already got four freaking kids, and who knows how a new one will throw things off."

"Who knows what she's been through and whether or not you can handle her damage. Or what happens if someone comes for her one day. What do you do if you love this kid and someone else shows up with a claim on her?" Alex said softly. "Adoption is hard. It's harder when you're talking about adopting an older kid. I've adopted two, and I will tell you that I don't love them any less than Vivi."

Cooper and Hunter were Alex's adopted sons, and Vivian the miracle baby he and his wife Eve hadn't even dreamed about.

"I'm not scared of adopting. Everything is peaceful right now. As peaceful as it can be with Kala around." He looked back to that sad-eyed little girl. How would he feel if this had happened to his Kala or his Kenzie? "And this could bring chaos we don't need."

"Or a peace you didn't realize you were lacking," Alex countered. "You know this, man. We can't see the future, can't predict what's going to happen. We make the best choices we can and then hold on through the storm. Whatever you choose, I'll back you up. She's not going to be alone. We just have to find the right family for her. How about you talk to Charlotte and I'll get the Lost Boys together on a call."

"You know what Charlie's going to say." It didn't matter what the Lost Boys decided. Charlie would want what was best for Natasha, and she would think it was them.

Alex handed him a fork. "Yes, and I know what you'll say when you've had more than ten minutes to think about it. But Ian, you do not have to take on this responsibility. It's not your burden."

He looked back at the girl. Sometimes truths slid into place, and there was nothing he could do to deny them. He'd known shortly after he'd met Charlotte Denisovitch that she would hold his heart for the rest of time. He'd known when he'd lost her the first time that he couldn't go on with life the way he had before. Those pivotal moments happened, and there was no fighting them.

"She's coming home with us," he said quietly.

"I know that," Alex said. "So eat your pad thai and I'll go grab a couple of beers and we'll get Mitch on the phone."

"And Adam." He wanted Adam in on this. "Ask Adam and Chelsea to come up. Tash is going to need paperwork. The Russians closed adoptions to the US years ago. She'll need a more friendly passport, and we'll need cash to get her out."

He liked Hutch, and Hutch could probably do all of it, but this was his…fuck. He was already thinking of her as his kid, and he wanted the best. Adam and Chelsea were the best.

"Congratulations, Dad," Alex said with a shit-eating grin.

He got the feeling the fifth time wouldn't be as easy as the other four.

* * * *

"I knew I was on the right track."

Ian stared at his wife. She was looking at the documents and information Kelsey Owens had sent over. "Do you know the woman who sent it?"

Charlie shook her head. She looked pretty in her comfy pj's, with her hair up in a messy bun, but then she always looked pretty to him. "Never heard of her before."

There was a crash somewhere in the house immediately followed by a little girl shouting, "I'm okay!"

To her credit, Charlie didn't even look up. Until they smelled fire or heard a pain scream, they pretty much stayed calm. It was the only way to survive their twins.

Would they get along with Tasha? Did he have any right to bring a traumatized girl into his chaos?

"She claims she's working for an interested party," he explained.

That got Charlie's gaze up. "A relative? I didn't think Sasha had any family left."

"I didn't either. She swears whoever she works for isn't going to show up and claim Tasha."

Charlie's lips quirked up. "Tasha?"

He shrugged. "It's easier to say than Natasha. I'm thinking mob."

"Of course you are. You know I've had Dusan looking into this. He found no connections at all." Charlie looked back to the screen as she talked about her cousin, who happened to run the Denisovitch syndicate. "He looked into who sold out Sasha and killed his wife when she went looking for him. He believes that was all SVR. He didn't find any mob connections at all, and yes, I believe he would have told me if his group had been hired to do it."

SVR was the shiny new name for the KGB, but that was all window dressing. They were the same old intelligence agency. Ruthless. Cutthroat. Willing to slice off an arm to protect the body. "They don't need to bring in the mob. They can kill fine on their own."

"This woman knows what she's doing." Charlie clicked through the documents. "Solo sent me some good shit, but this is superlative. The records she found show a perfect through line. You can see where they changed her name."

Kelsey Owens had included photos and medical records to prove Natasha Smirnova was Natasha Federova. Adam and Chelsea had authenticated the documents and photos.

"Yes, I'm worried she's too good."

"I might say the same, but Solo found a lot of this, too, and we've verified it. No, you're looking for a way out. Your paranoia is stirring up a storm in that head of yours." She closed the laptop and reached out to put a hand over his. "That magnificent brain of yours is going through every possible rotten scenario. Tell me the worst one you've come up with."

"We adopt her and she's so fucked up it fucks up our kids," he offered. There were no lies between him and his wife. He didn't prevaricate or try to hide the dark parts of his soul. What he'd found was they could get through almost anything if they were honest and open about what bothered them. Charlie talked to him when motherhood felt like a chain around her, and he got her through the hard moments so they could enjoy the happy ones.

"We can do that all on our own," Charlie said. "Try again."

He wasn't sure what his wife was looking for, but he had a whole list to run down. "Okay, our kids are a nightmare, and they traumatize her further."

"The girls are awesome, and they'll be delighted to have a sister," Charlie countered. "Try again."

Fuck. She was going to force him to look deep. "What if I can't love her the way I love my own kids?"

Her expression softened, and she moved to ease herself onto his lap. "You have the biggest heart in the world, Ian Taggart. There's a place for everyone who deserves it in there. All you have to do is be patient, and I think you'll find that loving a child is the easy part. Here is the only question that matters. Are we the best family for her?"

"I already have Mitch working with Adam and Chelsea to make sure everything is legal," he admitted, wrapping his arm around her. "Well, as legal as this adoption can be. I'm worried about whoever this client of Kelsey's is though."

Charlie leaned her head against his shoulder. "Yeah, that's my big worry too. We'll love her and someone will come to take her away from us. But it's not a reason to sit back and leave her on her own."

He already knew what he would do. "If anyone shows up, I'll fight."

"I know you will, baby, and that's merely one of the reasons you're an excellent father," she said with a sigh.

He loved these moments when he could sit here and be with her, breathe this woman in. "I'm only a father because you wanted kids."

She snorted, a sound he still found magical. "Sure, because you weren't a caretaker before. You didn't change the course of your life and form a whole company to give your family and friends a place to be, a job to do. You've been a father since you were a kid. It's who you are deep inside, and this will be no different."

He let his hand start to drift up to her breast because she was getting way too serious for him. "Oh, it'll be different. Tash will probably be easier to deal with than Liam was after he got blown up and had to go on the run. Whiny Irishman."

She rolled her eyes. "You are a great dad, and if you *honka honka* me right now you're going to ruin this shirt because my milk came in and there's a ton of it, buddy."

But he liked a good *honka honka*. "See, kids ruin everything."

"Dad, Kala's been listening in, and she says we're getting a new sister to make up for the fact that Mom keeps having boys. Is she right?" Monster Number Two stood in front of him, her strawberry blonde hair in pigtails and the dog by her side.

He was going to have to do something about Monster Number One's need to listen in on everything. "Kala!"

"I didn't do it!"

He could hear small feet running across the hardwoods.

Charlie sighed and kissed his cheek. "Well, we should talk about this as a family then."

There was another crashing sound. "Okay, I did do that. Mom, a bunch of books fell but they didn't hit anything except the printer."

They'd just bought that printer.

"She's got to be easier than those two," Charlie whispered.

The baby monitor lit up as a keening cry was heard. Travis was awake.

"You know you would be an even better dad if you could breastfeed," she said as she got up.

"Ewww, that would be gross. Dad's got hair there and stuff." Kenzie was still looking at them. "What's our sister's name? Does she like My Little Pony?"

He stood. "You go feed our boy, and I'll handle the monsters. Come on, Kenz. Let's find your sister and we'll talk."

171

He'd found talking was an important dad skill.

And so was patience.

* * * *

Paris, France
Three weeks later

It was surreal being here. The Velvet Collar. Where his real life had begun. He'd looked across that crowded dungeon and fate had come for him.

"You're thinking about her."

Unfortunately, his baby wasn't the one here with him. His sister-in-law was. Charlie was home with the new baby while their toddler was with his brother and sister-in-law. He'd made the trip to Paris to pick up Tasha in a private jet he'd borrowed from another of his sister-in-laws. He had four brothers, and they'd all married well. Erin could take out a man with one shot. Grace could organize the world and keep it running smooth as silk. Mia had billions of dollars and a jet. She was really his favorite.

And Chelsea. Charlie's sister had been the reason she'd walked away from him the first time, but now they were solid. Oh, she still called him Satan from time to time, but they were good, he and Chelsea.

"I can't walk into this place and not think about her," Ian said. He was oddly emotional about being in The Velvet Collar again. Of course he'd also had some business to deal with. He and Chelsea had updated Ezra and Solo on what had happened since she'd been arrested by Levi Green and Ezra had rushed in and saved his ex-wife.

Now they were hiding here, and Ian was preparing to move them to Italy in a few days. "Tell me you can walk into The Garden and not think of Simon."

Chelsea tilted her head up, and the grin on her face proved how much she'd changed since she'd gotten married. "Not even once. It was the first place we played. And now I don't even mind the Chelsea in Chelsea jokes. Though it would have been easier on me if Damon had settled down in some other part of London." She sobered as they walked back out into the lobby. "Are you ready for this?"

"We've been working with a family therapist, someone Kai recommended. We've talked a lot about how to integrate Tasha into our family." He would have told her all of this on the nine-hour plane trip if she hadn't managed to sleep the entire time. He'd envied that nap mightily. Chelsea had cuddled up with his monsters, and the three of them had slept most of the trip from Dallas to Paris.

Ian had sat up and thought of all the many ways he could murder Levi Green. He'd alphabetized them. Arsenic, bludgeoning, C4 shoved up his asshole without lube…

"That wasn't what I meant. I know you're ready for Natasha," Chelsea said. "If there is one thing you can do it's raise awesome kids."

"A compliment? Who are you and what did you do with my sister-in-law?" He leaned against the big front desk that was the main part of the lobby.

She wrinkled her nose his way. "Hubby and kiddo happened. I'm a new, mature Chelsea Weston. And I was talking about Levi Green and whatever Agency asshole he's about to bring in here. Are you going to kill him in front of your new daughter?"

"No, but I'd like to. I hate the fact that they'll be in the same room. I know he didn't pull the trigger, but that fucker killed her dad." Maybe he should. It would solve a lot of problems if he took Levi's head off. The girls could play soccer with it, and honestly, Tasha was Russian. They understood the fine art of revenge from a young age.

"I can handle this if you want to call the woman who's bringing Tasha here and tell her to meet us at the airport instead," Chelsea offered.

He shook his head. "No. This is better. This will help out Solo and Ezra. Solo sent us some very important intel about Tasha." She'd basically verified everything they'd gotten from Kelsey Owens, but he'd felt better having it come from a known source. "Besides, I want him to know I'm watching."

The bell that let the attendant know someone was outside rang, and Ian felt his heart clench because he was pretty sure it wasn't Levi. He walked over to the stairs that led up to Rene's apartments. Rene was the man who owned The Velvet Collar. Ian had sent Kala and Kenzie upstairs with Rene and his wife while he and Chelsea had talked to

Solo and Ezra. They were holed up in a safe room hidden away in the dungeon.

"Hey, Rene. She's here. Can you send my girls down?" Ian called up and he heard a soft feminine gasp and knew the girls had been trying to listen in again.

Little spies in training, and he was their favorite subject.

Chelsea opened the door, and he saw Tasha in person for the first time. She was far too thin, wearing a plain dress that hung off her and shoes that looked like they pinched her feet.

His girls loved pinks and vibrant blues and greens. Even their sneakers were crazy colors. Every item Tasha wore seemed to have been chosen for practicality and probably cost.

Like those years after his father had walked out on them and he and Sean had to wear whatever fit. They'd taken hand-me-downs and worn T-shirts that had seen better days. Alex had shared clothes with him.

He was thrown right back to that day when he'd realized he had to take care of his whole world. He'd been sixteen, and it had scared the shit out of him.

She'd been five when her world had changed. Five fucking years old.

"Hey, you've got a scary face on, and I know it's because you're pissed as shit that she's obviously undernourished and no one's taken care of her the way she should be," Chelsea said under her breath. "But you're going to look mean to her, and she doesn't need that."

He took a deep breath because his sister-in-law was one hundred percent right. He had to let his anger go because this girl didn't need it.

Kala and Kenzie had made their way down and stood on either side of him, staring at the girl who was supposed to be their new sister. They were such opposites. Two American princesses who'd never known a moment's hardship and the Russian orphan. They stared at each other across the lobby, an ocean of difference between them.

Had he been wrong to bring them?

"Is that her?" Kenzie asked.

"Duh," Kala replied. "I don't think they would bring another girl in. She looks sad."

Kenzie's lips curved up. "Because she doesn't have a sister. But now she will, and she'll be happier."

Even Kala didn't seem to have a comeback for that. "Yeah."

The stern-looking woman the orphanage had sent to bring Tasha from Russia to France looked down at the girl. The orphanage had been more than happy to be bribed with a godawful amount of money. It probably hadn't hurt that the head of the Denisovitch syndicate had brokered the deal. Tasha now had proof of her Ukrainian citizenship, and the adoption was perfectly legal.

Mostly.

The woman from the orphanage pointed his way and told Tasha that he was her new father and she was to go with him now.

Fuck. He stayed back and let Chelsea take over. If anyone knew how it felt to be stripped out of a life she knew and thrown into another one, it was his sister-in-law.

"She doesn't look like she wants to come with us." Kenzie was frowning again.

"It's because she's scared." Kala seemed to consider the situation. "If I were her, I would be scared, too. I would miss my mom and dad, and I would think Dad is big and scary and kind of mean-looking. She doesn't know him yet."

She was six. Yep. She was six and he was going to have so much trouble with her because smart kids always had trouble. She was smart enough to see a lot of the world for what it was and not mature enough to handle the emotions she would feel.

Chelsea seemed to be saying all the right things. The girl was watching her with clear brown eyes. Ian had to smile when Chelsea promised Tasha that he wasn't as scary as he looked, that he was a marshmallow on the inside, and she would learn to manipulate him very quickly.

She would. All his girls did. All little girls should have a man in their life who loved and protected them, some kind of father figure. So should little boys. And sometimes that father figure wasn't a man. Protection didn't have to come from some dude with testosterone.

But this girl would have him. And she would have her Uncle Sean and Uncle Case and Aunt Erin.

Tasha set down the tiny suitcase she was carrying and turned his way. He watched as she steeled herself and forced herself to walk over to him. She was so small, and he was sure he loomed over her like some massive monster she might have to slay.

He dropped down to one knee, but he still was taller than she was. Up close he could see how frail she seemed. There was worry in her eyes that no child should have.

"Did you know my father?" she asked, her eyes grave.

She'd asked the question in Russian, so he replied in her language. "I did. He was a good man, and I will honor him by taking care of you and giving you a good life. I know you're scared, but no one is going to hurt you. My wife is very eager to meet you. She is looking forward to having a new daughter to spoil."

Tasha frowned.

Kenzie giggled while Kala shook her head and stepped toward Tasha. She spoke flawless Russian because her mother had spoken it to her from the day she was born. "Dad's Russian isn't very good. He didn't mean spoil that way. He meant give you presents and cookies and stuff."

"Isn't that what I said?" Maybe his Russian wasn't as good as he thought.

Kenzie's eyes were light as she replied in English. "You said spoil like rot. Like a potato."

He winced and went back to his apparently bad Russian. "My wife lived most of her life in Russia. She's perfect, and she won't let you rot like a potato. I promise."

That got the faintest hint of a smile from Tasha and then she nodded. "I will be going with you then."

Such a brave girl, and her English seemed pretty good. Good enough that he switched. "I'm glad. We're going to take care of you. These are my little monsters. They speak better Russian than I do, so you can plot with them. If you can't tell them apart, use a marker in their sleep. It's what I do."

"Dad!" His girls had the in-synch thing down.

Then Kala was trying to get her sister to make sure there wasn't a Sharpie mark behind her ear, and Tasha was watching her new sisters with something like wonder. Kenzie took Tasha's hand and started talking about the plane they would be going in and how they would have lunch and cookies and everything.

There was another ring, and Ian felt his spine straighten because he had another job to do.

Not kill Levi Green. He nodded Chelsea's way to let her know he was ready.

Not tearing out his throat would be his first job as Tasha's dad, and he meant to do it right.

* * * *

Six hours later he was fairly sure they were going to make it. The paperwork was all in order. Mitch was meeting them in immigration in case they needed a lawyer. Just a couple more hours and they would have gotten past the worst of it.

He would be shocked if anyone in immigration spoke Ukrainian. They would assume the Russian was Ukrainian and not ask about it. Tasha could answer rudimentary questions in English.

It was going to be all right.

"You have your thinking face on." Chelsea was sitting across from him while the girls were on the other side of the aisle. The flight attendant had seemed happy to bring the girls lunch, complete with cookies and tea in little china cups he'd been assured the Lawless clan wouldn't miss if they broke.

"Just going over everything that can possibly go wrong."

Chelsea yawned. "Nothing is going to go wrong. Adam's monitoring immigration. The paperwork is already through, and they're expecting her. There are no flags, and there won't be because Adam will erase those suckers if they show up. He won't let you down."

Adam was one of his oldest friends. They gave each other hell, but he trusted Adam with his family, and Adam did the same for him.

"The girls seem to be getting along." Chelsea unbuckled her belt and sat up. "They've been talking about Seth and Travis. Natasha told them how much she loves babies. She said she was allowed to help with the babies at the orphanage."

Of course she had. She'd been free labor.

"And you look scary again." Chelsea stood. "I'm going to find some coffee, and you need to eat something. I'll make you a sandwich, and you can pretend it's Levi Green's heart or something."

He grunted. "Nah, I bet the fucker tastes like craft beer and sorrow." He looked up at his sister-in-law. "Thank you, Chelsea. For everything."

She smiled. "You've gotten so polite in your old age. I'll be right back, weirdo."

He glanced over, and it looked like the girls had started a movie.

A couple of hours to go and then he'd be back at home and he could sleep. He was going to have jet lag from hell since he'd been in the air for two days, but he wasn't going to be able to sleep until they were home and they'd made it through the hard part.

Except when they got home the hard part started.

He'd taken a couple of weeks off when Travis had been born. He was going to have to take more because his family needed him.

Alex and Liam could handle the office, but damn he felt like he was letting them down.

But sometimes a man had to choose his family over everything else. Everything.

He would focus on monitoring the situation with Ezra and Solo. It seemed like his ploy with Drake had worked, and they were heading back to England to continue the search. That was it. He could do a lot of that work from home, and in a few weeks it would all be settled. He was pretty damn sure Ezra and Solo were working their problems out because that tiny room they'd been in had smelled like sex, so they would probably both need jobs and he would be left with another freaking couple who would whine about assignments. *No, Ian. We can't be split up for six weeks, and what do you mean one of us is going to have to flirt to get information?*

He needed more single dudes. They never minded flirting for info. Of course, it almost never worked. It always worked for the women he hired because dudes were dumb.

God, what he could have done with twenty Kayla Summers. Naturally she'd married her client, and now he was left with Erin, who would rather shove her fist up a dude's ass than talk to him.

Also, his brother got cranky when he suggested sending her in as a diversion.

Yeah, he would come up with a staffing plan while he was on…a little bile rose in his throat…paternity leave.

"Mr. Taggart." A quiet voice pulled him out of his thoughts.

He looked to his left, and Tasha was standing there. She'd slipped out of her seat while Kenzie and Kala were staring at a screen.

He tried to give her his best "I wasn't just thinking about brutally murdering someone" face. "Hey. How was your lunch? Do you need something else?"

He asked the question in his best Russian, which was going to get so much better because he wasn't going to be lazy about it anymore. He would join in on the plan he and Charlie had put in place. Charlie thought it would be good to split the day up. In the morning they spoke Russian and nothing else to the kids. At night they switched to English, and they helped Tasha learn to speak it.

She sat down in the seat Chelsea had occupied, her little face completely serious. "I would like to talk to you about helping with the boys. Your daughters spoke of younger children."

Her Russian was very formal. He hoped his was a bit more relaxed. And right. "Yes, we have two boys. Seth is three, and Travis is almost three months old."

She nodded as though processing that information. "I help with the babies in the orphanage. I am good with them. I do not mind changing diapers, and I can feed them as well so you and your wife shall have more time to yourself."

He was missing something here. "Natasha, you don't have to help with the babies. You can play with them, of course, but there's no pressure on you. My wife and I can handle them."

Her jaw tightened, and she seemed to think about that. "Then I shall clean. I am good with this, too."

"When you get settled in we can talk about chores," he replied. "Kala and Kenzie have some. They set the table for dinner and they clear it. They feed the dog. You'll like him. He's big but he's very gentle. The only thing you have to worry about with Bud are his farts."

He said the words, hoping to get a smile out of her, but now she seemed almost on the verge of tears.

"I can do good work."

"I'm sure you can, but we're going to relax and let you settle in."

"I do not want to do…certain things, Mr. Taggart."

A chill crept across his skin because he didn't like the way that sounded. "What did they say you would have to do?"

"The other children…they say there is only one reason an American would take me in. I am old, and no one my age leaves except for bad reasons." She met his eyes, strength there, and wariness. "I do not wish to do these things. But I am good at cleaning."

He had to force himself to breathe because he was caught between impotent rage and an aching sorrow. It was everything he'd feared— this well of emotion he only felt for the people he loved. He had to suck it up and deal with the first part of the problem. "I did not lie to you, Natasha. I knew your father, and he is why we're taking you in. When we get back to our house, I'm going to show you pictures to prove that what I say is true. I am not going to make you do anything…no bad things. Ever. Tasha, did they make you do bad things at the orphanage?"

"No, but the older girls tell me this. They tell me Americans are bad and will probably hurt me."

It was good to know mean girls were the same across the globe. "They lied to you. I know you're scared, and I can't tell you how much that makes my heart ache. We want you to be our daughter. Just like Kenzie and Kala. You don't have to earn your keep beyond the few chores we'll ask you to do and trying hard in school."

Her lips pursed. "They tell me I must call you Papa, but you are not my papa."

There was the fire she would need. Good. It hadn't been beaten out of her, and he would stoke that ember. Despite what he joked about, he didn't want to raise kids who never questioned him. He was their dad not their god, and teaching them to be strong and independent meant they would all butt heads from time to time. Teaching them how to fight was one of his main jobs in life. "I'm not today, but one day I will earn the right to be your dad. I will work very hard to earn that title. Do you understand?"

A single tear fell from her eyes, rolling across her cheek. "You are an odd man."

He wanted to wipe that tear away, but he wasn't going to push her. He would be patient, and the hugs would come someday. One day she would hold his hand because she would trust that he would never hurt her, that he owed her affection and comfort.

"You are not the first to point that out, Tash." He sat back.

"Hey, you're missing the best part." Kenzie took her new sister's hand.

Tasha let her guide her back to their seats. She slid the headphones back on, and he noticed she reached for Kenzie's hand again.

"You need some Scotch to go with this sandwich?" Chelsea sighed as she handed him a plate.

He glanced up at her, setting the plate on the tray at his side. "You heard what she's scared of?"

She nodded. "Yes. I heard a scared little girl, and I heard you handle it beautifully. Ian...that was...I'm going to say something, and you should listen to me because I won't ever admit I said it."

"Okay." He was worried she was about to tell him he'd said something terrible he hadn't meant to say and that he should give up on the Russian.

"I wish Charlotte and I had someone like you when we were her age." Chelsea sniffled and then sighed. "You're a good dad, and she's lucky. Now we will forget we had this moment."

He smiled up at her. "Forgotten. And I'll skip the Scotch. I think I'll be pretty saintly for a while. She needs to trust me before she figures out what a flawed person I am."

Patience. He was going to need so much of it. Patience and some faith that he could earn her trust.

* * * *

"She doesn't want her own room." Charlie stepped inside their bedroom and closed the door behind her.

It was hours after he'd managed to get through the airport. Immigration had been easy. They'd checked the paperwork, asked a couple of questions, and waved him through.

God, he was glad he hadn't murdered all the people he'd thought he should. Sometimes they came in handy, and having a couple of politicians who owed him had likely saved him a lot of trouble. "Well, it's not exactly a great room at this point. It's pretty much a bed and a desk and a bookcase without any books yet."

He was on the bed, his whole body sinking into the mattress.

Home. He'd been all over the world, and nothing ever felt as good as this bed with this woman beside him. But then his Charlie knew how to turn something simple like walls and ceilings and rooms into a home.

Charlie had been waiting for their arrival. The whole house had smelled like cookies, and she'd planned a big dinner. Tasha had been surprised when Charlie had asked if she would help shape the pelmeni. She'd had Tasha talking as all the girls made the little meat-filled dumplings.

He'd sat and rocked Travis and let Seth treat him like a jungle gym and wondered when he could safely go to bed since he'd been awake for almost thirty-six hours.

And then he'd gotten the news that Solo had fled. Beck had fucked up. Oh, that wasn't in the report, but Beck had definitely fucked up.

"I thought it would be fun to let her shop for the stuff she wants." Charlie had changed into pajama bottoms and a T-shirt, and he wondered how fast he could get it off her.

If only he could move. His muscles didn't seem to want to work.

"Turns out we'll have to do a lot of shopping because she had exactly three dresses and five pairs of underwear in that suitcase." Charlie shook her head as she pumped out the body lotion she used every night.

Lavender. He usually got hard when he watched her smooth the lotion over that gorgeous skin of hers. Today he could only yawn and appreciate her on an aesthetic level. It was disconcerting.

"Baby, I'm dying and leaving you with five kids."

The most brilliant smile came over her face, and she climbed onto the bed. "Sweetie, you've been awake for almost two days, and your body has been in an airplane for almost the entire time."

She wasn't thinking about how grave the situation was. "I used to be able to make a way longer trip in the back of a cargo plane, jump out of the fucking plane, kill four dudes, catch another cargo plane, and when I got home, I went out and partied."

"And what did you do on the cargo planes?"

He sighed. "I slept. I used to be able to sleep anywhere."

She put her hand on his chest. "Now you're old, and you have a ridiculously comfortable mattress that supports your spine and these soft sheets and a gorgeous wife who keeps you warm."

182

"Are you trying to say I got soft, Charlie?"

"Never," she vowed and laid down beside him. "You also didn't worry as much then."

And he hadn't had much of a life. He'd had work, and having stinky kids was so much more fun. "Nah, I got soft. I like soft beds and soft blankets, and I definitely like how soft you are." He managed to get his arm around her. This was where he wanted to be. "We've got to teach that little girl how to be soft, too."

She cuddled close. "It's going to take time. She seemed okay with me, but she watched me when she thought I wasn't looking. She stole a knife. Not a sharp one. A butter knife. I saw her put it in her suitcase. She didn't even know to put it under her pillow. I made her move it."

He chuckled. "How did she take that?"

"She was a bit surprised. I told her when I had to go to my father's place in Russia, I was scared, and I didn't even have a knife and if I'd had one, I would have put it under my pillow so I could get to it if I needed to," Charlie explained. "I did it while the girls were brushing their teeth. She needs it for comfort. She's not going to hurt the girls."

He'd seen nothing in her behavior to make him think she would hurt anyone, but he could understand her fear. She'd pretty much clung to the girls all day. "You think she wants to stay in Kala and Kenzie's room in case we try to hurt her?"

"I think they feel safe to her," Charlie said quietly. "And we don't yet. Though showing her pictures of her father helped a bit. I wish he'd smiled more. And don't you have a single one where he wasn't drinking?"

Nope. That had pretty much been what Sasha had done the last couple of years of his life. He hadn't been a laid-back, happy guy.

He wondered what kind of a father he'd been. He'd had so little time with her. He hadn't gotten to know how obnoxious she would be, how much he would genuinely like the person she was becoming despite, or maybe because, of the obnoxiousness.

"If I had known we were going to end up with his daughter, I would have taken some better shots. Instead I had Owen and Tucker fucking around with their phones, so we're lucky any of them are suitable to be seen by children." He yawned again. He needed to break out of this exhaustion so he could fuck his wife. He didn't even have to wear a condom anymore since he'd gotten his balls scooped out. This wasn't fair.

"This is all going to be okay," Charlie promised. "I'm going to keep her with me for a couple of weeks. We'll get her new clothes and show her around, and then she'll go to school. You'll see in a few weeks things are going to normalize."

Her hand moved over his chest, stroking him, soothing him. "You don't think that thing in Wuhan is going to be a big deal?"

There was a bunch of talk about some new virus, but then wasn't there always?

Charlie sighed. "I think we had Ebola right here in Dallas a few years back and it turned out okay. I mean, how bad could it get?"

Yeah, they always said there was a pandemic right around the corner and they always took care of it. He yawned again. "Baby, you're going to have to do the work tonight."

She huffed and sat up. "Sleep, Ian." She kissed him and then turned out the light, climbing under the covers. "We'll have a lot to do in the morning."

He closed his eyes and warmth surrounded him.

He was home.

* * * *

Month One

"What do you mean school is closed?" Charlie paced the floor. "Avery, how could they close the schools? We need the schools. I just got them in school."

Ian sat at the breakfast table, strangely fascinated by how neatly Seth ate. He was three and tried to use a baby fork on Cheerios.

Bud whined, sitting under the high chair.

"Yeah, I don't think he's going to help you," Ian told him. The poor dog wouldn't starve because the girls were still messy.

"Why can't we go to school?" Kenzie was still in her pj's.

Charlie kept up her pacing. "How is that supposed to work? I can't get them to sit down long enough to tie their shoes, much less do an actual school lesson."

"You're still going to school. You'll just do it from home." The situation was worse than he'd thought. The world was changing. He could feel it. Perhaps not changing, exactly, but the dangers that were always there seemed to be pulsing to the surface. Charlie was upset the schools were closing, but he didn't mind keeping the girls close. At least until he got a lay of the land.

"But I like home," Kala complained. "Home is where I don't have to do schoolwork."

Tasha had gotten dressed. She looked oddly incongruous in her unicorn T-shirt and pink jeans. It had been weeks and she was still wary.

She'd started school ten days before, and it seemed to have made her even more quiet than usual.

"How about you, Tash? You upset about missing a couple of weeks of school?" He wanted to know where her head was.

Tasha shrugged and gently bounced Travis's seat. Travis kicked his legs and looked up at her with a worshipful stare. Tasha paid a lot of attention to the boys. Seth toddled after her because she always found a way to include him.

She was such a good kid. He just had to find a way to reach her.

"The other kids make fun of her," Kenzie said.

Tasha went a bright red. "I do not care about this. They do not matter."

Suddenly a lot of things made sense. "Is this why Kala threw dirt at the second grade boys?"

That had been a fun call, and all Kala had been willing to say was she didn't like those boys. It had gotten her detention. For his kindergartener.

"They made fun of her accent and she cried, and no one makes my sister cry but me," Kala announced.

"You do not make me cry," Tasha said with a hint of a smile that disappeared when she looked up at him. "I am working on my accent. I think my English is good enough that we do not have to speak Russian anymore."

Oh, he was not letting that happen to her. "There is nothing wrong with your accent. And those boys are dumb. They can only speak one language. It's important to speak at least two, and how will Seth and

Travis learn if you don't help them?"

If there was one thing he'd learned, it was that Tasha felt most comfortable when she was helping someone else. It was a trait that he and Charlie had talked a lot about. It was wonderful to want to help, but Tash had to learn how to be okay with the things she needed, too. Her selflessness was a survival tactic. But it could be useful at times. He wasn't going to allow some asshole eight-year-olds to make her give up her heritage.

"I can help them." Tasha started singing to Travis, a Russian lullaby.

Maybe a couple of weeks off would be good for her.

He winked Kala's way. "I knew there was something behind that particular incident."

Kala smiled, a rare occurrence. "I won't let them make fun of her. It's not fair, and the teachers don't do anything about it. All they do is talk. They said we should mind our own business and let the second grade teachers handle it, but she's my sister."

Tasha didn't look over, but she relaxed as though hearing the words helped make them real.

He leaned over. "Let me know if anything else happens. And never let them tell you she's not your business. She's my business, too. Hey, since you're not going to school today, what do you say we watch some movies?"

He could pop some corn, take the kiddos into the media room, and give Charlie a couple of hours to mourn the fact that they were about to get to homeschool three kids while dealing with a toddler and a baby, and McKay-Taggart wasn't closing down. If anything the need for security would go through the roof, and he would probably get called in to consult. A lot.

"Tasha's never seen a Marvel movie." Kenzie was clapping her hands.

Oh, he'd been looking for something they could do together. Charlie had the advantage on him. She baked and shopped, and Tasha seemed to enjoy doing both.

He shot things, and she wasn't ready for that. But she might like a bunch of sarcastic superheroes saving the world. "Oh, we're going to have some fun."

* * * *

Month Three

Ian slammed the door to his SUV and practically bent down and kissed the ground.

Then he realized the ground was where Bud peed and decided to just be happy he was home.

One week in New York consulting with three different government embassies, plus time with some Agency assholes dealing with Ezra Fain's issues and the fact that Kim Solomon had disappeared off the face of the flipping earth, had led to two weeks in quarantine. In a motel outside of Dallas. With Adam, who watched some really strange TV and talked too much about pie.

Like he didn't know what Adam meant by pie. Two weeks of listening to Adam bemoan his horniness and he'd been ready to kill the man himself.

It would take forever for him to get back in a halfway decent mood. Maybe he should decompress.

The door came open and Kenzie and Kala started running toward him yelling *Daddy*. Seth toddled after them, a wide grin on his face, and Bud was bounding his way, too. Charlie stood on the porch, Travis on her hip and Tasha at her side.

Nope. No decompression time. He let himself be tackled by his kiddos, and his mood changed entirely.

This was what he'd missed. This was his whole soul, and it came to life.

He found himself on his back on that grass the damn dog had probably peed on, hugging his kids and rolling around like he wasn't old and rickety. He wasn't when he was with them.

"We missed you," Kenzie said.

Seth bounced on his gut like it was a trampoline.

"You were gone for so long," Kala complained.

"I'm staying home for a while." He'd learned how to do most of his work over the Internet. The last few months had been a lot of figuring shit out, but they were starting to find their way.

Charlie smiled her goddess smile as she stood over him. "It's good to have you home, babe. So good. Is Adam alive?"

"Barely." He sat up, hefting Seth high. He'd grown in the last few weeks, and so had Travis. "I'm so glad to be home." He looked Tasha's way. "How many movies did you watch while I was gone?"

She shook her head. "No Marvel movies. I thought I would wait for you."

She wasn't hugging him, but that was progress.

"Then we should plan on *Guardians of the Galaxy* tonight," he promised. "You're going to love Groot."

She gave him a smile. "Miss Charlotte and I made lemon bars for you."

He stood, carrying Seth up with him. "I'm looking forward to that."

So they were still Mr. Ian and Miss Charlotte. He could wait a bit longer.

Charlie held his hand as the girls ran back into the house, shouting. "I think you'll find I've got some pie for you, too." She winked his way. "Serena and I have spent a lot of time talking about how we should greet our husbands with some pie."

Now that was a plan he could agree to.

* * * *

Month Four

"Is it Thursday?" Charlie stared out into the backyard. "Because I thought yesterday was Thursday."

"Nope." He was right there with her. "It's Thursday."

He was pretty sure every day was Thursday now.

* * * *

Month Five

Thursday. It was always Thursday.

188

* * * *

Month Seven

Thursday with sourdough.

* * * *

Month Eight

Masks sucked and it was Thursday again, and now he had to go out into the fucking world for a physical. He hated doctors.

* * * *

Month Nine

"Yes, I'll have that report finished within the week. I think your security is up to date and there shouldn't be any issues traveling to the site. Michael and Deke will escort you, and they'll make a boots-on-ground assessment then." Ian stared at the screen, the same way he had every day for the last couple of months.

The Zoom call cut out, and he shot off a quick email.

"Where are Michael and Deke going?" Charlie set a load of laundry down on the bed.

Because his office was now in the bedroom. The actual home office he'd been sure he would never have to use was now a distant dream that had three different laptops in various stages of decay that served as "school."

The girls were still sharing a bedroom, and they'd converted the one meant for Tasha into a playroom complete with a crafting table, pink floofy bean bags, and glitter everywhere. He was pretty sure the girls were made of glitter at this point.

"Los Angeles," he replied, putting his headset aside. His next virtual meeting wasn't for another thirty minutes. "Hutch is already out there, and there's some concern with cybersecurity for one of our clients. He's here in Dallas, and given the nature of his job, he wants security as he goes out to deal with it."

She winced, likely because she knew which company they were talking about. "Tell them to be careful."

It was a big pharma company working on a vaccine. It was shocking how even though the company was working in concert with several other companies, there were still people trying to sabotage them.

Foreign actors, or even domestic ones, who wanted to sow chaos. He wasn't letting it happen because he freaking wanted to get out of this house one day. He loved this house, but damn…

There was the sound of something crashing and breaking and then utter silence.

The silence was what really scared him.

They both took off running down the hallway, past Travis sleeping in his crib and Seth in his playpen, holding on to the edge so he could try to see what had happened.

All three girls stood in the kitchen, one of the everyday dishes smashed on the floor between them.

"Okay, no one move." Charlie sighed in obvious relief. "I'll get the broom. Kenz, you especially stay where you are. You don't have shoes on. I thought something terrible had happened."

Something had happened, but Charlie was missing it.

"I did it," Kala said. "I dropped the plate. I was trying to get some cake and I slipped."

No, she hadn't. She was a good liar, but he could see through her right now. Kenzie wasn't good at all, and she was looking at Tash, who had gone a pasty white.

Fuck. How careful had she been all these months? She wore what Charlie told her to wear, helped around the house, never complained, and she'd made one wrong move and now she thought it would all fall apart.

"Tash? Was it you?" He had a point to make. They were all on edge, and he was about to piss his wife off and probably everyone would shame him for being an unsafe dad and shit, but this needed to happen.

Tears rolled. "Yes, Mr. Ian. It was me. I wanted the cake, and the plate slipped out of my hand."

Her accent had softened a bit over the months, but it was back in full force now. And she'd forgotten it was afternoon and they'd shifted to English. He wasn't going to call her out on that.

"If I told you it's okay, would you believe me?" he asked quietly, replying to her in Russian since it was the language she fell back on when she was scared.

Tasha nodded. "Of course."

Liar.

He picked up a dish off the counter where it had been drying and let it slip out of his hand, crashing to the floor.

"It's only a dish, sweetheart. It's not going to get you in trouble. You are more important than any dish. You are my daughter." He enunciated each word, certain he was getting it right. His Russian had improved even as Tash's English got better.

Tasha's eyes had gone wide and she gasped.

"Ian, what the..." Charlie stopped and then seemed to process what had happened. She sighed. "Oh, well, it was time for new dishes anyway."

She picked up a cereal bowl, and it joined the ruins.

Kala was tossing down a plate before Ian could stop her, glee in her eyes. "Can we do them all?"

He walked over and picked up Kenzie because she'd been good and hadn't moved even though he could see plainly she hated being left out of the destruction. He let her select a dish and do her own damage.

He moved her out of the way and set her on the rug before he got to one knee in front of Tasha. "Mistakes will happen, daughter. You will not lose your place in this family for any reason, much less a couple of broken dishes. You need to feel safe enough to make mistakes and know you won't be hurt for them. I just want you to think about that. Now help your...help Miss Charlie clean up and then we'll all have a piece of cake."

He was about to stand when she shocked him by throwing her arms around him and bursting into tears.

She was crying. Tasha didn't cry. She was stoic, and now she was sobbing and she hadn't asked him for comfort. She'd simply gone on instinct and hugged him.

He wrapped his arms around her and let her cry.

When he looked up, his wife was crying, too.

Progress was a beautiful thing.

* * * *

Month Ten

Ian woke. He sat straight up in bed, absolutely certain that someone was watching him.

It was an instinct, a cold prickle up his spine, and he lay there for a moment listening, his eyes shut because if someone was in the room he wouldn't give himself away.

He was still, but all he heard was the hum from the ceiling fan and Charlie sighing in her sleep.

Was he being paranoid? He hadn't been sleeping well since the doctor had told him he would have to go through testing to figure out what was wrong with his heart.

His heart. Fuck. He couldn't have a heart attack in the middle of a pandemic.

There was nothing to worry about. He was still sleeping and this was a dream, and wouldn't it be nice to walk outside? It was a lovely night. He could go out to the back porch and sit for a while and everything would be okay.

He found himself sitting up in bed before he even questioned it. What the hell was he doing? He started to crawl back under the covers, but the urge to go outside overwhelmed him.

Something was wrong, but he still dragged on pajama bottoms and pulled a T-shirt over his head. He still found himself walking down the hallway. The world seemed surreal as he unlocked the security system and let himself out on the patio.

"Hello, Tag," a deep voice said.

Ah, he was dreaming. He had to be because Sasha was standing in his backyard, dressed all in black and without a bullet hole in sight.

He was sure Kai would tell him this dream was a long time coming. It had only been last month that he'd made his breakthrough with Tasha. Somehow the long days of this seemingly never-ending pandemic had worked to bond them all as a family in a way he wondered might not have been possible without it. They'd been forced to go through this together, forced to focus on their family every single day, and Tasha had become a part of them. She smiled more, laughed often, and she'd started joking around. Just this morning she'd saucily told Charlie that when she went back to school, Charlie would miss her because of all the free labor.

That front was going well. He was worried it was all about to fall apart.

So it wasn't surprising that he would dream about Tasha's biological father.

It was a bit surprising that the man's eyes seemed to glow, but again, his brain was kind of fucked up. "Hey, Sasha. How's the afterlife?"

Sasha's lips turned up in a smile Ian had never seen before. Sasha smirked. He never looked happy, but now there was something peaceful about the man. "Well, it is far more active than I would have imagined. Why do I always find myself in the middle of wars? I think it is my fate. How is my little fish?"

Ian sighed and sat down at the big table they had by the pool. Though it was winter, December in Texas could go any of a dozen ways. It was a warm night, the moon full overhead. "She's good. She's settled in and seems happy. She's…man, I have no idea how we functioned without her. She's the peacekeeper. We're all tired of being stuck in the house, but it's made us closer. It's a weird time, but I think we needed it."

Sasha looked toward the house as though he could see inside. "She seems very happy. I've looked in on her once before. She seems happier now. Healthier. I wanted to see her one last time before I go."

"Have you been hanging around to watch over her?" It was a sweet thought, that Sasha could be sure his darling girl was all right.

"It's more complicated than that. So is the world, though you shouldn't worry about that part." Sasha sat down across from him. "I must move forward. I hoped to stay a while longer, but we can't anymore. It's time to leave this plane."

And move on to the afterlife. To something like heaven. Ian wasn't sure he believed in the whole harps and angels thing, but he believed something happened, and he didn't think it was bad. Punishment was meant for this life. He couldn't imagine a god on high sentencing souls to eternal damnation.

After all, what was God if not a father?

"I hope you find peace," Ian said. "You should know your brothers have."

"They are good?" Sasha asked the question softly, as though he'd prayed for the right answer.

Ian nodded. "They're all good. Jax and River are in Bliss. Owen and Rebecca and Robert and Ariel are still at The Garden for now, but Rebecca's probably going back to research work when she can. Hey, Tucker went into a coma, and when he came out he found a girl."

Sasha laughed, a booming sound that would definitely wake up the neighborhood if this wasn't a dream. "Tucker could always find a girl. The problem was in keeping one."

"Well, he'd already knocked this one up," Ian allowed. "He did not get a proper lecture on condom usage. Roni showed up at the door of The Garden with a two-year-old and the coolest mom ever. I mean it. Sandra rocks. She's mean as shit, and twice as sexually aggressive. I'm pretty sure this Agency wunderkind named Drake lost his virginity to her."

Sasha sat back. "Oh, it's good to know they're happy. I've missed them. They are good men. They deserve the world."

"Hey, since you're obviously some manifestation of my worries or hopes or some shit, maybe I can ask you some questions," Ian began. As long as he was here, he might as well give the whole talking to himself a try.

"Is that what I am?" Sasha chuckled and sat back. "I've got a few minutes. Ask me anything."

"Do you have any idea where Solo is?" It was hard trying to find a person when the world had shut down. Adam had been monitoring the situation in every way he could.

"Solo is missing?" Sasha frowned. "I assumed she and Ezra would fix their problems."

"Damn, I was hoping I knew something I was overlooking." Sometimes the truth was down deep, down where he apparently kept the people in his life who'd died.

"I'm not all-seeing, though I do keep up with the people who are truly important to me," Sasha admitted. "Sometimes in a way they would likely find…invasive, but I make no apologies. Now it is my turn to ask you a question."

"Okay." It was cool to see this side of Sasha, even though he was aware this was all in his head.

"It would have been easy to hand us over to the authorities." Sasha was staring at him, his skin pale in the moonlight. "I understand why you took in Robert. He'd been with Theo for a long time. But why the rest of us? I wasn't particularly grateful."

It had been one of the easier things he'd done. "You went through something unimaginable. I've been in bad places in my life. I've been tortured before. I don't talk about the things I saw when I worked for the Agency, but it was bad. And every single time I had a bedrock to fall back on. I had my memories. I had everything I'd learned before. In the beginning it was my brother and Alex. I couldn't let them down. After I met my Charlie…it was always her. Even when I thought she was dead, that woman lifted me up. You were sent to hell without anything to lift you up. How could I give you over to a group who would at best subject you to tests, and at worst complete the doctor's work?"

"You are a good man, Taggart. Without you and Damon and Ezra, we would have truly been lost. I wish… It's hard to even find the words. I wish to thank you and Charlotte and your children for taking in my girl. I don't know what would have happened to her if you had not," Sasha said quietly. The words seemed to come with a warmth to them, a sensation Ian felt in his soul.

Gratitude. He could feel it.

"She's a wonderful girl. She's kind and thoughtful and she's smart. I'm not sure how she came from you." Sarcasm was his go-to when things felt too real.

Even in a dream.

Sasha's eyes glowed, but it seemed like a benevolent thing. Like some gift death had given him, along with the peace Ian sensed. "She got all her goodness from her mother. And now she will learn from you and Charlotte. Teach her well. Never let her forget that she was loved by so many people."

"When we can travel again, you should know I intend to take care of the men who did this to you," Ian vowed.

Sasha shook his head and reached into the jacket he was wearing, pulling out a bottle. "No, my brother. I do not need vengeance from you. I am past that, and I need you to protect my daughter. Fate will take care of those men."

That didn't sound like him. Except maybe he'd started to realize that he owed Sasha more than vengeance. "This is the weirdest dream."

"Have you figured out what it is about?" Sasha asked, as though deeply curious.

"I think I'm rationalizing a lot of things. I think I've had the majority of this godawful year to reflect on the fact that those kids and that woman inside the house are the center of my universe. I have to put them first, even before my own needs."

"Then it's been a good year, but I think you've known this for a long time. I think what you've found is that your heart is bigger than you could have imagined."

"Let's hope not because I had to have this stupid physical, and they're going to do this ultrasound of my..." It hit him why he was having weird dreams. "I'm anxious about the results. I put off going to the doctor, and this is my psyche telling me I shouldn't worry. It's age. That's all. I'm supposed to have the test done tomorrow. Charlie's freaked out. I don't want to go because then we'll all worry I'll get infected with this fucking virus."

"Yes, that seems like an excellent reason to have a dream about a dead man," Sasha mused as he held the bottle up. "I am a man who tries to pay his debts, and sometimes that means...keeping track of people I owe and helping them out a bit. Now, let us drink. This is a special liquor. My people call it the blood of life."

At least in his dreams he got some cool alcohol. "Scotch?"

"Something like it. Have a taste." Sasha uncorked the bottle.

He took a long swig. The liquor was rich, like the darkest, smoothest chocolate. It warmed him and sent a feeling of peace through his body.

Everything would be all right. He wasn't fucking it all up. His family would get through this and he would have the test to make his wife happy and...

He would be okay. Everything would be all right because he had them.

Sasha stood and recorked the bottle when Ian passed it back to him.

Ian followed suit. "You're not drinking? That's definitely not the Sasha I know."

Sasha tucked the bottle in his coat again. "No. I don't need to anymore. Go back to bed now, Ian. I have my own journey to make and my own lost boys and girl to take care of. I learned that from you. Sometimes the kindness we show affects the world in ways we could never have imagined. Your kindness might save two worlds one day." He glanced toward the house. "I will miss her so."

"She doesn't call me dad." There was a sorrow about Sasha he had to acknowledge.

Sasha turned and gave him the saddest smile. "She will. She will, and you will have earned it. I will be a distant star for her, something she looks up to but can never reach. You are the sun. We talk about the beauty of the stars and complain about the sun because it is right there. It is ordinary to us. But ordinary things are the ones that give us life, that we build ourselves around. We ignore such things because they're always there. You and Charlotte will be her sun. Good-bye, Tag. And don't worry about the test. I think you'll find your heart is as strong as it ever was."

Sasha seemed to fade into the darkness.

Ian moved through the house and got back into bed.

And then he woke up with a start.

What a weird dream.

Charlie yawned and cuddled close to him. "You okay?"

He rolled her over. That had been a weird dream, but he was awake now and kind of horny. He felt good. Damn good. He rubbed himself against her, loving every soft inch of her skin. "I'm excellent, and you are gorgeous. Come here, baby."

He kissed his wife and let that crazy dream go.

* * * *

Month Eleven

"Ha." Ian turned in his chair, aware there was a big grin on his face. And a magnificent sense of relief running through him. "I've got the heart of a twenty-year-old athlete."

Charlie moved from her seat. She'd been next to him during the virtual appointment. He'd tried to convince her that no doctor tells him he needs a heart transplant during a telemedicine call. Even in the middle of a pandemic surge, they would have gone into an office for that news. She'd been so worried.

He'd been oddly calm about the whole thing. He was usually a pessimistic son of a bitch, but he'd known this would be all right.

"Well, you definitely have the libido to match." She lowered her lips to his. "I can't tell you how relieved I am. The doctor seemed so worried before."

"And now he's not." He didn't know why, but the last few weeks he'd felt fucking incredible. He'd had more energy than he'd had in years. The truth was he'd started worrying there really was something wrong with his heart, but it turned out he'd been right all along.

He *was* invincible.

Charlie sighed and dropped her head to his. "I love you, Ian."

"And as soon as we can, you're going to love me at Sanctum." The vaccine would be here soon and the world would open up again. A few months more.

There was a knock on the door.

"Come in," Charlie called.

The door opened and all their kids were there, led by Tash, who had Travis on her hip. She held the fourteen-month-old with the hands of an expert, and he clung to his big sister. Kenzie was holding Seth's hand, and Kala brought up the rear, a worried look on her face.

They knew.

Damn it. He'd tried to keep the whole "my heart needs to be checked out" thing on the down-low.

"Is Dad okay?"

Then his heart did constrict, and he had to take a deep breath because Tasha had asked the question.

Charlie slid off his lap and reached for their oldest daughter's hand. "Yes, sweetie. Your dad is great. We talked to the doctor and his heart is in amazing condition. He's healthy and going to be with us for a very long time."

He watched them all sigh in obvious relief.

"That's good news, Mom. We were all worried about him." Tasha smiled, a bright, happy expression. "And it's good because he promised we could watch *Ant Man* again. I'll go make some popcorn."

She turned with the surety of a child who wouldn't get turned down, who knew her dad would stop the world to watch a movie with her.

The kids walked out talking about snacks, and Charlie turned, tears rolling down her cheeks. "She called me Mom."

He drew her into his arms, his heart fuller than it had been before.

It had taken awhile, but their girl was finally home.

8

Countdown: A Glimpse of a Possible Future

Countdown takes place sometime in the future.

Deep in the Himalayas

Ben Parker fired, taking down the last of the security. The black-clad guard hit the floor with a thud and Ben breathed a long sigh of relief. There had been twelve, a ridiculous number for a facility that was supposedly used to study the effects of climate change high in the Himalayas. But then Ben's higher-ups in the CFI knew what was really going on in this remote site deep in Nepal.

The "climate" scientists were actually virologists and engineers who had seemingly made evil their minors in college. Or greed, perhaps, but given what they were brewing up here, he had to think it was pure evil.

A new delivery system for anthrax was being researched in this complex, and Canada was going to make damn sure that was one research project that didn't get completed.

Ben was silent for a moment, waiting for any sound to reach his ear. The floors in this part of the complex were metal, and any sudden movement rattled. Nothing. It appeared the intelligence had been correct and the facility had been evacuated except for security personnel and a few lead scientists. Now all he had to do was find the big bad guy and he could call it a day.

He touched the comm system. It was sleek and small, nothing more than a dot that sat on the outer edge of his left ear. He could walk around with it all day and no one would notice. "Tim, are you there? I'm past the inner perimeter. I need the code to get into the lab."

A garbled sound came over the line.

One of the best reasons for a whacko terrorist to hide a lab in the middle of the Himalayas was the fact that technology sometimes went awry out here. It tended to give the bad guys an edge. He stared at the door in front of him. It was massive and made of four-inch-thick steel. He wasn't going to kick that sucker in no matter how many leg days he'd suffered through.

He knew he should have brought some damn C-4, but no, his handler was worried they would blow up the anthrax and kill the population of Nepal. There was no optimism left in his world.

He had one shot, and damn but he hadn't wanted to take it. He'd wanted to get this thing done before the other team showed up. It would have made things infinitely easier, but it looked like there was no way around it. He hadn't come across anyone with the key to the inner sanctum. Behind that door was the part of the building not even security got into.

He glanced around, touching his comm again. "Tell me the damn Americans came through. I can't move forward without a code. I wasn't able to find anyone with the proper key card. You were right. All the scientists are gone. Huisman's in there somewhere. I think he's crazy enough to go down with the ship, eh?"

"Americans...code...coming. Sorry, there's a storm. Moving in...five...hang..." The line went dead.

Outside, the wind was whipping through the mountains. Tim and the team were roughly ten thousand feet below. He'd been forced to climb the damn mountain to get to the facility. He'd started in the dark, taken hours of moving quietly and steadily so they didn't see him coming. Though they were no longer worried about being seen, Ben didn't see his skinny-ass tech hauling butt up the mountain any time soon.

He stared at the door that separated him from the prize. From what he'd learned about the facility, this door led to the promised land—to the laboratory and the private office and residence of the man who had started this all. Dr. Huisman was in there somewhere, working on his plans.

The Chinese had gotten a foothold in North America, and Europe was rattling sabers. The world was changing rapidly, and it was a renaissance time for the spy. Ever since the Mexican revolution had sent the entire continent into chaos, Ben had known he would wind up here. Maybe not this particular location, but in times when the whole world was on the brink, there was always some asshole willing to push them all over.

The world was a powder keg, and if this new threat got in the wrong hands, Ben was worried it would blow sky-high.

And now he was literally one door away from reaching the prize, and the Americans hadn't come through with the code. They'd had one job. One.

He heard a slight squeak coming from the hallway to his left. He brought up his gun, ready to take out whoever came down that hall. Had he missed someone? Had their intelligence been off?

One breath in and he was focused.

And then he wasn't. A glimpse of pink hair made him stop. He lowered the gun because shooting this particular player wasn't what he wanted to do.

Nope. He sometimes wanted to throttle her, but mostly his intentions were far more sexual.

The woman he knew as Ms. Magenta stood at the end of the hall, dressed all in white for a change. She had on a huge white parka, but he knew what it hid—curves and hips and breasts he couldn't get out of his head.

The Magenta name was her play on her agency's time-honored tradition of calling its operatives Mr. Black or Mr. Green, or some other color that was meant to protect the operative's true identity. The woman in front of him was roughly five foot eight in flats, and when she wore heels like she had on the mission in Macau, she could look him straight in the eyes.

Let other men covet petite, delicate females. He wanted this one. She was the alpha female, cool and competent and often at odds with him. Maggie. Since he didn't know her real name, he called her Maggie.

He stared at her for a moment, trying to figure out which Maggie he was dealing with. Sometimes she showed up and he could feel how dangerous she was, how reckless and ruthless. Other times she nearly melted in his arms, coming so close to kissing him that he'd ached with the loss.

"Ben, I'm sorry I'm late." She strode up to him, pulling back the hood of her parka and setting free all that pink hair that was sort of her signature. He'd seen her with almost every color of the rainbow, including her natural reddish blonde. There was something about the softness of her face that made him relax. She wasn't here to fight. "We had trouble with the helo, but it looks like you handled everything with your usual aplomb. That was a lot of bodies out there, buddy."

He loved that slight Texas twang that came out when she wasn't thinking too hard. He loved that it came out more and more when they were alone. But he frowned because they weren't supposed to be alone today. The US was still friendly with Canada, but the last thing he wanted was Maggie walking out of here with the prize.

The prize, in this case, was something he firmly intended to destroy.

"I didn't realize you were late because you're not supposed to be here at all," he returned.

She stopped a few feet away from him, her blue eyes narrowing. Ah, there was the dangerous girl. "You know we were responsible for getting the code. How did you think I would get it to you?"

"Text works." If she was here, she had a mission and it was likely to get that formula for the Agency.

She reached into her pocket and pulled out a card. "You need this along with the code. I took it off one of Huisman's men last night at a bar. He's still sleeping it off, so I doubt he'll miss it. Now, if you don't mind, I'll open that door and we can be home in time for dinner."

Since they were on a completely different continent from home, he took it as pure sarcasm. She seemed to breathe sarcasm at times.

What was his play? He could fight her for the card, but she wouldn't give him the code. He could argue that she wasn't going with him, perhaps even slip in and lock her out.

And then she would take his balls off, and that wasn't how he wanted her to get introduced to his balls. He would have to get in, find the formula, and destroy it before they ever left here.

"Did you get the vaccine?" If they hadn't inoculated her against inhalation anthrax, there was zero way he was taking her with him.

She rolled those gorgeous eyes of hers. "Of course. Do you think I have a death wish?"

He'd seen her jump out of a plane at nearly 35,000 feet, so yes, he often thought she did. Of course, he'd jumped out after her because they were about to be murdered and she'd taken the only parachute.

Maybe he was the one with a death wish. His dick seemed incredibly stupid.

"All right, I'm going first," he said. "I don't know if Huisman is behind that door or not. According to our intelligence, he hasn't left the base in a week, but he sent home the rest of the non-security employees a few days ago. Be careful, eh? He might be a doctor, but he gave up on his Hippocratic oath a long time ago. He will be armed, and he won't hesitate to kill you. Stay behind me."

She moved to the door, flashing the key card and punching in a five-digit code. "You know I love it when you say 'eh.' And hey, if you want to get murdered first, who am I to stop you? What's wrong with the comms? I can't get my team on the line."

So hers wasn't working either. It was good to know they were completely blind. "Apparently the storm is wreaking havoc on our electronics. Stay behind me."

He started to move through the room, catching sight of the SIG Sauer in her right hand. The whole three years he'd worked with her off and on, she'd always used that weapon, though there were far more technologically advanced guns out there. She always claimed if it had been good enough for her father, it was good enough for her.

The door closed behind her and he turned on the light. "According to the plans we stole, this is where Huisman works."

"This outer section is part of his office. The lab is in the back. It's a level-four biosafety lab, so we'll have to change if we go in there," she explained.

Did she think he was a moron? "Yes, I got that intel. And we don't have to change at all. I'll deal with it, and you'll stay out here and watch for any stragglers. And Huisman. I haven't found him yet. He's got to be here somewhere."

She stopped in the middle of the hallway, one hand on her hip. "I'm not going to sit out here like a good little girl and wait for you. I can bet what would happen. You would go in and the formula would mysteriously disappear."

He wasn't playing these games with her. He strode down the

hallway. Huisman's compound was multi-tiered, but this was definitely the level with the most security.

So why were the doors all open?

"If you think I'm going to allow something that deadly to fall into your country's hands, you don't know me," she insisted as she followed him.

The door to the lab was closed, but there was a green light blinking above, indicating that it wasn't locked. The lab was on one end of the hall and, if he was correct, Huisman's office was on the other. Perhaps he should check the office first. He didn't want to get caught with his pants down.

"I don't know you at all, sweetheart. I don't even know your real name. The only thing I know is that you'll do anything for your country, including turning over a weapon of mass destruction when you would be better off destroying the formula." He strode down the hallway, well aware that they were making far too much noise. He couldn't seem to help it around her. "And don't even talk to me about our countries. Let's see which one is known for being involved in every war it can send its troops into, and which one is known for maple syrup and delicious donuts."

"We have excellent donuts, too," she shot back. "And maple syrup. Have you never been to Vermont? Name me one thing Canada has that America doesn't. Face facts. You're nothing but America North, buddy."

She irritated him to no freaking end. So why did he dream about her at night? Why did every woman he slept with morph into her at some point? He was young, fit, and in a job that seemed to attract women even though he couldn't talk about it. Somehow they seemed to know he was dangerous, and it drew them to him. He should be having the time of his life, but no, all he could think about was a woman with pink hair who challenged him at every turn. "You know what we have that you don't, baby? It's called common sense. Sweet, sane common sense. Which is precisely why you're not stealing this formula."

He stopped at the doorway. Not because he was worried about Huisman getting the jump on them.

They weren't alone. Not that it mattered.

"Is he dead?" Maggie moved in behind him.

Yep. Dr. Emmanuel Huisman was totally dead on the floor of his office. Unless he'd managed to fake the bullet hole to his left temple. Ben kicked the revolver away from the bad doctor's hand anyway. Never hurt to be cautious in his line of work. More than one person had come back from the "dead" and tried to kill him.

"He must have decided to kill himself rather than face the Agency." Maggie stared down at him.

"Maybe he knew he was facing CFI." Canadian Foreign Intelligence. His group.

She laughed. "You've been around for five years, buddy. You're not known for being particularly ferocious when it comes to dealing with prisoners. You do tend to give them donuts and hope they like you enough to talk."

There was another thing his country had on hers. Niceness. The Canadian version of the CIA hadn't existed until five years before, when the Chinese and Russians had started moving in on South America and Mexico.

Maybe they weren't great at all things torture, but damn it, he wasn't going to allow his country to go down.

He stopped and stared at the desk in front of him. Huisman's office was totally different from the utilitarian rooms outside it. This office was luxurious and built for comfort. There were several laptops and a big, sturdy desktop that likely held the secrets of this facility. A monitor sat on the desk, a sticky note hastily attached to the side. It was barely clinging there.

Play Me

"I don't think we should go down that rabbit hole," Maggie said, her boot tapping against the floor. "Let's get into the lab and get out of here. If he wanted to monologue like a good villain, he should have stayed alive."

Somehow Ben couldn't see it going so smoothly. Huisman was the kind of man who tended to get what he wanted. If he wanted them to listen, he would have found a way.

Still, he agreed that he wasn't simply going to stand there and comply. He glanced around and saw there was another door. There was a room beyond the office.

He stepped in and found something the reports hadn't mentioned.

Huisman had a beautifully decadent bedroom. He should have known the fucker wasn't sleeping on some military-grade cot. The whole space was white and cream-colored, dominated by a massive four-poster bed. He had to wonder what it had cost to get that gorgeous monstrosity up a mountain.

Was that a fucking Picasso above the bed?

"What is that?" Maggie stepped in behind him.

She wasn't talking about the bed. Right there in the middle of the room was a large piece of equipment with tons of wires and compartments attached. On top of it sat a digital clock.

The door behind them slid closed with a nasty hiss, and Ben watched in horror as the clock blinked to life.

1:00:00

0:59:59

0:59:58

"Shit. It's a bomb," Maggie said.

Yes, the other quality the Americans possessed was the unquestionable ability to state the obvious.

He turned and tried to open the door. It held firm. "Try the key card."

She waved it over the security box. Nothing. Well, not nothing. They got nothing from the door. It didn't budge, merely blinked red to let them know it wasn't opening. But a monitor did slip down from the ceiling. It was perfectly placed to be seen from the bed. Ben moved back, taking in the monitor that was now full of Huisman's self-satisfied smile.

"Welcome, Benjamin," the man on the monitor said. He spoke in softly accented English, French being his native tongue. "I figured you wouldn't follow my very reasonable orders, so I had to set a bit of a trap to get you to hear me out. If you are not Benjamin Parker of Canadian intelligence, I apologize. But I think it will be you. You and the American girl. I seem to find you together so very often. Welcome. You finally found me. I applaud you, and you've managed to catch me at a delicate time. Even now you're at work in the outside perimeter, taking out my soldiers. I went cheap on the mercenaries. I suppose thrift really was my downfall. The good news is the bomb you are currently sharing space with is not cheap. It's quite expensive, filled with all the best uranium China could get to me. It's certainly enough to blow the top off this mountain. And it will be enough to send my enriched and hearty anthrax all over the country of Nepal."

"What the fuck did Nepal do to him?" Maggie asked.

Huisman wasn't finished. "Why do I care about Nepal, you might ask? I don't, but the Chinese want it destroyed and they paid me an enormous amount of money to do it. The explosion will destabilize this part of the world. In addition to blowing off the top of this mountain, I've rigged something special up there. When my new anthrax hits the upper atmosphere, it will breed and form clouds. It will rain down on the people of this region. Imagine that. Not acid rain. Anthrax rain that only the Chinese and their select friends will be immune to. It will seep into the soil. Perhaps my new bacteria will continue to breed. It will be a brave new world, my friends. Unfortunately, you and I will not live to see it. I think I'll go out on a high note, but I wanted to leave you a bit of time to contemplate the end of your existence. This is my final gift to you, Benjamin. I give you the gift of time. What will you do with the final hour of your life? I think you will be like a rat on a sinking ship, scratching and panicking to save your own pathetic life. You see, there are worse things than dying. *Au revoir, mon ami.*"

Ben felt her hand slip into his. He squeezed it tight.

They were so fucked.

41:34

The clock kept ticking.

"I think we should cut the blue wire." Maggie had been carefully inspecting the bomb that would likely end their lives. "The only problem is I'm fairly certain this sucker has a couple of land mines attached. I don't mean that literally, of course, but I think bad crap could happen if I clip the wrong wire. The red wire goes to something that looks like it's empty, so it's probably a gas."

"I wouldn't put it past him to release some sarin on us if we did something wrong." He could see what she was talking about. The bomb was a complete mess of wires. It would take hours to figure out where each of them went. Hours they didn't have.

Maggie sat up, pushing her hot-pink hair out of her face. She'd gotten out of the massive parka she'd been wearing and underneath had been a white jumpsuit that would have looked utilitarian on someone else. It just made her look like a freaking walking wet dream. "I could use a little optimism."

"I don't have any when it comes to that bomb. I think we should try to work on the comms. Neither one of us is a bomb expert." He'd tried everything he could to get that damn door open. It wasn't budging, and he'd nearly taken off his own head by trying to shoot the locking mechanism. Luckily, he was excellent with some forms of technology. He touched the ultralight tablet he carried with him at all times and felt a thrill go through him as the TV screen switched from Huisman's face to a computer screen. "I'm in his computer system."

She stood, her eyes going wide. "How did you manage that? Can you get the door open?"

Probably not, since he'd shot the mechanism. Yeah, not his best moment. He started typing on the tablet. "The TV is a smart screen. It should be able to connect to any system with a signal. Huisman sprang for the best. The satellite connection is still working. It looks like he's shut down electrical to all the doors. No one can get in or out."

"Send out a message before his handlers figure out they should shut down the satellite." She was close to him again. He could smell the citrus scent of her shampoo. He lied to himself, trying to force his brain away from dangerous territory. She wasn't his type. He liked normal women. Women who didn't jump out of planes and have pink hair. Women who weren't incredibly skilled assassins. Women who didn't make his heart pound the way this one did.

He quickly typed a message to his handler. Tim was in a camp at the base of the mountain, and they would all need to evacuate as quickly as possible. He sent it off but couldn't get through to Tim's mobile. He passed Maggie the tablet.

"Thanks," she said, turning away slightly. "At least I can warn my team."

"Where are they?" He knew next to nothing about her team. He'd only dealt with her.

"They're probably with Tim by now," she said. "They were taking the helo down the mountain after they dropped me off. My partner was worried about losing the bird. It's brand new and it's capable of getting up to almost thirty thousand feet, but it's struggling with the storm. Langley will murder us if we crash that chopper. It's their baby, and we might or might not have had permission to take it out for this op."

Somehow it didn't surprise him. She was likely a massive pain in the ass to her boss. "You stole a helo?"

She finished typing and looked back up at him. "I think they will discover that we were simply mistaken about which helo we were supposed to take. It was really early, and that requisition form can be hard to read before I've had a cup of coffee."

"Let me see if I can affect this bomb from here." He took the tablet from her and started poking around the system. "I have no idea how you get away with that shit. If I did it, I would be fired."

"It helps to have friends. We work with some of the best Special Ops teams in the world, and I happen to have grown up with some of those guys. I'm sure if times weren't what they are those relationships would cost me plenty, but I'm incredibly valuable for them now. My helo pilot used to steal cookies from my mom's cookie jar. Though I'm not the only one who seems to have connections. Why did Huisman call you friend?" If she was upset about the fact that they were locked in a room with a bomb big enough to take out a mountain, she didn't show it. She made a slow circle around the room, trailing her hand over the comforter on the bed. "Or more specifically *mon ami*."

"Because he's an asshole." He didn't want to go into this. It wasn't any of her business. He should leave it at that, but he found himself going on. "We were friends when we were kids."

Why had he said that?

"I knew he was from Canada," she said, sitting at the end of the bed. "I didn't realize you knew him."

Frustration welled inside him as he pored over the system. Any way he went, he got blocked. Huisman had been a brilliant doctor, but he'd known computer systems, too. He might have gone cheap on the mercenaries hired to protect him, but he'd been smart enough to hire the best when it came to setting up his cyber security systems. Of course, it wasn't like Ben himself was some brilliant hacker. He knew just enough to think he could do things he obviously couldn't. That was why he had Tim. But he was worried Tim wouldn't be able to get into a closed system.

It was up to him. The whole fucking fate of this region was up to him.

"Hey, it's okay." She was suddenly behind him, her hands on his shoulders. "None of this is your fault. Unless Huisman was your secret lover and you cheated on him and that's why he hates the world."

He rounded on her. This was not the time to joke. "He was not my secret lover."

She shrugged, the motion making her breasts move. Gorgeous fucking breasts. Those breasts made his mouth water. They made his brain soft, because he was looking down the barrel of a massive, uranium-enriched gun, and all he could think about was how he could see a hint of nipple through that white shirt. And it wasn't cold in here. It might be freezing outside, but Huisman had managed to keep it nice and toasty in his evil lair.

"I always wondered."

He turned, forgetting about the tablet for a moment. "You wondered if I was gay? I'm not gay. What exactly gave you the impression that I'm gay? If you say it's because I'm Canadian, I swear I'll be done with you."

Her lips curled up in the sexiest smile. "That sounds like something my dad would say. He's pretty *rah-rah* USA. Spent some time in the military. But no, your Canadianness doesn't make me question your sexuality, merely your choice of bacon."

She was so frustrating, and he suddenly got the idea that he should show her just how not gay he was. "My choice of bacon is fine. It leads to far less heart disease than yours. Let me explain a few things to you, sweetheart. There's nothing wrong with homosexuality. It's a perfectly natural state. My natural state is different. I like women. I like breasts and hips and pussies. I really like soft, welcoming pussies, especially when they're attached to smart, sexy, dangerous women."

She held her ground and, yes, those nipples were definitely out, and that had not a thing to do with the temperature. "Well, we've worked together a couple of times now and you've never once hit on me. It makes a girl think."

So arrogant. "So if a man doesn't hit on you, he's obviously gay? Maybe you're not my type."

"Oh, I'm you're type. Don't get me wrong, Ben. I can be arrogant, but I'm self-aware, too. I know perfectly well that I'm not every man's type. I'm a brat of the highest order, and I was probably raised to have ridiculously high standards, but we're alike, you and I. If you prefer women, I'm your natural mate."

What was she trying to do? They had less than forty minutes before the world blew up and she was hitting on him? She wanted to do this now? "Natural mate? In your world do natural mates take the last parachute and leave the other to die? Do they shoot their mate in the shoulder? How about the throwdown in the alley in Beijing when you kicked me in the balls and stole the only invite to that auction the cartel was having?"

She rolled those gorgeous blue eyes. "Don't be so dramatic. I took the parachute because I knew damn well you would follow me. If I hadn't, you would have stood there and talked that asshole to death. Excuse me for getting bored. And I shot you through the shoulder because that was the only way to kill the bad guy. His heart was behind your shoulder. I knew what I was doing and I wasn't about to let him drag you away and use you as a human shield. As for the auction... I know you won't believe me but I felt bad about that. I should have found another way but it worked out. That invite led to us all getting valuable intelligence. I'm sorry about...well, I'm just sorry."

He tried to keep his eyes on the monitor, but he could feel her moving behind him. "You halfway sound like you care, Maggie."

"I did and I do," she said quietly. "You're not going to be able to untangle that mess, Ben. We don't have near enough time."

She cared? About him? "I need some optimism."

That was the moment the lights went out. They were plunged into complete darkness. Ben reached out, putting the tablet down.

He stepped back, turning and reaching out for her. "Maggie?"

"I'm here." She moved close to him, bumping up against his chest. Her arms went around him. "I don't want to lose you. I can't see a thing."

He couldn't see a damn thing either, but he could already feel something. A chill went through the room. If the power had gone out, then the climate control would go as well. It was possible the venting had opened and they were about to get a big dose of what it meant to be twenty-three thousand feet above sea level.

The truth was even if he could get them out, it wouldn't matter now. They could try to climb down, but their time was running out, and this was the kind of climb that took hours and hours without the aid of a helicopter.

And they couldn't hack into a system when the wireless was down.

He held her for a moment, taking in the gravity of the situation. His eyes adjusted and he realized something was still working. "Is the timer still ticking down?"

"Yes." She laid her head on his shoulder, the same one she'd shot. "It's on some kind of battery, but if I try to clip it, it looks like it triggers the system."

Naturally.

"And the sensor that connects it to the bomb on top of the mountain is very likely battery operated, too." It's what he would do. Huisman would have left nothing to chance. He'd set everything up perfectly. He'd even left them in the dark.

Like rats on a sinking ship.

How did he want to spend the last half hour of his life?

"I think I can see enough to get around now." Maggie took a step back. He heard her boots move across the floor. "Damn it. Well, the power going out didn't kill the security system. That door is not budging."

Because the man on the other side of it would have been very careful. Had Huisman hurried and hustled to make this happen? Had he realized he was going down and scrambled to catch the hunter in a trap of his own? Or had this always been his plan?

Ben rather thought it was the latter.

He heard a long sigh and then a single stream of light cut through the darkness. Maggie moved through the room, toward the big four-poster bed. She opened the nightstand and started going through it.

"Oh, look. The good doctor believed in safe sex," she murmured. "And a shocking amount of lube. Who needs that much lube? Ah, there we go."

She set down the small flashlight and there was the scratching sound of a match striking. She lit the candles that had decorated the room.

"Do you think he used this place as his pleasure palace?" Maggie asked as she filled the room with soft light.

Ben realized that he hadn't moved. Not an inch. Since that moment when Huisman's words had whispered through his brain—*how will you spend your last hour?*—he'd been locked in place, his focus shifting from survival to something else.

Her.

She turned, her pink hair still somehow so vibrant in the candlelight. It had softened all of her other features. "You okay?"

It was a ridiculous question. They were trapped inside a mountain that was going to blow up and decimate a whole lot of the population of their planet. He was not okay. "No."

Maggie stepped in front of him. "You need to have a little faith. We're stuck. There's nothing we can do, but our people know what's going on. They won't let this happen. I assure you that my team is taking that state-of-the-art helo up the mountain right now, and they will move that bomb or they will find a way to ensure that it doesn't go off. They're the best. They won't let me down."

"But there's no way for them to stop the bomb that's five feet away from us."

She glanced over at it and sighed. "No. I don't think they can, and they know what their priorities are. I've already assessed this and the most likely outcome is that my team takes out the big bomb and we die in here anyway."

"Yes, I think you're right." He wasn't going down like a desperate rat. He'd known this would be his fate. He would die on a mission, trying to save his country—the world, really. He reached out and did what came naturally. He touched her, touched that spun-sugar hair of hers. It was ridiculously soft against his skin. "I wish you weren't here with me."

"That's funny because I was thinking that there was no place I would rather be." She stepped in closer, tilting her head slightly up. "You took your time, Ben. You're not good at reading signals because I've been sending them out forever."

He let his hands sink into her hair, the sense of anticipation flooding his system. Yes, this was the way he would spend the last moments of his life. With her. Warm and happy with her. "Your signals suck, baby. All you ever had to do was this."

He lowered his head and brushed his lips over hers. So long. He'd waited forever to feel those velvet-soft lips under his. He moved slowly despite the fact that there was a bomb ticking down the time. It didn't matter anymore. That clock could move on and he would stay here, doing this, kissing her and exploring her like he'd wanted to from the first moment. Oddly enough, now that he was here, time seemed to slow and the destination wasn't half as important as the journey. If the world blew up, at least their bodies would mingle. No one would be able to tell the difference between them. In that moment, he was all right. It was a better fate than any other he'd been offered.

She moved with him, her mouth flowering open at the mere hint of his tongue. She welcomed him inside, her hands going to his hips. He felt her sigh as he deepened the kiss. Their bodies brushed each other and then she moved against him, bringing her breasts to his chest as she wrapped her arms around him.

Had they been anywhere else, he wouldn't have trusted the moment. He would have been on his guard, thinking she was trying to distract him. She was, but he wanted this distraction.

No. It wasn't the distraction he wanted, and he hoped she wasn't using sex simply to get her mind off the fact that they were going to die.

"Maggie, I'm crazy about you. I've wanted to touch you since the moment I saw you. Well, most of the time," he whispered against her mouth. He dragged his tongue across her lower lip, loving the way she shuddered in his arms. "Sometimes it's like you're a different person."

She shook her head. "Don't think about that. That was all work. This is different, Ben. I want you so badly sometimes I can't stand it. My friends know it, too. They know you're the reason I haven't had a damn boyfriend in a year."

He kissed her again, drugged by her softness, the feeling of being able to lose himself in her. He took her mouth over and over again, thanking Huisman for being so slavishly devoted to his own comfort that he would have a bedroom built for sex even on this remote mountain.

He let his hands roam over her back and down to that perfect ass he thought about all the time. Maggie was fit and strong, but she had curves in all the right places. Her backside fit into the palms of his hands like it'd been made for him. He pulled her close, letting her feel what she did to him. "Do you have any idea how hard it is to work with you? I get this any time you're around."

She frowned at him. "Even when I'm busting your balls?"

"Okay, so there are times when you seem more pissed off than others." Sometimes she seemed deeply dismissive of him, as though she didn't remember or care about the times when they'd talked and worked together in harmony. Those tended to be the times he had to watch because he ended up shot or kicked in the balls. "I often wonder who hurt you."

Her hands moved up his chest. "One day I'll explain everything, but for now, please kiss me again, Ben."

One day would have to be had in Heaven or Hell, or wherever operatives went after they got their asses blown to bits, but he wasn't about to argue with her now. He gave in and kissed her again, their tongues sliding against each other.

He moved from her mouth to her cheek and down toward her neck. He wanted to kiss her everywhere, but that damn jumpsuit she wore covered her well, and he couldn't find the zipper. "Baby, I want to see you. I want to touch you. I know we don't have much time, but I want to spend every single second we have left getting inside you. It's all I want now."

He wanted her more than breathing. If the door opened at this point, he would ignore it. He wouldn't waste his time trying to flee. He would spend it wrapping himself up in her.

She stepped back, the sweetest smile on her face. He loved seeing her like this. This was the Maggie who haunted his dreams. Not that she wasn't competent in the field, but this side of the woman seemed devoted to working with him instead of showing him what a dumbass he was.

"You know we have all the best toys." She turned slowly, and he could see there wasn't a zipper anywhere and yet it was plastered to her body. It fit perfectly. "Nanites. They conform to whoever's wearing them. They're also resistant to bullets and weapons. Oh, push hard enough and you can still get a knife through there, but it gives me some protection."

Yes, the Americans did have all the best tech. "How do I get it off you?"

He didn't give a damn about how it worked except to get her naked. Normally he would ask a hundred questions because he'd never seen nanite tech like this before, but he couldn't care less. He was all about finally seeing how gorgeous she truly was.

"It's easy," she said. "It's voice-activated. Undress."

The white jumpsuit flowed down her body like a metallic cascade, unveiling her skin. Her hair spilled around her shoulders, falling almost to her nipples. The sight of her breasts made his dick harden even further. How hard could he get before he died from it? It didn't matter because he was watching as the nanites retreated and showed him her hips and the gorgeous spot between her legs. Her pussy was smooth and bare, and he could see the glistening arousal there. Even the damn boots she was wearing disappeared into a cube that formed at her feet. She reached down and placed it on the nightstand. "Cute, huh?"

That wasn't the word he would use. "I take it that voice control is only for you. Because I could find a definite use for that. Damn, but you're gorgeous. Come here. It's cold and I don't want you to feel the chill for even a second."

"I didn't notice. I'm perfectly warm." She moved toward him, slowly, as though well aware of his eyes on her. "And I would never give you that code. I know what you would do with it."

He would have her naked whenever the mood sparked him, and it would spark him a lot. He would keep her on her toes, and the second they had any privacy at all, he would find a corner and give the command that would have her naked. "I don't have clothes that undress themselves. I think I need you to help me."

She moved right in, her hands going to the bottom of his sweater. "I should have known you would be needy. Lucky for you, I don't mind a little work."

She eased her hands under the sweater and thermals he was wearing underneath. Ben bit back a moan the minute he felt her hands on his flesh. She slid them up, running along his abs and up to his chest, and he was happy he'd kept up a hardcore gym routine because this woman deserved a lover who could keep up with her. He stared down at her while she stared up.

He wished he hadn't wasted so much time. They'd been on a

dozen ops together over the past three years, and now he wished he'd kissed her the first time they'd met.

She dragged the layers over his head and tossed them to the side. Then her hands were on him, palms flat on his chest as she leaned over and kissed the curve of his neck. Yeah, he wasn't feeling the chill anymore. A delicious heat stroked through his body as he allowed her to explore. She cuddled up against him, her nipples rubbing. He cradled the back of her neck as she kissed her way down his torso. She stopped briefly at the scar on his left shoulder, the bullet wound now raised and white.

"So sorry about that, babe." She kissed the scar and then ran her tongue around it before continuing down.

When she dropped to her knees, it took everything he had not to come then and there. There was something almost formal about the way she did it, as though she was offering him something he didn't entirely understand. He wasn't about to turn it down though. He watched in breathless anticipation as she unbuckled his belt and eased down the heavy fabric of his slacks and thermals. They'd kept him warm, but now the heat in her eyes would do the trick.

She glanced down as his cock came free. He bit back the need to beg her to touch him. He didn't care how much time was left on that fucking clock. He wasn't going to make this some rushed thing. It was their first time.

Their only time.

"I knew you would be beautiful, Ben. I win that bet."

He was about to ask her what she meant by that, but she leaned forward and gripped his cock in her hand. When she tongued his cockhead, he gasped and fought the urge to come. Nope. Wasn't happening.

She sucked the head behind those sinful lips of hers, and he thought he was going to die. Heat sparked through his system, and he felt his balls drawing up. That was all it took. She was so gorgeous, so hot and perfect that it was a fight to stay calm.

Her tongue whirled around his cock, and he let his hands find her hair, sinking in and drawing her closer.

"Take more." He wasn't going to come in her mouth. No. He wanted to get inside her body, wanted so badly to feel that sweet pussy sucking him inside. But he would know her mouth, too. Fully.

"You have no idea what that deep voice does to me. One day we're going to have a long talk about my personal kinks, but for now just know that I can take orders. I want to please you."

Fuck, that did something for him. It made his heart speed up and his dick throb. He had a sudden vision of tying her up and torturing her body in the sweetest way. He would make her come again and again, and only when she begged him would he find his own release and relent. Then she would be his. His own spy girl with pink hair and cherry lips. She would fight against everyone except him because she would know he would protect and care for her.

Oh, the life they could have had.

"You please me in every single way, baby. Now take me. Suck me hard and fast and don't stop until I tell you to."

She licked her lips and settled back down, sucking him in long passes. So good. It felt so good, but he couldn't let it last. Her mouth moved over him, infusing him with energy. It hummed through his body and made him feel more alive than he'd ever felt before. He pushed into her mouth, taking control and feeling the moment when she surrendered. She let him use her mouth, sucking him hard and submitting in a way that nearly sent him over the edge.

This was what she wanted. She was trying to show him what she wanted from him. He tugged on her hair, just enough so she would feel it.

She came off him, her face tilting up and showing him red, gloriously swollen lips. Her blue eyes stared up at him as she waited.

She was waiting for him to take control. The idea made his cock jump, and it damn straight made him want to show her exactly how good he could make this.

"Get on the bed and spread your legs for me. I want to see that pretty pussy before I eat it like a starving man." Something about her brought out the dirty talk. Sex before this had been good but polite. He'd been taught to be respectful and gentlemanly, but now he realized he could be both. He could respect the hell out of her and give her every dirty, filthy fantasy he'd ever had.

He kicked out of his boots, watching her while she spread herself on the bed. Her hair made a halo around her, but there the angelic references ended. She was a siren, calling a man to temptation, and he didn't care if it all led to tragedy.

"Touch yourself. I want you to rub your little clit and get it hot and ready for me. I want that pussy wet. I want to lick that pussy and get cream all over my tongue. Do you understand me?"

"You're killing me." She drew her hand down her body until she found her pussy and brushed manicured fingers over the pearl of her clitoris.

Ben stepped out of his pants and stroked his cock as he looked down at her. She was the sexiest thing he'd ever seen. So feminine and perfect. Sure, she had scars, but so did he. Those scars marked them, and if he'd had time, he would map her body. He would kiss every inch of her, moving from scar to scar and having the story of each one so he could know her soul as well as he would learn her flesh.

He climbed on the bed with her. "Give me a taste."

Maggie offered up her fingers, and he brought them to his lips, sucking them inside. He was perfectly satisfied with the way she flushed. He sucked on her fingers, drawing the taste of her inside and letting it coat his tongue.

"You taste perfect, but I'm going to need more." He leaned over and took her mouth, giving the taste of her own arousal back to her before kissing his way down her body.

Her hands fisted in the covers as he sucked on one nipple and then the other, laving them with his affection. Her breasts were so beautifully sensitive, responding to him by puckering up.

He could stay there forever, but their time was limited so he kissed his way over the soft swell of her belly and down to where he'd wanted to be since the moment he'd laid eyes on her.

He breathed her in, the smell of her sex lighting a fire inside him.

"Please, Ben." The words came out of her mouth on a low moan as she spread her legs even further.

What happened next would definitely please Ben. He lowered his mouth and covered her pussy. He settled in, loving the way she tasted, and he could feel her shaking under him. She was already so close. He could taste it, sense it in her little whimpers and cries. Her hands came up, fingers tangling in his hair, trying to keep him in a place he had absolutely no intention of leaving. Not until he was sure she'd been satisfied.

This was everything he'd wanted from her and more. He settled in, grinding his tongue over her clit as he eased his finger into her. She was so tight. Those muscles of hers clenched around him as he started to fuck her in time to the rhythm of his tongue. He curled his finger up inside her, looking for that sweet spot.

Her whole body stiffened and she came around him, her arousal flooding his senses.

And now it was his time. He got to his knees, stroking his cock. He glanced over at the condoms, but damn it, it was the end of the fucking world. Still, force of habit had him reaching out and opening the packet before he could really consider the fact that it didn't matter.

Then nothing mattered except the woman underneath him. Her skin had flushed to a gorgeous pink, and he couldn't deny himself a second longer.

He pressed in, working his way in inch by inch. He couldn't breathe, couldn't think past the next thrust. She was silky and perfect around him. So tight he could barely move, but also slick and ready to take him. He pulled back out, her muscles sucking at him and sending a thrill through him like never before.

This was good. This was right. Finally the right woman at the right time.

It was perfection.

He fucked her hard, rubbing his pelvis over her clit and watching every expression on her face. Her eyes would widen with each thrust, and she would clutch him when he retreated. He could feel the way her nails bit into the skin of his back, and it hurt so much that he wouldn't wake up in the morning and stretch and feel that pain and know she'd been right here with him.

He wanted tomorrow with her. All the fucking tomorrows.

He wanted to take this one moment and make it stretch forever, make it last until he couldn't breathe, couldn't take another single second.

But he was only human and long before he wanted it to end, he felt her tighten around him, her pussy milking his cock as she flushed again and called out his name.

He couldn't fight it. His balls drew up and his spine tingled. He gritted his teeth as he came harder than he'd ever come before. He unleashed himself and pounded inside her, the need to mark her as his own a primitive and undeniable instinct.

Pleasure coursed through him, and he held himself tight against her, giving up everything he had.

He dropped down on top of her, giving her his weight as the blood pounded through his system in a pleasurable way. Her hands came up and she stroked his hair, sighing as she cuddled close to him. He buried his face against her neck and let peace flood him.

How could it all be ending when he'd just found her? He'd spent his whole adult life fighting for his country, but something had been missing, something hadn't been whole inside him, and now he knew what had always been missing.

Her.

A long moment passed and he realized she was shaking a bit. Cold. The cold suddenly bit into him.

"Baby, let's get under the covers. I want to hold you." He wanted to spend every second in her arms.

She smiled and kissed him briefly. "I can get with that. But go and get rid of that condom first. I do not want that slipping off and going everywhere. Sticky is not the new black."

Even here she teased him. He kissed her again and reluctantly pushed off her. "I'll be right back. Get under the covers. I want you warm."

Her lips curled up. "Yes, sir."

Something about the way she said *sir* made his cock spark all over again. He moved toward the door that would likely lead to either a bathroom or closet. He didn't care which. It wasn't like there would be some cleaning crew that would get embarrassed if he tossed a condom where Huisman stored his suits and shoes.

He glanced down and couldn't miss the red lights shining in the dim.

3:10

God. Three minutes. He opened the door and found himself in what seemed to be a gorgeous bathroom. The room was in shadows, the only light coming from the candles Maggie had lit. He pulled the condom off and dropped it in the trash and then tried the sink. The water still worked.

He wanted to touch her again, with clean hands. There wasn't time to make love, but he could hold her. He could cuddle her close and kiss her over and over until the end.

Make love. He'd never used those words with the act before. He'd had sex, fucked, gotten laid, but he'd never made love.

He loved Maggie. She was the one woman in the world who held a piece of his soul, and he was about to lose her.

He forced the dark thought back because he wasn't going to panic. There wasn't anything that panic would solve, and he would spend his final moments in peace.

He would spend them with her.

He strode back out, barely registering the clock as he moved to her.

2:37

Two minutes and thirty-seven seconds left to hold her, to love her.

She was under the covers and she drew them back, welcoming him in. He immediately pulled her into his arms.

"I hate that I wasted all this time," he whispered, kissing her forehead. "I should have made a move, should have told you that first time that I thought you were the most gorgeous thing I'd ever seen, but you seemed so cold."

"About that," she began. She rubbed her cheek against his chest like a kitten looking for affection. "I'm glad you didn't because it would have been awkward."

"The second time I saw you I wanted to kiss you. Do you remember?"

She smiled against his chest. "I remember. We were in Croatia trying to track down that bomb maker and we had to pretend to be lovers. You danced with me."

Such a sweet memory. He'd thought she was gorgeous the first time, but the second time they'd worked together something had been utterly different. Something had slipped into place that had been missing before. "Your hair was flaming red and you were wearing that ridiculous green dress that had every man in the room panting after you."

"Including you?"

"Oh, so including me. That was when I knew I wanted you. You were distant before and then we clicked." They'd danced all night and brought that man down. Together.

Her head came up. "I should explain that. Why I seemed like two different people at times. Ben, I want to be honest with you."

Their time was running out. So fast. God, he needed more time with her. She looked over and her face fell.

1:10

She shook her head and wrapped her arms around him. "It doesn't matter. Just know that I always wanted you. I knew it from the moment I saw you. I knew you were the one for me and even though it was complicated, I was always going to end up right here. With you. This is how we end, Ben Parker. We end together."

He held on to her and found her lips with his. He kissed her again and again, this time with no expectations of anything but to die in her arms. His cock thickened, but he could ignore it in favor of telling her how gorgeous she was, how lucky he'd been to meet her, to know her.

To love her.

She wrapped her arms around him and held on.

For way longer than a minute.

What the hell was going on? He glanced over and the clock read *0:00*.

It held for one second and then another.

And that was when he heard the clang of someone knocking on the door.

"I'm coming in. Dear god, please cover up and don't be doing something that will make me vomit," a familiar voice said.

"Oh, shit." Maggie turned and practically leapt out of bed.

The door came open and he was facing...well, he was facing a second Maggie, except her hair was a brilliant purple.

"Okay, sis, there's good news and bad news," Second Maggie said.

Maggie was reaching for her clothes cube. "I take it the good news is that we didn't blow up, and that's awesome. How did you manage to shut down the bombs?"

"I didn't," Second Maggie said. "Tris did. He and that Canadian dude worked some serious mojo while Coop and I took the helo up and tried to take the bomb somewhere safe. Luckily we didn't need to because the techies came through. By the way, the comm problem was totally one way. We could hear everything, and also, there are cameras that fed out even after the power went off, so way to make a sex tape, sis. Dad's probably getting hold of that one, you know." She finally looked his way. "He's going to kill you, dude. And you should know that it was totally me who shot you and kicked you in the balls."

Yes, he could see that now. Damn it. She was twins. His head was kind of reeling because they weren't dead, and now there were two of her and apparently she had some crazed father who wouldn't appreciate his sexual performance.

"Maggie?"

She was dressed again, the nanites covering her gorgeous body in an instant. She gave him a brilliant smile. "It's Kenzie. Kenzie Taggart."

His brain caught on that last name, and his stomach kind of took a deep dive. That last name was iconic in his world. It couldn't be a coincidence. "Taggart? Tell me he's not your father."

She sighed and rolled her eyes and looked like that perfect brat she'd called herself. "He's not that bad."

Ian Taggart was known as the single scariest dude in the whole of the intelligence community, and apparently he'd just made passionate, end-of-time love to the man's daughter. And it had been caught on camera.

The other Kenzie grinned but managed to make it slightly sinister. "Oh, he's so going to want to meet you, dude. Now let's go because we still have a crazy scientist to hunt down. I have no idea how he managed it, but he took a helo off the mountain twenty minutes ago while we were trying to make sure he didn't blow up the world."

Ben stood, not caring that he was naked. "Huisman is dead. His body is out there in the office."

"Nope," the twin said. "He faked it all and got out with the formula. We're starting from scratch. I believe you're wanted in a debrief and then our agencies are going to form a team. That should be fun now that little sister scratched her itch."

Maggie...Kenzie frowned her sister's way. "He wasn't an itch. You know that, Kala."

Kala sent her what seemed to be a sad smile. "I know. But we have to move. We have to get that helo back or Coop will be in trouble."

Kala winked at him. "And nice package, Parker. I'm glad I didn't wreck it."

Kenzie turned his way and rushed to him. "I have to go, but I'll see you soon, Ben."

She kissed him briefly and then walked out the door.

Ben stood there utterly shocked.

"Hey, clothes, man." Tim walked in the room. "You might have made a sex tape, but I don't need to see it up close and in person."

"Sorry." He was still looking at the door she'd walked through. "My clothes don't work on their own. Start talking. I want to hear everything."

Tim started the debrief as Ben dressed, but his mind was on something else. Someone else.

The game wasn't over. Huisman was still out there, but that was secondary in Ben's brain.

Kenzie Taggart could run. She could try to hide behind her legendary family, but he knew one thing.

That woman would be his.

Author's Note

I'm often asked by generous readers how they can help get the word out about a book they enjoyed. There are so many ways to help an author you like. Leave a review. If your e-reader allows you to lend a book to a friend, please share it. Go to Goodreads and connect with others. Recommend the books you love because stories are meant to be shared. Thank you so much for reading this book and for supporting all the authors you love!

Sign up for Lexi Blake's newsletter
and be entered to win a $25 gift certificate
to the bookseller of your choice.

Join us for news, fun, and exclusive content
including free short stories.

There's a new contest every month!

Go to www.LexiBlake.net to subscribe.

Catch up with other couples in the Masters and Mercenaries World!

Master Bits & Mercenary Bites
The Secret Recipes of Topped
Short Stories and Slices of Life by Lexi Blake
Recipes by Suzanne M. Johnson

Top restaurant has become the hot spot in Dallas for elevated comfort food—and a side of spicy romance. Run by executive chef Sean Taggart, Top is the premiere fictional destination for gourmet food. Join creator, *New York Times* bestselling author Lexi Blake, and Southern food expert Suzanne Johnson as they guide you through the world of Masters and Mercenaries via the secret recipes behind the food served in Top.

But what would a gourmet meal be without some company? Spend an evening with your favorite characters from McKay-Taggart as they celebrate the special moments that make up their happily ever afters. Learn how to make Sean's specialty dishes and Macon's desserts while exploring the private lives of the characters who make up the world. From Charlie and Ian's next demon spawn to a change in path for Simon and Chelsea, these are the times that bind us together, the moments that make us a family.

Good meals, good times, good friends.

Bon appétit!

* * * *

Master Bits & Mercenary Bites~ Girls Night
Short Stories & Slices of Life by Lexi Blake
Recipes from Suzanne M. Johnson

From the creators of *Master Bits and Mercenary Bites*, *New York Times* bestselling author Lexi Blake and Southern food expert and *USA Today* bestselling author Suzanne Johnson, comes a new look at the

Masters and Mercenaries world—*Girls Night*.

Join us for easy to cook, delicious recipes and stay for the stories of the women of McKay-Taggart. From slow cooker special dinners to cocktails that will elevate your game, Suzanne will show you that easy can be delicious.

Lexi dives into what happens after happily ever after. Charlie and Ian try to have a night out—but their kids prove that anything can happen when Taggarts are involved. Faith and Ten get a gift they never expected. Karina and Derek go on a stakeout. And Serena finds the meaning of Bliss. All these stories and more explore what it means to be a wife, a mother, a woman navigating love and responsibility.

Good meals, good times, good friends.

Bon appétit!

Treasured
A Masters and Mercenaries Novella
By Lexi Blake

David Hawthorne has a great life. His job as a professor at a prestigious Dallas college is everything he hoped for. Now that his brother is back from the Navy, life seems to be settling down. All he needs to do is finish the book he's working on and his tenure will be assured. When he gets invited to interview a reclusive expert, he knows he's gotten lucky. But being the stepson of Sean Taggart comes with its drawbacks, including an overprotective mom who sends a security detail to keep him safe. He doesn't need a bodyguard, but when Tessa Santiago shows up on his doorstep, the idea of her giving him close cover doesn't seem so bad.

Tessa has always excelled at most anything she tried, except romance. The whole relationship thing just didn't work out for her. She's not looking for love, and she's certainly not looking for it with an academic who happens to be connected to her boss's family. The last thing she wants is to escort an overly pampered pretentious man-child around South America to ensure he doesn't get into trouble. Still, there's something about David that calls to her. In addition to watching his back, she will have to avoid falling into the trap of soulful eyes and a deep voice that gets her heart racing.

But when the seemingly simple mission turns into a treacherous race for a hidden artifact, David and Tess know this assignment could cost them far more than their jobs. If they can overcome the odds, the lost treasure might not be their most valuable reward.

The Dom Identity
Masters and Mercenaries: Reloaded, Book 2
By Lexi Blake
Coming September 14, 2021

A man with everything

Michael Malone seems to have it all. A wealthy, loving family. A job that fulfills him. Friends he can count on. But something is missing. He's spent years watching his brother and close friends get married and start families, but it hasn't happened for him. When an assignment comes up to investigate fallen Hollywood star Vanessa Hale, he jumps at the chance. She's gorgeous and potentially deadly. Playing the spy game with her might be just the thing to take his mind off his troubles.

A woman with nothing left to lose

Vanessa Hale had big dreams that ended in scandal. She returned home with nothing but heartache and the desire to find her sister's killer. The trail points to someone at Lodge Corp, so taking a job with Julian Lodge's mysterious company is her best option for finding the truth. While she hunts for a killer during the day, she hopes to find some solace at night in The Club. Meeting the gorgeous, sexy and seemingly kind Michael Malone, their chemistry sparks in a way she's never felt before, and Vanessa thinks maybe her luck has finally changed.

A love that might save them both

When Michael's true motives are revealed, she will have to find a way to forgive his betrayal. The killer has made Vanessa their next target. Working together and stopping this monster is the only chance for them to have the real love they both deserve.

About Lexi Blake

New York Times bestselling author Lexi Blake lives in North Texas with her husband and three kids. Since starting her publishing journey in 2010, she's sold over three million copies of her books. She began writing at a young age, concentrating on plays and journalism. It wasn't until she started writing romance that she found success. She likes to find humor in the strangest places and believes in happy endings.

Connect with Lexi online:

Facebook: Lexi Blake
Twitter: authorlexiblake
Website: www.LexiBlake.net
Instagram: lexiblakeauthor

CPSIA information can be obtained
at www.ICGtesting.com
Printed in the USA
LVHW101651270123
738093LV00002B/220